Plastic Man

Plastic Man

A Novel of the Sixties

Dan Culberson

Copyright © 2008 by Dan Culberson.
Cover photo by Gayle Swanson with digital enhancement by Lynne Vigue

ISBN:	Hardcover	978-1-4363-2027-6
	Softcover	978-1-4363-2026-9

All rights reserved. No part of this book may be reproduced or transmitted in any form or by any means, electronic or mechanical, including photocopying, recording, or by any information storage and retrieval system, without permission in writing from the copyright owner.

This is a work of fiction. Names, characters, places and incidents either are the product of the author's imagination or are used fictitiously, and any resemblance to any actual persons, living or dead, events, or locales is entirely coincidental.

This book was printed in the United States of America.

To order additional copies of this book, contact:
Xlibris Corporation
1-888-795-4274
www.Xlibris.com
Orders@Xlibris.com
32426

CONTENTS

ONE:	*I've never seen the sea*..9	
TWO:	*The pillow of fog burns away by eight o'clock* 20	
THREE:	*The old mustached man brakes the truck to a clanking stop* 28	
FOUR:	*The time we sent T.K. to Cleveland had been a good drunk* 38	
FIVE:	*The café's walls are decorated with gayly colored posters* 46	
SIX:	*Robin never forgave me for the way she said I had acted*....57	
SEVEN:	*We discussed Rape's death for some time after that*.............71	
EIGHT:	*T.K. wondered about his sanity the time he went with the Catholic girl*..80	
NINE:	*My ride lets me out in a little Utah town* 90	
TEN:	*I am kind of interested in how the jail looks, having never been in one before*...97	
ELEVEN:	*The sheriff stands on one foot leaning against his desk* 104	
TWELVE:	*"So I figured, what the hell, you know?"*...........................118	
THIRTEEN:	*A really good-looking stud Negro walked into the house* 130	
FOURTEEN:	*The Place, as I said, is a small cubbyhole cellar* 146	
FIFTEEN:	*I pull the car over to the side of the road*........................155	
SIXTEEN:	*I go on in to Las Vegas* 161	
SEVENTEEN:	*Going over this unbelievable bit of business at the time, I can't help thinking about Bido* 169	
EIGHTEEN:	*The two days I spend with Lorraine are wonderful* 181	
NINETEEN:	*I realize that I still haven't seen the ocean* 195	
TWENTY:	*I am awake before any of the others* 201	

Dedication

To all the people who came of age and lived through the Sixties, both those who remember that decade and those who don't, but especially to those who didn't survive that tumultuous decade.

ONE

I've never seen the sea

I've never seen the sea.

Oh, I've probably seen thousands of pictures of oceans in my life, and I've probably seen the sea spread across the wide screen fives of thousands of times in the movies and watched it roll tens of thousands of times within the tiny confines of television, and, therefore, I know what the ocean looks like, even though I've never seen it in real life. I would recognize it if I saw it.

I like to imagine the ocean, though. I like to imagine its huge vastness, its rolling spilling wonderment, its tangy salty smell seducing my nostrils and causing them to flare in a vain attempt to become saturated with the sea's vapors. I like to imagine the sea's numbing coldness, which, if you stand in it not far from shore, causes you to forget everything else in the world except the cold, comforting insensibility enveloping your thighs. I like to imagine its powerful roar.

But I've never seen the sea. I'm a stranger in a world of oceans. I'm a foreigner in a world of water. I haven't felt its physical presence or sensed its swirl around my thighs. I haven't tried to hold it in my cupped hands or tasted its salt on my tongue. I've never smelled it. I've never experienced it.

So, I decided to experience it. I decided to leave Colorado and go to California, the land of opportunity and ocean. I decided to see the sea.

It is two-and-a-half years after the start of the decade, and what will happen to my generation on its quest, what will happen to the nation for a decade will change my life, our lives, its life forever. We may never recover. I have never recovered.

We live in a world of subversive order, a world full of madness, and yet afraid of madness. Even in this age of anti-conformity, you can still shock your friends. They become upset if you do something rationally that seems to be irrational to them. An irrational act done irrationally is accepted, because that is the point. But a rational irrational act is disturbing. Disorder has to follow pre-established, accepted norms. Therefore, some of my friends thought I was crazy.

"You're crazy," Dayo said. "You've utterly lost it. You are absolutely out of your mind! . . . You're joking, aren't you?"

He stared at me, his eyes peering out of his face, searching my face and my eyes to tell whether or not I was joking, but no one can tell when I'm joking except when I say that I'm joking. And you can never believe anything I say . . . including that last remark. Dayo finally decided that I wasn't joking.

"No, you're not joking. You're crazy."

"Look, Dayo. My sanity is not what we're discussing. I've already made up my mind. All I want you to do is take care of my things while I'm gone, okay? I'm not telling anyone else, because I don't want anyone else to know until after I'm gone. I don't want to have to go through a whole mess of explanations that won't make sense to anyone but me. I know what I'm doing, and that's all I care about right now."

He shook his head unbelievingly, his long dark hair swaying back and forth across his forehead. Then, throwing his hands up into the air in mock beseechment of the gods, he sat down.

"Thanks a lot. What's the matter with you, Hud? You're going to graduate in three months—probably with honors. And you want to drop out now? Call it quits? After all this time? You're crazy!"

Dayo will never understand. Even today, in his self-designed, mondo unique house in Albuquerque, Dayo will never understand. No one can ever understand the rational irrational act of a romantic. Except other romantics.

Why can no one ever understand anyone else? Understanding your own self, we do fairly well. Of course, sometimes your mind withholds information from you and your elf, causing you to make a mistake in elf-judgment, forcing you to backtrack and reevaluate your elf. For the most part, we can understand our own elves. But trying to figure out someone else's elf is the problem. Give up. It's no use.

I wandered slowly around the room, trying to think of something that would satisfy Dayo. Books in their bookcases, pictures in their frames. Walls, windows, doors, floors, desks, chests, ceiling closing in on me, stagnant air choking me, burning me, sticking in my throat. I was suffocating and can't help my elf. I want to dive through the window glass and escape. I want to be free. How do I explain to him something I can't really explain to myself? How can I make him understand when I don't even understand. Do I even want to understand?

"Look, Dayo. I can't expect you to understand. That's why I'm not even going to try to explain it. Perhaps I'm not even sure, myself. As a matter of fact, I know I'm not. All I know is, I've got to get away. It's no good, anymore. I know that's a cliché, and you know how I hate clichés, and I know you know I know you know. But I don't care about school right now. I don't care about graduating. I just feel there's something more important to do with my life. I just don't care. I've had it. I'm leaving. I'm dropping out. And I wanted to tell you, so you and Theo can take care of my things while I'm gone. I might be back. I don't know for sure if I ever will, but I might come back."

Be back. Be back. I'll be back. Be back. I promise. I'll come back.

"Does Diane's death have anything to do with this?"

Dayo's question will haunt me for the rest of my life. That question will terrify me to California and back. A simple question and a simple answer that Dayo has a right to know. *Does Diane's death have anything to do with this?*

He asks the question softly with a thunder that fills every crack in the room, that smacks against the far wall and bounces back against me so hard that I start remembering again. I don't answer him right away, because I can't. I can't be sure what noise will come out of my throat. So the tapping of my fingers beats nervously around the room, trying to force the thunder away, trying to calm my fears and shove them under the door.

The study stares at me and won't let me think clearly. I want to say yes, or no, or maybe, and then run away. But I can't decide which one is the right answer. I am afraid to say anything. I know that I won't cry, but I can't be sure how steady my voice will be, and all the time Dayo waits, embarrassed, looking at his watch, and I can hear his watch ticking, clicking at a galloping pace that keeps picking up speed, that keeps racing faster and faster until I think my face will burst and my wheels and springs will fly all over the room. Yes, no, maybe. Yes! No! Maybe! Yes, no, maybe. Yes! No! Maybe!

"Look, of course Diane's death has something to do with it. Everyone's death has something to do with it. Everybody has something to do with it. You do, Theo does . . . T.K. . . . Bido . . . everybody here and everybody there. But no one person and no one thing has anything to do with it. Just me. I'm the one. Call it a quest. So, don't try to look for a simple, logical reason. There isn't any." *Blame it on the nation. Blame it on society.*

That doesn't satisfy him.

"Okay, I'm crazy," I say. "I admit it."

His face shows that he is slowly accepting the truth of what I am trying to tell him. I am really leaving. I am really quitting school just three months before graduation and taking off, dropping out, leaving all my possessions behind—save one: I am taking my memories with me.

And I am not upset about it. I am very calm, very rational. I don't care anymore, because suddenly nothing seems worth caring about anymore. A few friends, maybe, but I might come back. And my leaving won't disrupt their lives any, but my staying will destroy mine.

"And you won't even say where you're going? Or how long you'll be gone?"

Sit down and relax. Trust yourself. The worst part is over, because now he understands. Now he will accept the fact of a stupid, noble, idiotic act. You've finally talked him into it. Now it's only a matter of talking your elf into it. You've reached the point where you can't turn back. The river of no return. The failsafe point. You've gone too far now, and you couldn't return if you wanted to, because now there's no returning. You've already taken the hardest step, the first step, and each successive step will be easier as you go along. You've already started on your way.

"I don't know how long I'll be gone. But, I'm going West. California. I don't want to tell you exactly where. I can't, really, because I'm not even sure, myself. But I don't want anyone else to know. I want to be completely separate from everything. The only things I want with me are my memories, and I'm even going to try to forget them. I know no one would follow me, but I want the complete freedom of the feeling of aloneness. I'm going to go away, see what's there, and then I might come back."

Dayo sits there silently in the afternoon sunlight trying to understand, and I try to make him understand, and if I can't make him understand, at least I can try to make him try not to try to understand.

"Don't worry, okay? Nothing's wrong with me. Really. I'm not crazy. Everything's perfectly all right. Maybe I just want a rest. Maybe I just want to stretch the bounds of my limits. Maybe I just want to stretch the bounds of everybody's limits. Maybe I just want to save the world. Hell, maybe Diane's death really has affected me, but I'm not crazy, psychotic, paranoid, split, freaked out, slipping, fading, insane, daft, or touched. A little 'weird,' maybe, but none of those other things. I'm all right, Jack, really. I might be back in a month or so, and everything will be just as it was before. You probably won't even realize I'm gone. Now, that's going to hurt, if you don't! But, I'll understand."

I leave early the next morning. I don't want the knowledge of my leaving to get around while I'm around, because I just want to leave quietly. I didn't tell Dayo not to say anything, because I know he wouldn't be able to stay silent anyway, and I want to avoid having to try to explain to twenty different people what it's all about.

What's it all about? I don't know. What's it all about . . . .

So, I leave the house at five-thirty the next morning. I left Dayo enough money to pay my portion of the rent I will miss until the end of the semester, and he continued studying. Theo came in late during the night from a date, stumbling around in the dark muttering to himself, shushing the dogs, throwing his clothes all over the living room and the bedroom, finally flopping into his bed, tossing all over it, kicking out the cat, trying to be quiet. All the time Dayo and I were half-awake/half-asleep, not being able to decide whether to wake up or go back to sleep.

We will have that problem all our young-adult lives, my generation: what to decide what to do. What decision to decide to make. Shall I get out of school and take my chances in the Army and maybe get killed in Vietnam or shall I try to stay in until I'm too old for the draft. Shall I give up my freedom and get married and stay out of the Army or shall I take my chances with a wife and whatever that might bring. Shall I become branded as a radical and join with others in support of my ideals and try to stop the idiocy of the nation or shall I chicken out, join the establishment, wear a suit, and silently cry at night. Shall I kill my elf now or shall I kill my elf later.

As I tippy-toe creakingly to the front door, I am met by the dogs, wagging their merry little behinds in anticipation of a walk, and I have to squeeze out the door. Both of them look up at me through the glass in the front door as I stand on the outside looking in, and who ever said dogs don't show emotion? I know they know. They know I'm not going for a walk. They know I'm going away. They know I'm going to see the sea. Cassius begins whining until clumsy Clytemnestra starts tumbling with him, and as I walk off the porch, Cassius is chasing Cly into the kitchen.

A thick wet fog has crept up on Boulder during the night, and from the top of Flagstaff Mountain, which isn't a mountain, the view must look like a huge gray pillow flopped down on the floor of the plains, propped up against the foothills. Everything is strangely quiet as only a fog can make it quiet, muffling and surrounding everything with a mist so thick that walking through it is like moving through your own cold, gray world. My footsteps click weirdly, as if they are detached from me as I walk quickly up to the Hill, that bit of Boulder just across the street from the campus of the University.

As I turn up Broadway, a lonely police car passes by, going on down the hill to the central part of town, its headlights not making any headway in the fog. I am chilly, and I clench my hands in the pockets of my ski parka to keep them warm. I haven't brought anything with me. I don't want to be troubled with a suitcase, with a bag, with a backpack, with a Dopp kit, with even a comb. I can get along without anything. I am carrying nothing. Wanting nothing, needing nothing. Using nothing.

I have money. I'm not stupid. I may be crazy, but I'm not stupid. I cleaned out my savings account yesterday. Money, the root of all evil, will get me where I want to go. Money, the essence of all goodness, can buy me anything I want. And right now I want to buy . . . not forgetfulness . . . just awayness. I want to take a break. I want to break out of the Fifties and show the world some excitement. I want to lose my inhibitions. I want to step off from the world for a while and take another look at life and at how it should be lived. I want to stop doing what the bastards want me to do and do what I want to do and do what I think is right and should be done. I want to shake off the dizziness of boredom.

The fog causes everything to be in silhouette. The trees, just now beginning to show small green buds, are reduced to mere black outlines enveloped by the gray fog. Farther away they are faded to gray. Beyond that they are nothing. They cease to exist beyond the threshold of my vision. They no longer be beyond the edges of my being.

Cars suddenly take form out of the mist, parked against the curb, waiting for the daylight and the sun to burn away the fog. Now you don't see them; now you do. Now you don't again. I wonder if this is a fitting departure from this edifice of higher learning where I have spent more than three-and-a-half years, but I don't bother with the bother of the analogy.

I become vaguely aware of a form in the fog walking ahead of me. It is a formless form, and I can't tell exactly what it is. I assume it is somebody walking along the sidewalk ahead of me, but I can't hear any footsteps other than my own strange clickings. I am walking rather fast, and yet I can't overtake it. Eventually the form silently disappears into the mist, melts away, and I never see it again.

I wonder what it had been—if anything. Perhaps it had been a person, perhaps. Perhaps not. I prefer to think that it hadn't been a person. It had been a lonely, wandering ghost, searching for a dream. And it-he-she-it is allowed to search only in the fog, where it can't be seen, and where it can flit about as fast and as silently as a little bat. I wonder what dream it is searching for. Perhaps it doesn't even want to find its dream, for that would mean the end of the ghost's existence. For, once ghosts find their dream, then they have to melt away into the mist, and then they can sleep peacefully, restfully, until all the world melts into mist.

Perhaps I am that ghost, p'raps not. Perhaps we are all that ghost. Perhaps ghosts don't even exist in the foggy, foggy dew.

Why is it, I wonder, we are always searching for something? Why is it, I ponder, we can never know who we are? Or even what we are searching for? The whole gang seemed always to be searching for something. Each individual in the group always searching for each individual's something or other. Each individual sometimes searching for another individual, like Gaga searched for Dayo.

"Why won't he pay any attention to me?" she asked me that day.

We had all gone up to the waterfall in Eldorado Canyon for swimming and drinking.

"I know I'm not beautiful, but I'm not ugly, either."

"Gaga," I said in my most bullshit fatherly manner, "you've got to be patient with Dayo. He's basically shy, poor guy."

I rolled over onto my stomach, feeling hot granite against my belly and being careful not to spill my beer.

"He's basically a man," she sniffed.

Diane, next to me, laughed. "Don't tell me you're man hungry."

Gaga sighed. "No, I'm not man hungry. But Dayo's different. He makes my ovaries itch."

The basically shy object of our conversation was at the time building a dam across the stream with the help of T.K. and Rape. Or rather, they were trying to build a dam. They wanted to test their power against nature, but the mountain-rushing water was too swift, and they were having trouble getting their rocks to stay put. (No jokes from the future—please.) The water was icy-cold fresh from the still snowy Rocky Mountains high above us, but the guys moved vigorously, laughing as they tried to shove large boulders around in the plunging water. The roar of the waterfall just below them completely enveloped and stamped us, dulling our senses along with the stream-cooled beer.

Theo, Gaga, Diane, and I had rathered sleep than build a dam, and we lay on an overhanging rock, soaking up the sun and occasionally looking down at them encouragingly to see how they were doing, and jeering, and tossing down a beer which T.K. pierced with the churchkey suspended from the perpetual string around his neck.

I thought Theo was asleep, but he popped one eye open, squinted into the sun, and asked, "Where's Bido?"

"Guess."

He leaned up on an elbow, looked around, and dropped back on his towel.

"Yeah, I see Myrna's not around, either."

"They said they were going to pick flowers," Gaga said, opening another beer and frowning at the golden liquid which spilled on her hand and trickled down to her fingertips where she lapped it up like a cat with her flicking tongue.

"I think that's rather symbolic, picking flowers," I said.

"Yes," Gaga sighed rather too dramatically, "I wish Dayo would ask me to go pick some flowers."

"Do I detect a note of double meaning there, my Dear?" Theo asked from his rock above us.

"Yes," she said, looking down at her meager chest, encased in her blue swimsuit. "Be still my heart, B-flat my chest . . . ."

"Well," she said, looking up, "he could at least ask me out more often, couldn't he?"

"*Help!*"

We looked down just in time to see T.K.'s long legs being swept over the waterfall. He had been working too close to the edge and got caught by the swift current. We all scrambled down over the huge tumbled rocks along the edge of the stream. Rape and Dayo were already down there, wading in the chest-high water, but seeing no sign of T.K. Just bubbling water and the insensate waterfall.

Gaga and Diane were frightened. The waterfall was only fifteen feet high, but T.K. could have struck his head on a submerged rock in the stream bed, since he had chosen to go over head first. However, the water in the pool immediately below the waterfall was about five feet deep. We waited patiently, somewhat anxiously, for him to come up. He didn't. You always hate for an accident to spoil a perfectly good day.

"I'll look for him," Dayo said, as he waded farther out into the pool.

"Be careful!" Gaga cried. "Don't you get hurt, too!"

Dayo shot back at her that quizzical, comical disgusted look that he has perfected and pantented, just before he suddenly disappeared from sight. Seconds later he reappeared, spewing water, his brown hair streaming down his face into his eyes. Gaga screamed when he went under, and she waded out into the water to help him.

"I stepped in a hole. Be careful."

"Hey!" I yelled. "What about T.K.?"

"Oh, yeah," Dayo remembered. He started stumbling around again, searching for T.K.'s lifeless body pinned to the submerged rocks by the crushing water.

Rape said in a bored, slightly concerned voice, "I hope he's not dead."

"Yeah, me, too," Theo said, draining the last of the beer from his can. "He owed me some money I'll probably never see again."

"Theo!" Diane said disgustedly. "How can you say such a thing? I'm ashamed of you."

"Yeah!" yelled a voice that sounded suspiciously like T.K.'s. "How can you say such a thing?"

It was T.K.'s.

Dayo stopped searching and looked toward the waterfall. Gaga had just reached him and was trying to look toward the waterfall, too, but she was having trouble standing up and instead grabbed hold of Dayo, almost pulling him under again. The water was up to her nose.

"Okay!" I yelled. "Where are you, you idiot?"

"I'm behind the waterfall, you idiot," T.K. yelled back. "There's a kind of cave back here!"

T.K. came flying through the waterfall and disappeared into the pool. He shot up again, hooting and splashing water on everyone and chasing Dayo and Gaga around the pool in animated slow motion. We all then had to inspect the cave behind the waterfall, and it turned out to be more of a shallow concavity than a cave, just barely room enough to stand on a ledge and keep from getting drowned by the water crashing down from above.

In years to come, we will sadly discover that most of the caves we so excitedly hoped to discover will turn out to be only shallow concavities with just barely enough room to stand and keep from getting drowned. Is that all there is?

When we had finally saturated our outsides, we climbed back up to the rocks and started saturating our insides and drying off in the sun. It was a good day to get drunk.

"This is a good day to get drunk," Dayo said redundantly.

"Dayo," Gaga purred, "don't you ever think of anything else." She let one shoulder strap of her bathing suit slip seductively off her shoulder.

"Yeah," Dayo said, looking her full in the eyes. "Food. We got any?"

Gaga pulled her strap up. "Oh, *cocoa!*" she cried.

"No, no!" we all chorused. "*Caca*, Gaga. *Caca!*"

"Hey, is there any beer left?"

Bido and Myrna had finally come out of the woods.

Gaga wished that Dayo would come out of the woods, or take her into them, either one or the other. Actually, they only kidded each other half kiddingly. She wasn't that sex crazy and he wasn't that girl shy.

He was scared to death of them.

Theo and I had given up trying to get Dayo to take out girls. He would sometimes get a date only if it was a special occasion. Whenever our fraternity would have a formal dance, he would get a date, or for a special party he might show up with some strange girl, or Gaga, or both, but between formals and special parties it was pretty barren country for the girls, as far as Dayo was concerned.

"As far as I'm concerned, I can do without them," he said early one morning. "They either don't want to do anything, or they want to do too much."

"Yeah," I replied, not paying any attention to him.

We were going through our early-every-morning ritual. We both had an eight-o'clock class Monday through Friday, and we would get up at seven-thirty, leaving us just enough time to eat a bowl of soggy-eyed cereal flakes staring back up at us. Dayo sat on one side of the kitchen table, I sat on the other, and the box of cereal sat between us.

"Aren't there any in-between girls around anymore? I'm not a prude, but Jesus Christ I've got morals."

"Yeah, sure," I replied and continued reading.

Dayo, giving up trying to start a conversation, began reading his side. I had the back of the box this morning, which took me longer to get through.

"They've got a pretty good offer back here."

"Oh, yeah? What do they give you?"

"A set of some plastic frogmen that go up and down in the bathtub. Come in different colors."

"We already have those. We got the larger size from the shredded-wheat company."

"Yeah, I know. I played with them about a week ago when I took my bath. But these have little spear guns that really shoot."

We continued eating in soggy silence, in cereal installments.

"Aren't you finished yet?" he asked impatiently. "We haven't got much time left."

"Just a minute . . . . Okay."

Dayo turned the cereal box around and began reading the back. All I had now was the front, and I could finish that in less than five seconds.

"I'll sure be glad when we finish this cereal, so we can get a new box to read," I said, killing time.

"Yeah. It's been about a week now with this one, hasn't it?" Dayo said, reviving it. "Theo just hasn't been pulling his weight."

After we finished the cereal and the box-reading, we put the dishes in the sink to be washed later—in a couple of days if they were lucky—and collected our books to leave. The campus was only ten blocks away, but Dayo's car took longer than anyone else's, especially if it happened to be parked the wrong way. "A-Frame," his old black Model A Ford, was in perfect condition in every respect save one. For some strange reason, it could turn only to the left. So, before we could go anywhere, we had to plan our course carefully, planning, plotting, calculating, eliminating all right turns. One mistake, and instead of simply making a right turn, we had to go completely around an extra block, three left turns in a row, four extra blocks out of the way.

"Why don't you get rid of this junk heap?"

"Shut up. You'll hurt her feelings."

Dayo fired up the engine.

"We're off! We're off!" I yelled.

"We're all off!" Dayo yelled back.

"Now we're getting some off!" we both yelled in unison.

We went through this ritual every time we got into a car together to go somewhere. Perhaps we didn't want A-Frame to get nervous during those first few critical moments. What would we do without rituals to make us feel comfortable and secure?

Having to go to classes every morning made it easier, though, because we had two regular routes worked out from constant use, depending on whether Dayo had parked facing east or facing west the night before.

Dayo always claimed he could fix A-Frame for practically nothing, but he never really gave it any serious thought. After all, he also claimed, his car had character. It was more than just a cold hunk of metal. And it presented a challenge every time he got into it to go anywhere: He never knew for sure if he was going to get there. Especially on streets such as Broadway, which curves when it gets to the Hill. Dayo could negotiate it getting out of town, but trying to go downtown on Broadway was another matter. He just couldn't do it without going around those extra blocks.

TWO

The pillow of fog burns away by eight o'clock

The pillow of fog burns away by eight o'clock, and I am about five miles south of Boulder, still on foot, on the road to Golden. The sun has come up out of the plains behind Denver and is floating slowly up into the sky, watching this lonely figure hiking along this lonely road. I am beginning to think I will have to walk all the way to Golden when I hear my salvation. The clankety-clanking increases and an old, battered black pickup truck comes rumbling along behind me. I turn and wave, and the truck pulls up ahead of me and stops beside the highway in a cloud of gravel and dust. The old man sticks his white mustache and his battered once-white cowboy hat out the window at me.

"Going to Golden?"

"Yes," I answer, jogging up to the truck. "Going to Golden."

"Hop in."

I hop in and through a change of grinding gears we rattle off down the highway. He winds her up and manages to get forty miles an hour out of the antique, sixty going downhill. The old man sucks his mustache and squints ahead. He looks like an old cowboy who could tell a tale or two.

"Pretty early to be out hitching," he says.

"I wanted to get a head start," I reply, trying to be congenial.

He quickly takes his eyes off the road and looks at me suspiciously.

"Oh?"

"A head start on the hitching."

"Oh."

We ride on in silence. The road between Boulder and Golden plays tag with the foothills, darting in and out of the hogbacks and whipping over the mesa to allow a quick glance of Denver's crown towers off to the east, sprawled over the plains in the distance and glinting in the morning sun. They don't call her the "Queen City of the Plains" for nothing. Then the highway skirts behind a hogback again to remind you that you are at the foot of the Rockies and you have no business watching the boring fruited plains when you can be gazing up in awe at the proud, snow-capped purple Rocky Mountain majesties. We pass a hogback that looks as if it could be the remains of a petrified 5000-foot dinosaur, the rock outcropping on top curving gently as its spine, its huge body now covered with grass and wild flowers, its head buried deep in the coarse sand.

"I'm only going as far as Golden," the old cowboy says.

"That's fine. Golden's fine."

His chin and head move up and down in barely perceptible nods. His mustache is wet where he has sucked it on the sides of his mouth, and the white hairs are plastered down to his chin.

"You going on further?" he asks.

I think. What should I say?

"Yes. I'm going on quite a bit farther. I'm going to Tlapallan."

He thinks.

"Oh. Don't know that place."

I'm going to Tlapallan, I think. Tlapallan, Valhalla, the Happy Hunting Grounds, Paradise, call it anything you want, in any language, any myth. It's all a myth—heaven or hell—and it doesn't make any difference. It just doesn't make any difference anymore. Besides, as T.K. said, what's in a name? What's in a word?

"What's in a word?" T.K. said. "A word is just a symbol, made up of little disinterested letters, just simple little symbols all. A word can't be dirty by itself. It's the person's own thoughts behind the word that's dirty. It's the person's own mind that's dirty, not the word."

We were drinking coffee in a little cafe on the Hill, killing time between classes. T.K. was telling me about his latest project, a term paper on dirty words.

"Not just dirty words, exactly," he corrected, "but the dirty sayings written in rest rooms. The *graffiti* of the *populi*. There's a whole wealth of research material around this campus, and I won't have to spend hours in that damn stuffy library doing research."

"No, you'll just have to spend hours in a damn stinky toilet."

"What the hell? I have to go in there anyway. And not 'toilet.' '*Toilets.*' Plural. I'm going to inspect every damn head in every damn building on campus. This is going to be an exhaustive, complete report. No word shall escape my eye."

"What about pictures?" I said. "Are you going to include the pictures, too?"

"Say! I never thought of that." He straightened up in the booth and sipped his coffee thoughtfully. "Yeah, why not? I'll include all the pictures, too. They're just as vital a part of rest-room literature as all the words and poems. The ones that are scratched in the paint, I'll make pencil rubbings of, just like the archaeologists do with caveman drawings and tombstones. The ones that are drawn, I'll have to make sketches of. Maybe I can get Theo to do them for me. Man! This is going to be the best damn term paper this school has ever seen!"

"At least it ought to keep you from failing sociology," I said. "But you might want to be careful about you and Theo being in the same stall together while he's sketching them for you."

"Yeah." He slumped back into the booth, setting his mug back onto the ring on the tabletop. "It'll be too crowded, won't it? I'll have to stand outside and give directions. Got to be careful. If this paper doesn't make it, I don't make it."

A week later, I saw T.K. in The Sink.

"How's the paper going?" I yelled above the roar.

"Great. Great," he replied around a bottle of Coors. "It couldn't be better."

He finished a swallow and added, "Well, maybe it could be better in just one little respect."

"What's that?"

"I haven't exactly started yet. But don't worry! I've got lots of ideas, and I've been doing a lot of research."

"Yeah? Where?"

"Well . . . I just came out of the head back there."

The next time I saw him, T.K. was lying on the grass in front of Hellems waiting for his next class.

"Hi, T.K."

"Hi, Hud. Rest your wearies. Pull up a piece of grass."

"So, what's the latest with you?"

"Oh, nothing much. I failed sociology."

"Already? Before the finals?"

"The final won't do me any good. I got a zero on my term paper. The professor thought it was obscene and chewed me out in front of the class and sent me to see the Dean."

"Was it that bad?"

"Hell, no! It was the best damn paper I've ever written. But . . . well . . . I guess I was just too explicit. But that was the whole point! And the drawings didn't help, either. The damn prof is just too conservative. He doesn't see that a whole brave new world is coming. He's from too far back into yesterday, if you ask me! But the thing that makes me so damn mad," he said, "is the fact that I put so damn much work into it for nothing. I mean, I really worked my ass off. Damn near got it shot off, too."

"What do you mean?"

"Well, I figured I would go a little bit further than I had originally intended. You know, give it a little more perspective. I decided that I wouldn't just have dirty sayings and pictures from men's rest rooms. I was going to collect all the ones I could get from the girls' rest rooms, too."

"You mean, they write them, too?"

"Hell, yes! Man, some of them are dirtier than ours! Anyway, I couldn't figure out how I was going to be able to sneak in them, and I asked Gaga if she would do it for me. She said I was crazy and a dirty old man, besides. She said it would almost be like breaking a confidence to do something like that against her fellow men."

"'Women.'"

"Yeah, 'women.' So I had to do it myself."

I turned from the short swaying skirts I had been watching and looked at him. With T.K., you could never really be sure when he was being serious and when he was putting you on. I decided he was being serious.

"You mean, you went around going into girls' rest rooms to collect your dirty sayings and poems and pictures?"

"Hell, yes. At first I thought about going in disguise. You know, dressed up like a girl. I asked Gaga if she would loan me a dress, then, and she said I was really crazy and worse than a dirty old man—a dirty *young* man and maybe a little queer, too, and not just in the head. Hey! That's a play on words! 'In the head,' get it? Anyway, I'm not sure she'll talk to me anymore."

"Well, what did you do?"

"Well, I finally decided that I probably couldn't find a girl tall enough to fit me anyhow—that's a play on words, too—and besides, I didn't like the idea of having to shave my legs."

"What about your goatee?"

"Hell, *no*! I'm never going to shave my '*tee*'! I was just going to have to be a woman with a little facial hair."

"My god, you *are* crazy!"

"No, listen. I'm serious. Anyway, I discarded the disguise idea and decided I'd just sneak in late at night when no one else was around."

"And that's how you almost got your ass shot off."

"Yeah," he answered in all seriousness. "That's how I almost got my ass shot off. What with this window-peeping Tom running around the sorority houses lately, the cops would have probably figured I was him."

"'He.' You mean, you got caught?"

"Yeah, 'he.' No, I didn't get caught, but I damn near did. I was in Hellems Annex and about thirty minutes before they lock up for the night, I ducked into the girls' john. No one was around, and I thought it was safe. I didn't think there was anyone around on the whole damn floor."

"But there was, huh?"

"Well, I don't know where the hell they came from, but they did. I was in the only stall, busily copying down these obscenities when I heard two girls talking out in the hall. 'Christ,' I said, 'I'm a dead pussy.' They were coming right in and there wasn't anything I could do. So I quickly locked the stall door and sat down on the toilet seat with my feet up in the air so they couldn't see them. They walked right in and damned if one didn't want to use the john. She needed to go real bad, too, and she really cussed a purple-green streak when she couldn't get the door open. I would have blushed if I hadn't already been surrounded by the evidence of girls' obscenities."

"Yeah, I'll bet."

"So, when she gave up trying to get the door open, damned if she didn't try to crawl under it."

"You're kidding."

"No, I'm serious. She stuck her arm under and tried to reach the latch. Jesus, I was scared. She almost touched me. '*Well, Jesus Christ on a crutch!*' she yelled. '*What the hell do they want me to do? Pee in the sink?*' And damned if she didn't."

"T.K., you're out of your mind."

"No, honest. This is all true. They finally left, and I was so shook up I almost got locked in the building overnight. I tell you, I was really nervous as hell whenever I went into a girls' head after that."

The bells boomed and everyone on the lawn hopped up and trotted off to class. Pavlov's dogs, we.

"And all that work didn't help you any, huh?" I asked as we scampered inside the building.

"Hell, no. The damn prof said the thing was obscene. He won't even let me back into the class."

"Later, T.K."

"Later, Hud."

If anyone could tell a good story, it was T.K. He just had a way about him that made him a good story teller. He threw himself into the thick of the tale, and he always came out the winner. He could take the most serious, factual, true story in the world and make it sound as if he had made it up on the spot. Theo told him this one night at the Gondolier.

"T.K., you're a lying son of a bitch."

"No, really. This is an honest-to-God true story. I read it in my history book. A damn trapper ate himself."

"Look," Theo said, "I've heard of eating, and I've heard of eating other people, and I've heard of eating your *date*. But I never heard about anyone who ate him*self*. It's just not healthy, and damn near physically impossible."

We went down to the Gondolier practically every night for coffee, garlic bread, and brilliant conversation. It's close to the campus on Broadway and not too far from where Dayo, Theo, and I live. T.K. had wandered in and immediately began telling us about some queer trapper he had been reading about.

"No, he wasn't queer! He was hungry! Really, there was this trapper out in the plains of Wyoming or Colorado or somewhere. He'd had a pretty rough time. Lost his horse or something. His food, too. Or maybe he had already eaten it. Anyway, he was practically starving."

"Why didn't he trap something?" Dayo asked.

"He lost his traps, too," T.K. said. "I don't know. The Indians were chasing him or something. Anyway, he didn't have any food. He had gone for over two weeks or so without any food. Maybe without water, too. He had tried some buffalo chips, but he didn't like the taste."

"T.K., why don't you go home?"

"When the chips are down, some people can eat anything," Dayo said.

"Dayo, who don't you go home?"

"Look, for Chris'sakes! I'm not making this up. If I had my book with me, I'd show you in print."

"Yeah, yeah, sure. And if it's in a book, it must be true."

"Anyway, he was without food. Maybe he'd already eaten his horse, I don't know. You know, the French eat their horses. Anyway, the only thing left to eat was himself."

"I think I'm going to be deathly ill," I said.

"Hang on," Theo muttered. "I don't think we've come to the best part yet."

"Hell, no," T.K. said. "So he built himself a big fire from the buffalo chips he didn't like the taste of—."

"Where did he get the matches?" I asked.

"He was a frontiersman," Dayo said, "a trader and a trapper. He didn't need matches. They could make fires by rubbing two sticks together, just like the Indians."

"Where did he get the sticks?" Theo asked. "I thought he was out on the plains."

"Hey! Do you guys want to hear this story or not?"

"No!"

"No!"

"No!"

"So, anyway, he got his buffalo-chip fire going real good and hot."

"And smelly," Dayo said.

"Is it smelly?" I asked. "I've never smelled a buffalo-chip fire."

"You haven't?" Theo asked. "Well, when I lived on the farm as a little kid, we used to—."

"Hey, you guys! Do you want to hear this story of not?"

"No!" we said, together this time.

"So he built this big fire," T.K. continued, "and right when it was going real good and hot and smelly, he took out his big buffalo knife and sliced off his left arm."

"What are you talking about?" Dayo said. "He would never have been able to cut off his own arm!"

"He was a big trapper, for Chris'sakes!" T.K. yelled.

"Why didn't he bleed to death?" Theo asked. "Or did he use the blood for drinking and recycle it?"

"God, you're getting sickening," T.K. said. "That's what the fire was for. Right after he cut off his arm, he shoved his stump into the fire to sear it shut."

"And then what happened?" I asked.

"He passed out."

"He passed out in the fire?" Dayo asked. "And he didn't burn up?"

"No. The fire burned out. How long do you think buffalo chips can burn?"

"I don't know," I said. "I've never burned any."

"Really?" Theo asked. "Well, when I lived on the farm as a little kid, we used to—."

"Get out of here!" Dayo said. "You didn't have any buffaloes on your farm."

"It could have been a buffalo farm, for all you know," Theo said. "Anyway, we had cows."

"So what happened when he came to?" I asked.

"So when he came to, the funniest thing had happened," T.K. said.

"What?" Dayo said. "He didn't like the taste of his arm, either?"

"No!" T.K. said. "He didn't even get a chance to taste it. When he came to, the only thing left of his arm was the bone. The damn buzzards had got to it before he even had a chance."

"T.K., why don't you go home?"

"No, really," he said. "This is a true story. It's right in my American history book."

"So, what did he do then," Dayo asked. "Cut off his other arm?"

"No. When he saw—. How the hell could he do that? When he saw he had gone to all that trouble for nothing, he just died."

"Get out of here!" Theo said. "If he died, then how come anyone knows the story so it can be in your history book?"

"Some other trappers came by shortly after he died. They saw his body and what was left of his arm, and they deduced what had happened."

"Naw, I think they just made it up," Theo said.

"I think the history-book writers made it up," Dayo said.

"What are you talking about?" T.K. snorted. "People don't make up history! History is true facts!"

In years to come, history will be rewritten in text books to suit the objectives of its authors or political and religious leaders. It's true. Come to think of it, everything is written to suit the objectives of its authors or political and religious leaders.

"Come on," I said. "Let's all go home."

THREE

*The old mustached man brakes
the truck to a clanking stop*

The old mustached man brakes the truck to a clanking stop in Golden and lets me out on the street that leads to the highway into the mountains. I walk quietly in the morning sun along the street, but I feel more like running as quickly as possible to get out of this town with the huge sign slung over main street, "Howdy Folks! Welcome to Golden Where the West Remains." I don't care for the kind of West that means nothing more than depressing cultural deprivation, whether or not it is self-inflicted. I don't blame Golden for its position, straddled between the mock civilization of Denver and the mock wilds of the mountains, making it a real frontier town, but I also don't condone the gloating in its backwardness. The fault is too common: if you can't correct your shortcomings, then call them attributes and in time you'll believe yourself.

The street has no sidewalks, and I have to walk along the side in the weeds. A few weathered, washed-out houses are stuck in the dirt alongside the road, but here and there a tree breaks the barrenness, or else an old battered Nash or Hudson. For some reason, out in the country you usually find an old Nash or Hudson abandoned along the way or silently rusting away in someone's backyard. Why these two cars? What did history have against them? Why couldn't they make it to the great junkpile graveyards of our nation, the lost burial grounds of these mighty mechanized elephants we call automobiles?

In years to come, the even more Westerny, tiny towns of Central City and Black Hawk will get to have legalized gambling in order to boost tourism, and Golden will get to modernize its highways and intersections so the tourists and natives can get through Golden without a glance of interest as they flash through from Denver to the mock-turtle towns of gambling glee.

I come to the junction with the main highway from Denver, which dashes by Golden as if trying to ignore it just before winding into the mountains, and I start walking along it, hands in my pockets. I have to be careful and keep walking, because "No person shall stand in a roadway for the purpose of soliciting a ride from the driver of any private vehicle" (13-5-60). (Translation: *No hitchhiking.*) Of course, the cops don't care if you're standing or walking. They don't make decisions, just like all bureaucratic bozos. They see you standing, they pick you up. They see you walking with your thumb out, they pick you up.

I don't want any encounters with the law this early in my journey. I might lose my nerve and go back. So, whenever I hear a car behind me, I turn to make sure it isn't the state patrol, then look in the other direction, and finally stick my thumb out.

The third car that comes by slams on the brakes and grinds to a skidding halt fifty yards from me, sliding off the blacktop onto the shoulder in a cloud of dust. Then it starts racing backwards toward me as I start running toward it. A hitchhiker can't appear too nonchalant, because the driver might change his mind by the time you stroll up to his parked car. But this driver appears to be more anxious than I am. The blue Chevy again roars to a skidding stop as I jump out of the way. Three young men are in the car, all in their early twenties, all seated in front.

"Buddy, you got a long, hard walk ahead of you if nobody picks you up, so you might as well get in," the guy riding shotgun says. He gets out of the car so I can climb into the back seat.

"Where you going?" the driver asks as he starts the car hopping back onto the pavement. I share the back seat with three radios, five lamps, an assortment of coats, suits and dresses, shirts and blouses, a typewriter, a cardboard box full of small appliances, and a white miniature poodle dog yapping its head off at me from down in the far corner on the floor.

"West," I answer. "Say, have you got any method for making your dog be a little less noisy?"

"Yeah," says Shotgun. "Give him a couple of quick kicks and he should shut up real good."

"Rather an expensive-looking dog to go around kicking," I say.

"Yeah!" laughs Middle, craning his neck around to look at me, only not being able to hold it twisted that way for long before having to turn back again toward the front. "What's your name, buddy?"

I stare at the back of his neck.

"Hud," I say. "Why?"

"Hey! Fellow! Take it easy," says Driver, also turning to look at me. "We just want to be friendly is all. If we're going to be riding together, we want to all be on a first-name basis, don't we? I'm Joe. What kind of name is Hud?"

I stare back at him, then finally smile. "Watch the road, Joe. It's really Hudson. Hudson Harrington Holyoke the third, Hud for short. Real high-class name."

"Okay, Hud for short," says Joe the driver, "meet Jim and Morey. And hang on back there, because you're probably going to go West faster than you *ever* hoped you would."

He is right. We have been going fast to begin with, but now he really concentrates, and the car picks up speed as we climb higher into the mountains. He pays no attention to the curves in the highway. He passes other cars going around blind curves, going uphill, and speeding through tunnels, squeezing in front of the passed car just in time to escape a honking, onrushing automobile, and the tortured tires squeal in pain with every bend. A few feet to the right—and then left—of the highway is the granite of a nearly perpendicular cliff. A few feet to the left—and then right—of the other lane is a sheer drop to the river, and we are protected only by the thin ribbon of steel of the guard rail running alongside us and matching our speed. The needle on the speedometer bounces around seventy whenever it gets a chance.

"Hey, Joe," I call over the noise of the barking dog, "you're not in any hurry, are you?"

Shotgun—Jim—turns around to watch me.

"Yeah, as a matter of fact, we are," he says. "We've got to get to Utah as soon as possible."

"Great," I say. "That's okay fine with me. But how about let's all get there in one piece, okay?"

"What's the matter, Hud for short," says Morey, straining his neck around and enjoying himself. "You're not scared, are you?"

"Me? Hell, no. I'm always this pale. A sickly child, I."

Morey smiles an unfriendly smile at me.

"You don't have a thing to worry about. Joe here drives race cars on weekends."

Joe reacts to this statement of applied fame by hunching even further over the wheel and squinting even more fiercely.

"Yeah, well, they have wrecks, too . . . only at faster speeds. Don't get me wrong. If it were just you guys, I wouldn't be worried. But I keep thinking, this is me sitting in the back seat . . . defenseless."

"Here," says Joe. "Take a swig of this. It'll help you relax."

A silver hip flask flies over the seat toward me. I unscrew the top and taste the stinging pain of whiskey.

"Thanks. A little early in the morning for me, but I'd rather it was me drinking this stuff than you. You just keep a steady eye on the road up there and I'll take care of this, Joe, old boy, old buddy, old friend, old chum."

"Don't worry about me," Joe says, looking back and grinning. "I've got another one."

He pulls a matching flask out from under his jacket, holds it up for proof, unscrews the lid while steering with his elbows, and takes a long swig from it, watering his eyes. Morey and Jim are enjoying themselves, watching me, and then Joe, and then back to me again. I settle back in the seat with the flask. Joe takes another long swig from his flask and then passes it on to Morey. Morey drinks and gives it to Jim. Jim raises the flask in salute to me and takes his turn. I half-smile and salute him back with my flask and take a drink. Then Jim passes the whiskey back to Joe.

"What's the matter, Hud?" Joe says, looking at me through the rearview mirror and smiling. "You don't seem to be in the mood for drinking."

"It's still a little early for me yet," I say. "It's not much later than before."

"Where in particular you heading out West?" Jim asks.

"As far as I can get, I guess. California. I hear there's a lot of interesting stuff happening out there. I'm in no real hurry, though. I've got all the time I want. How about you guys? What's in Utah?"

"Uh, Morey here's got a brother in Utah," he says. "We're taking some of his brother's stuff out to him from Denver. Aren't we, Morey?"

"Huh, huh! Yeah!" Morey laughs, as if he is enjoying a private joke.

"You know what I want to do?" Joe says suddenly. "I want to piss on that sign that marks the Continental Divide. I want to piss all over that sign. And then half my piss will run into the Pacific Ocean and half will run into the Atlantic. And then in no time it will spread to all the oceans of the world. Yeah, I'd like that. I think I'm going to piss all over that sign."

"You do that," Jim says. "You always were a real pisser."

Jim laughs obnoxiously at his own joke, just as all untalented people do to draw attention to their meagre talent. Morey is feeling happy and keeps trying to burst into song, but he gets stuck after the fourth word, and then he takes another swig from the flask to try to jostle his memory.

"Oh, Baby don't you . . . uh. Oh, Baby don't you . . . Hallelujah oh Baby don't you . . . . Hell, what's the song, Jim?"

"Forget it." Jim leans over and switches on the radio.

That's Morey's problem to begin with, however, and he keeps trying to remember under his breath.

"*Oh Baby don't you oh Baby don't you oh Baby don't you . . . .*"

The radio comes on in the middle of the news, but I don't pay any attention to it. I have given up drinking and am watching the passing cliffs and am thinking maybe I can get a little sleep. But the words, "white poodle," suddenly make me pay attention to what the announcer is saying.

"*. . . and in addition to the dog, the predawn burglars reportedly got away with a number of household furnishings, expensive jewels, and clothing. Denver police say the trio forced their way in through the kitchen window, apparently knowing that the owner was away. A neighbor reported the burglary after seeing the three young men leaving the ransacked house in a blue sedan. I'll be back with the weather after this word from our sponsor . . . .*"

Joe is concentrating on his driving, passing cars at every opportunity and driving as if his life depended on it. Morey is still trying to remember his song, and Jim is just staring out the side window. I am suddenly sober.

None of them gives any indication that he heard the radio. They don't even glance at each other. I take another look at all the objects I am sharing the back seat with. *What the hell do I do now?* The dog is carsick and has thrown up quietly on the floor, but at least he has stopped barking. *What the hell do I do now?*

"Say, uh, Joe old boy," I say very jovially but probably not convincingly. "How far's Idaho Springs?"

"About five miles," he answers, turning around to look at me intensely and ignoring the road. "Why?"

"Well, look. If it's all the same with you guys, I'll just get out there, okay? I'm not in quite as big a hurry as you guys apparently are, and I'd kind of like to just take my time, you know, watch the scenery? Anyway, I've got this aunt who lives there, and she's always writing me how whenever I come through, I'm supposed to stop by and say hi. You know, for coffee and cookies and stuff."

Jim slowly turns around and looks at me.

"Yeah?" he says, finally.

I stare back at him.

"Yeah."

He watches me with a slight smirk a few seconds longer, glances fleetingly at the objects in the back seat, and then turns to Joe.

"What do you think, Joe?"

"No skin off my nose. If he wants out, let him out. We're out of here, anyways."

"Hey, why don't we all stop?" Morey says. "I could use some cookies."

Joe saves me the trouble.

"No, that's okay. Remember? We got to get this stuff to your brother in Utah's."

"Oh, yeah."

Jim looks back at me once more and then turns around and stares through the windshield. No one says anything. Morey stops trying to remember his song. He senses that something is going on, and he looks from Joe to Jim, back to Joe, then tries to turn around and look at me. Jim turns off the radio, and the only sound in the car is the whine of the tires over the pavement, squealing occasionally when we take a curve in a racing corner, and the whimpering of the sick dog. My pulse pounds in my throat as I wait.

The highway bypasses Idaho Springs, but Joe pulls into a gas station at the turnoff. Jim gets out, and I push the seat forward in too much of a hurry, shoving Morey into the dashboard.

"Hey!"

"Well, Hud for short," Jim says unsmilingly, "it's too bad you don't want to go on to Utah with us. It could have been kicks."

"Yeah, well, you know how it is, Jim. This, uh, aunt of mine and all."

"Yeah, sure. Your aunt."

"Yeah . . . ."

"Well, so long," he says, getting back into the car. "It's been a slice. Good luck on your trip out West."

"Yeah, thanks. And good luck to you guys, too."

Morey waves as the car spits gravel out behind it and jumps back onto the pavement, then speeds up the road even faster than before. I don't even bother to look at the license-plate number. I just go into the diner next to the service station and order a cup of coffee.

I sit in front of a window, staring out at the highway and the passing cars, and I don't do anything. I sit and I stare and I do nothing.

Too much trouble to report them, anyway, I think.

Besides, I'm in a hurry.

And how do I even know for sure that they're the ones?

Hell, the way they're driving and drinking, they'll probably kill themselves before they get to the Divide, anyway.

Piss on them.

Hell! *I* could have been killed!

Like the time I could have been killed when we sent T.K. to Cleveland.

Rape drove one of the cars and nearly killed us all on the way to Denver. Rape, on top of everything else, had visions of someday becoming a sports-car race driver, and he barreled down the Denver-Boulder turnpike at a hundred miles an hour, yelling, singing, and drinking all the way. We thought nothing of his loony actions at the time, because we were all yelling, singing, and drinking, too.

We found out later that his right front tire was completely bald and could have blown out at any moment. At one hundred miles an hour we would have been smeared all over the highway like bad paint.

At the time, however, we couldn't have cared less.

"Hey, slow down, godammit," T.K. yelled from the back seat.

The top was down, and he kept trying to stand up, but the beer and the wind kept knocking him down, all feet and arms and beer can. This was before fall registration, and we had had a wild woodsie on Flagstaff Mountain and all got bombed out of our minds. After we took the girls back before their curfew and went by the fraternity house for our nightcaps, T.K. started sobbing and slobbering about some girl he had fallen madly in love with over the summer. She was from Cleveland and had gone to summer school at "Dear Old C.U."

"Get the hell up off the floor and pass the pitcher," Rape yelled from behind the couch.

"I don't want to," T.K. sobbed. "I want to see Ophelia."

"*Ophelia, Ophelia, o, how I want to feel ya*," I sang from the top of the piano.

"Shut up!" he yelled.

"All right then," I yelled back, "go and see her! But pass the goddam pitcher up before you go."

Before anyone knew what had happened, we were all at T.K.'s apartment helping him pack.

Rather, packing for him. He sat in a chair with his pitcher of beer stuck between his legs, trying to focus on what was going on around him.

"Hey, what shall I pack?" Bido said.

"One of everything," I yelled.

"Right toe! One of everything. One suitcase. Check! One underwear. Check! One undershirt. Check! One sock. Check! One shoe. Check! One check. Czech!"

"Don't forget a handkerchief," Dayo yelled from the bathroom. T.K.'s in the shower crying again."

"What the hell were you doing in the shower with your clothes on?" I asked T.K.

"I was going to take a shower before seeing Ophelia," he smiled.

"*Ophelia, Ophelia, o, how I want to feel ya,*" Bido sang.

"Shut up!" T.K. sobbed.

"To horse! To horse!" cried Rape, running in the front door. He stepped on the empty pitcher and fell on his face.

"Medic!" he screamed.

"Make up your mind! You want a horse or a medic?" Theo asked.

"Get him a horse doctor!" Dayo yelled.

"Hey!" cried T.K. "What about Ophelia?"

"*Ophelia, Ophelia, o, how I want to feel ya,*" we all sang.

Somehow along the way we acquired eight people for the bon voyage party, and so we took two cars. In all the confusion, however, we managed to take along only one can opener, and we had to pass it back and forth between the cars. The other car would pull up alongside and they would make opening motions for the churchkey, and Rape would nod and the two cars would edge closer together so I could hand the opener over to Murphy in the other car. T.K. claimed that since it was his can opener, he should go along with it to protect his interests, but no one would help him over the side, and he was in no shape to try it by himself.

Kids in the future will have no appreciation for the importance of the invention of the pop-top can. They will take for granted the ease with which they open their virgin beer and soda pop cans, each with its own comfortable ring for sensual penetration. I will still remember fondly how we were limited in our roving and rambling by the finite radius from the can opener—the "churchkey"—and how T.K. always had one on a string around his neck for his oft-occurring emergencies. I will also remember fondly when the first pop-tops entered our world. They were crude, metal tabs that you had to slide your thumb under to force up, and the rough metal edge soon gave you a drinking "badge of honor": cuts and scars criss-crossing the fleshy part of your thumb.

At three o'clock in the morning the airport was pretty empty, so Rape parked right in front and we all went running inside. No flight went straight to Cleveland, but one to Chicago left in thirty minutes. T.K. paid in cash. Otherwise, I doubt if he could have bought a ticket. I spied two stewardesses down the way and ran off chasing them, trying to get a date for the next time they were in town. They must not have liked the idea, however, because they ran into the ladies' room and blocked the door, so I went back to the gang, milling around the ticket counter.

"Hey," Dayo said. "Rape's going, too."

"Yeah, I couldn't stand to see the poor slob go up in his condition. Besides, I've got friends in Chicago. I'm only going that far. Who's going to take care of my wheels?"

"Christ!" Bido said. "This is getting exciting. I wish I could go."

Dayo grabbed me.

"Hud, I just got my check today from my dad. That'll get us to Chicago. Let's go, too."

"Yeah, that'll get us to Chicago, but how the hell do we get back?"

"Who cares? We'll worry about that when we get there. I'll loan you the money. Do you want to go?"

"Why not! Let's go!"

But the ticket seller had other ideas.

"I'm sorry, but I can't accept a two-party check," he said.

Dayo argued with him, trying to convince him that the party was over, but we could all see he was losing the battle. The fact that Dayo was dressed in a coat and tie, shorts, and barefooted didn't help his cause much. So, we resigned ourselves to just sending off Rape and T.K.

"Goodbye, goodbye! Don't forget to write!"

"Have a good time!"

"I'll take real good care of your car, Rape."

"If you don't get back in time, I'll register for you, T.K."

"Get her once for me!"

"It's a going-away party, Miss."

"*Ophelia, Ophelia, o, how we want to feel ya!*"

The plane taxied down the runway and took off into the night, carrying among its ten-odd passengers two of the oddest, both passed out. We waved goodbye once more and headed back to the cars. Just as we stepped out of the building, Murphy tripped and fell on the steps, breaking his glasses in two right at the nose bridge. All the way back to Boulder he kept trying to make the two pieces stay on his ears, saying to each of us in turn, "Hey, I broke my glasses. Hey, Hud, I broke my glasses. Hey, Dayo, I broke my glasses."

"Yeah, Murphy. Shut up."

Murphy had been having such a good time that he forgot to go crazy, like he always did in crowds.

The next day I showed the telegram to Theo and Dayo.

OPHELIA WOULDN'T SEE ME STOP SHE GOT MARRIED TWO DAYS AGO STOP WIRED DAD FOR MONEY STOP SEE YOU SOON I HOPE HELP STOP. T.K.

"Oh, well, easy come, easy go," Theo said.

T.K. was back in Boulder in two days, madly falling in love with the new crop of freshman girls. But Rape didn't show up for another week.

"Well, what did you do?" I asked him.

"Man, I swung."

"Yeah, well, how did you live? Where did you stay?"

"I shacked up with a couple of stewardess chicks who have an apartment right on the lake front. I met them at the airport in Chicago."

I believed him.

"It was beautiful, I kid you not. It was so beautiful I almost decided not to come back. Ever."

I believed him.

FOUR

The time we sent T.K. to Cleveland had been a good drunk

The time we sent T.K. to Cleveland had been a good drunk, all right, but none of the drunk-outs ever matched the ones we had during C.U. Days weekends. This particular weekend would come in the spring, and we would all be continuously drunk from Friday afternoon on, sometimes not sobering up until Monday or Tuesday in class. Murphy got so bombed once, he didn't come out of it until Wednesday in Psychology 101, a lecture to some two or three hundred students. Murphy suddenly reacquired his senses right in the middle of the mass of students, and he went berserk right there, as he always did when he found himself among a lot of people. Murphy wasn't even taking psychology at the time, so he never did figure out how he got there.

The C.U. Days weekend that I remember best was the one in my junior year. That was the weekend Diane and I made it for the first time. That was also the weekend that T.K. and I won the drinking contest at the Sink.

The Sink is a corner drinking establishment on the Hill which does a rousing business every Friday afternoon at Friday Afternoon Club, or F.A.C. for short. After classes every Friday everyone usually goes to either the Sink or Tulagi's, or the Tule for short, another drinking establishment on the Hill, but which is higher class, because it has a designated dance floor. At the Sink you don't try to evade the issue. You just go there to drink.

The place is always packed solid on Fridays anyway, but on the Friday of C.U. Days they stack them in on top of each other. Murphy always had to drink alone on Fridays, because he would have been reduced to a slobbering maniac if he'd tried to go to F.A.C. On the other hand, however, Bido was always there, because the place was so crowded you were forced to come into physical contact with practically everyone within shouting distance. Bido whiled away Friday afternoons drinking beer and squeezing past girls. He didn't particularly care whether he brushed up against their fronts, backs, or sides. "Frontal, backal, and sidal contact," he called it. Just as long as he made contact, he was happy.

The F.A.C. of C.U. Days of my junior year was even more crowded than usual, because of the drinking contest. All week long it had been advertised in the campus newspaper, the *Colorado Daily*. Phi Epsilon Phi, the sophomore men's honorary society, had challenged the Hammers, the junior men's honorary, to a drinking contest to see who were the best drinkers on campus.

By some strange quirk of fate, both T.K. and I happened to be in Hammers, which was enough right there to keep them from being officially recognized by the University. We had gone to the contest only with the intention to watch, cheer, and do a little side drinking on our own. However, the drinking team for the Hammers turned up two short, and T.K. and I were the only ones there who could fill in at post time.

"Christ," T.K. said, "I didn't want to start out C.U. Days *this* serious."

"Shut up," I said. "They're paying for the beer."

The contest consisted of five members on each team facing each other across a wooden picnic table in the back room of the Sink. At the signal to start, an umpire would fill up the nine-ounce cups with beer, and each team member had one minute to down his cup. This would continue for as long as possible, one cup of beer per minute, until only one man was left. When you couldn't go on any longer, you were out. And if you threw up, you were disqualified.

"Hell," T.K. said after dashing off the first one, "this is going to be a cinch. This'll be as smooth as perfect pussy."

"Wait until after about fifteen," I said.

One Hammer went out after only five cups. He had been drinking since noon and couldn't go on any further, he said, but he stayed around to coach us.

"Take the whole minute to drink it," he said. "Sip it slowly. Don't let any air bubbles form in your stomach, or you've had it."

A sizable crowd had gathered and was pressing in around us on all sides. The noise of the onlookers was becoming unbearable, everyone was offering advice, and the heat was rising because of the closeness so that I was developing sticky armpits. I tried to focus my attention only on the Phi Ep directly across from me and on T.K. sitting on my left. At ten cups my Phi Ep dropped out, evening up the sides again.

"You're doing good," the coach said, now drinking from his own beer bottle. "Keep it up."

"Keep it down, you mean," T.K. burped.

At fifteen cups the minute seemed like five seconds. We had a real struggle to get the whole cup down in time. It just wouldn't all pour down the throat, but had to be taken in tiny swallows. Another Hammer couldn't go on, dropping out, and then the Phi Ep across from T.K. couldn't get the seventeenth one to go down his throat. It all ran out the sides of his mouth and down his shirt while he desperately tried to swallow, but just couldn't, and he was disqualified.

By the time we hit twenty cups, T.K. and I were the only Hammers left, and three Phi Eps were still hanging in. The judges let us stop after the twentieth cup for five minutes to make a head call.

"I don't think I can go on any longer, Hud," T.K. wailed in the toilet. "I'm sure I've filled my stomach all the way up to the back of my throat."

"Then empty it," I said. "And then you can fill it back up again. That's what we're here for."

When we resumed the contest, only two Phi Eps were left. The other one had passed out when he stood up, falling backwards head first over the bench.

"Two to two," I said to T.K. "We can take them."

One Phi Ep dropped out after twenty-three cups, and the other one was looking green. I wasn't feeling so well, myself. I had a tremendous need to belch, and I knew that if I didn't, I wouldn't be able to last much longer.

Finally, at twenty-six cups, the last Phi Ep spewed his beer onto the table, and the Hammers were the winners. We were the best drinkers on campus, two to none.

But the crowd wanted us to go on. They wanted a single winner.

"I'm game if you are," T.K. moaned.

"I'll drink you under the table, you bastard."

I could just barely get the twenty-seventh down within the minute limit, and the question was moot as to whether or not it would stay down. The beer trickled around my lips inside my closed mouth, and I could barely swallow. My mouth was salivating like crazy, and I had to lower my head down to the edge of the table.

"He's throwing up! He's throwing up!" someone yelled.

"No, he's not," my coach said. "He's just spitting."

I brought up a huge, healthy, wet belch from out of the bowels of my stomach, clearing out all the air inside and settling the beer to the bottom, leaving plenty of space for more on top of it. I felt great now and could go on for at least another ten.

"Come on, you drunk bastard," I said to T.K. "Drink up."

At the end of twenty-nine cups of beer, T.K. couldn't keep the last one down. He had a sickly look on his face as he tried to force his mouth closed, but the beer slowly came back up all over the table and down his shirt.

"The winner!" my coach said, lifting my arm up in the air.

"Hooray! Hooray!" the crowd cheered and immediately dissipated.

"Are you okay, T.K.?"

"Hell, yes. Let's get back to the fraternity house and get something to eat."

We helped each other up and weaved our way through the throng of people, many of whom hadn't even been aware of the contest in the see-what-the-boys-in-the-back-room-will-have. Once outside, the going proved to be tougher, because we didn't have the crowd of people to guide us and hold us up by the mere presence of their congested bodies. We managed to stagger less than a block before T.K. fell down, pulling me on top of him by my arm. I climbed up by using the side of a men's clothing store, pulled T.K. up after me, and he immediately walked into the side of the building.

"All right," I said. "We're too drunk to walk. Let's ride."

"Are you kidding? We don't even have a car."

"No problem," I replied, and I stepped out into Broadway and hailed a passing Volkswagen. I raised my arm into the air as I stood right in front of it, and the VW screeched to a skidding halt just inches from my ankles. The driver was a somewhat surprised, confused young woman.

"What the hell? You guys trying to get killed or something?" she asked as we climbed in, T.K. sitting on my lap in the front seat.

"No, I want to confess," I said. "We're too drunk to walk, and we would humbly request a ride."

"How far are you going?"

"Five blocks," I said.

Five blocks later she dropped us off in front of the fraternity house. T.K. and I made it just in time for the dinner bell, sliding in through the dining-room doors and slipping into our seats under the watchful eye of the housemother. Dinner was shrimp, and we ate shrimps to our little hearts' contents, excusing ourselves every now and then to make a head call.

In years to come, the Sink will change into Herbie's Deli, because drugs, street people, fern bars, and revised liquor laws will cause the owner to close down and remodel the college hangout that sold more bottles of beer in the early Sixties than any other bar in America—700 cases on a typical Friday Afternoon Club. When you went into this new family bar, you missed the carved-up wooden tables, the wall murals with the busty women caricatures, the ceilings blackened by candles, the red heating pipes, the employees yelling "Watch your feet!" as they rolled kegs of 3.2 beer from the back to the front, the loud music drowning out calm conversation, but most of all you missed the Sink Burgers and the famous Hickory Sauce.

Hooray! The Sink will be back!

In more years to come, Herbie's Deli will change back into the Sink as nostalgia and two grown-up sons will cause the owner to close down and demodel the okay yuppie but not-quite-your-college-bitchin' hangout. The barn wood nailed over the surrealist caricatures will come down. The artist will be called back from California to restore what needs to be restored, and he will add a caricature of Robert Redford, rumored to have worked in the Sink during his brief stay at C.U. The carved-up table tops will be back, except for the ones that were sold for $15 apiece when the original Sink was closed. But the 3.2 beer will not be back, nor will the 18-year-old college drinkers, because Boulder will grow up with the rest of America, only much more slowly. Boulder will always believe *You can't have your beer and drink it, too.*

Tulagi's will try to break that belief in the Sixties and will sell more draft beer than anywhere else in America, until Boulder tries to grow up and repeals prohibition in 1968, which allows bars to serve hard liquor inside the city limits.

The Sink. Tulagi's. Known all over America. If you're a college kid.

That night I had a date with Diane, and since the dog track had just opened for the season and she had never been to the races, she pleaded and begged me to take her. I didn't particularly want to leave Boulder during C.U. Days, because something might happen that I didn't want to miss.

But she gave me that pleading look that girls can do so well, and we went to the races. Even though it was her first time, she won more money than I did just by picking dogs that looked cute to her, whereas I studied the records and the dogs' past races and compared weights and owners and bet a quiniela every race by baseballing three dogs. But I didn't hold Diane's beating me against her, because she said she would pay for something to eat after we got back to Boulder. We arrived about eleven, and by that time the riot had pretty much quieted down.

The noise was still loud—we could hear the rumbling undercurrent of the milling mob two blocks away and couldn't figure out what it was—and a large crowd of people were still left in the main block of the Hill.

The police had closed off both ends of the block and were just observing, standing behind their cars which were parked across the intersections. Occasionally a beer can would come flying through the darkness at them, but they just ignored it. They didn't want to cause any more trouble.

All the buildings were closed and dark, even Tulagi's—which was unusual. We learned that earlier the Tule had been so crowded that no one could get in or out. A mobile unit had parked on the street and started playing dance music for the crowd of people who were outside and couldn't get inside. Then the street had become too crowded with dancers and drunks, and the riot had naturally ensued.

Once it got started, they locked the front door of Tulagi's, so no one could *really* get in or out. Bido had just started in with his date, and she had made it in, but he got separated from her and didn't make it before they locked the door. He could watch her through the front window, but that was as close as they got until the door was unlocked again. But by that time most of the fun was over.

When we arrived, quite a large number of people were still around who were trying to keep the thing going, but we could tell that the climax had been reached and passed. A few students were also passed out in the middle of the street. One white girl, notorious for her campus-wide sexual escapades, was locked in the arms of two black football players on the curb, all of them passed out.

"Hell," I said, "we missed all the fun."

The next morning I went to pick up Diane early, because for the occasion of C.U. Days the Sink and the Tule opened at 5 a.m., and I wanted to get an early start.

Diane had taken an overnight and had signed out to Gaga's house. Gaga lived at home with her mother, not far from the campus. I knocked on the door, but no one answered. So I went in.

Diane was apparently in the bathroom and hadn't heard me at the door. No one else seemed to be home. So, being a great one for practical jokes, I decided to hide in Gaga's closet and surprise Diane when she came back into the bedroom.

I hid among all the dresses and shoes and sweaters and slacks, and I tried to keep the hangers from banging against each other. I waited about five minutes, and the place was becoming insufferably hot. *God*, I thought, *is this all worth it? Hurry up and come out of the damn bathroom!*

I heard the door of the bathroom open as someone came out. Then the bedroom door opened and closed.

Just as I was about to throw open the door and jump out and say *Boo!* and scare the living daylights out of her and then laugh and comfort her in my arms and see how far I could get, the door opened suddenly and I blinked, and Diane screamed and jumped, and then stood there saying, "Oh! Oh! Oh!"

She had been taking a shower and all she had on was a man's white shirt, which now clung to her still wet body, becoming transparent where it was wet. I was almost as surprised as she was.

"Oh, Hud! You scared me to death."

Then she clung to me, putting her arms around me, trying to calm down. I didn't mind the wetness and started patting her back, slowly moving my hand down to her well-turned bare rump, which I could see in the mirror behind her, peeping out at me below her shirt.

"My god!" she cried, suddenly remembering how she was dressed. "What are you doing here? Get out of here and let me get dressed!"

She stood back and pulled the shirt down with both hands, trying to hide her femininity, but only causing the shirt to stretch even tighter across her wet breasts.

I smiled at her.

"Surprise, surprise," and I started walking toward her, grinning even larger, with my hands held out in front of me like giant grabbers.

"Now, Hud," she warned me, backing away. "You know what I believe. You might as well just go into the living room right now and let me get dressed."

She didn't sound convincing to me at all. At least I couldn't allow myself to be stopped with that weak defense. She backed around the bed and I slowly pursued her.

"What's the matter, Diane," I said playfully. "I just want to kiss you hello."

"Yes," she laughed nervously. "Hello and a lot of other things."

I had her trapped up against the bed. The only way she could escape me was to jump over the bed or out the window.

"Now, stop it, Hud," she said, almost pleading.

I stalked up to her and slowly put my arms around her. I kissed her gently on the neck and felt the wetness of her breasts and the shirt against my chest.

"This isn't going to do you any good, Hud," she whispered, the forcefulness slowly escaping from her words.

She reluctantly kissed me back and then put her arms around my neck. She rubbed her body sensuously against my surprised and stirring groin.

"Oh, Hud . . . ."

We didn't have any trouble at all falling back onto the bed, and we made love for the very first time.

That was the day we all lost our innocence.

FIVE

The cafe's walls are decorated with gayly colored posters

The cafe's walls are decorated with gayly colored posters advertising the various ski resorts in the area. The bronzed, blond snow gods smile and glare and grimace into the piercing sun as they swoop down the slopes, and the delicious snow bunnies flash sparkling teeth as they stretch their taut trousers and sleek sweaters to the stretching point. Sex is poured over the mountains and dripped down the slopes like topping on a sundae. The sad part about the posters, however, is that no one in the cafe pays any attention to them. The few people besides myself in this twentieth century's answer to the roadside inn sit and stare into their coffee cups or else carry on half-hearted conversations with the waitress and their tablemates. But, then, they aren't the types to be interested in skiing, anyway. They are the types to be pumping the gas, splashing the coffee, and cleaning the rooms where all the skiers spend their time between slopes. To these locals, skiing holds no glamour. Or, perhaps, because they live right here among the skiing areas full time, they know how phony the posters are. The brightly colored paper holds no attraction for them.

Skiing will become a major booming tourist industry in Colorado, however. Future Olympic champions will come from here. A President's widow and her children will vacation here. A future President will build a second home here and spend his winter vacations skiing and his summer vacations wrecking havoc on the golf courses. A back-yard winter Olympics will even be turned down.

The price of equipment and lift tickets will reach heights unimaginable in 1963. The sport will become the leisure activity of the rich, the famous, and the carefree young. Tragedy will occasionally shake us out of our numbed reality when we will read about first-time skiers slamming into a tree and being knocked stone-cold dead or about experienced skiers getting caught in spring-time avalanches and being lost until the summer thaws or about unfortunate passengers being unlucky enough to be riding in a gondola that decides to snap its cables and spill its riders onto the rocks and snow and trees up and down the line.

Lawsuits will spring up over who is at fault for tragic and stupid accidents: the skier, the ski manufacturer, the other skier, the ski-lift-equipment manufacturer, the ski resort, the land owner, the U.S. Government, the gods, the Furies, the Fates, the Russians, the Arabs, the Texans. Reckless skiing will become a crime. What next? Reckless reading?

And future arguments will occupy future avid skiers' attention as they choose up sides and debate the merits, benefits, cost, freedom, peace, exercise, and beauty of downhill skiing versus cross-country skiing. Future flatlanders will even intrude in the state and dirty the snows by referring to their favorite water sport as "skiing" when in fact they mean water skiing. Fashions will change. The equipment will change. The slopes will change. The most popular resorts will change. Fashions will change back again. We will change.

I step out into the sunshine, ready to face the world once again. I figure my best bet is to hang around the gas station and ask the travelers who stop for fuel if they would mind taking me in the direction of Grand Junction. Asking them outright might get me a ride quicker than relying on the standard hitchhiker pose, trying to look unobtrusively obtrusive with my thumb sticking out like a sore thumb. I doubt if many people are asked outright for a ride from a hitchhiker, because you usually see them standing along the highway like a reminder of something you are trying to forget. And they embarrass you when they run up to the car after you have decided to pick them up and have stopped fifty yards beyond them. Personally, I never pick up hitchhikers unless they're female, young, and pretty. Because you can never tell *where* they have been.

Besides, hitchhiking in Colorado is illegal if you're standing in a roadway.

The first couple of cars don't pan out. Well, he'd like to, but he isn't going in that direction, one fellow says. And, sorry, but he makes a practice of never assisting panhandlers, another one says, and me without a pan to be seen on me. How did the original guys who handled pans get such a bad reputation? What did they do to get themselves so infamously immortalized? And what does panhandling have to do with hitchhiking, anyway?

Eventually a young, friendly lonely man offers to give me a lift. He's a traveling salesman for a blue-jean company, and he is going all the way to Grand Junction. He says he is happy to give me a ride.

"Sure, there's some pretty lonely stretches between here and the Junction. Be glad to have someone along I can talk to. Name's Johnson. Fred Johnson."

"Glad to meet you. Hud Holyoke." Extended hands. "I really appreciate the lift."

"Quite all right. Man in my business gets plenty tired of traveling alone. Good to have someone along to shoot the bull with for a change. Grand Junction your home?"

"No, just passing through. I'm headed for California, actually."

"California, huh? Real nice out there, so they say. You live out there?"

"No. I've never been there before. Thought I'd just go out and see it for myself. I hear there's a lot happening out there."

"Yeah? Kind of a long trip for someone with no suitcase. You're not running from anyone, are you?"

He laughs to show that he is just joking, but his eyes hold a nervous prisoner who thinks—just possibly—that maybe I really am running from something, and the frightened captive of the eyes doesn't know what he is going to do if I start any trouble.

"No, not that I know of. Not yet, anyway. All my stuff's back in Boulder. I go to school there. At least, I did. I thought I'd take about a month off and just bum around for a while. You know, sort of straighten things out in my mind. Kind of a sabbatical, maybe."

"Oh, I see," he says, relaxing again. "'Get your head straight,' as you kids say, right? Been having a little trouble with the grades, huh? Well, it's good to get away from things once in a while, but, you know, leaving school certainly won't bring them back up again."

Why not? Let him believe what he wants to. If he thinks it was grades—fine. Makes no difference to me. Don't make me no nevermind, neither.

"You're still traveling a little light to be bumming around for a month, though, aren't you?"

"Oh, I don't know. Bums don't carry much with them, do they? I've never seen a tramp with a suitcase."

"Yeah, I guess you're right. . . . Went to school around that area back there, myself. School of Mines, in Golden. Was going to be a big engineer, you know? Was going to build big bridges . . . big buildings. Ha! Here I am peddling blue jeans around the state to fat-assed store managers."

"Say," I say, "have you ever run into that farmer's daughter?"

I just want to change the subject. I don't want to talk about school. I don't want to start remembering again.

"Jesus, you must be the umpteenth person to ask me that," he says. But he enjoys the joke. "I've never had the chance, actually. Ha! My car never broke down!"

"Then you ought to break it down yourself," I say. "Around some lonely farmhouse. Just to see what happens."

"Well, I did stop alongside the road once to smash in my windshield for the insurance. Had a pit in it that I didn't like, so I stopped and hefted a good-sized rock into it to claim that some other car did it. Ha! Almost smashed in the whole damn windshield! The claims adjustor looked at me a little suspiciously, but I'd always given him good business, so what the heck did he care. Anyway, to get back to your lonely farmer's daughter, figure I'm just a little too old for that, anyway," he says sadly. "Besides," he winks, "don't think the little lady would like it."

So, what's the problem with that, I think. *Do you tell her every time you look up a pretty girl's dress or try to catch a glance at a sneaky nipple?* Some people make all their own problems and don't even know it.

"Ever do any skiing?" he asks.

His turn to change the subject.

"Yeah, I've been skiing, some. I'm not a racer or anything, but I can manage to come down the slope without falling down. Why?"

"Company's just coming out with some ski togs. A little variation in the line, you know? Never been skiing, myself. Lived in Colorado all my life and never been skiing. Actually, I've never been too hot to try it. Too easy to break a leg. That right?"

"Sure, it's easy. It's easy to drown in the bathtub, too. It's all in knowing how."

"Yeah, I guess you're right," he laughs once. "Oh, well, it's too expensive for me, anyway. Ha! Even after getting a discount on all the ski clothes.

The wheels drum a drowsy tune on the lonesome road ("*Look down, look down . . .*"), and the wind whistles wearily through the partially opened window. We are climbing toward the clouds.

"This Vail area we're coming to is getting to be a pretty good place to ski," I say.

"Yeah, and a pretty good place to get stranded, too. Almost had to spend a night in my car around here one time last winter. Couldn't get over the pass. Looked easy, too. Lucky for me a guy came along in a jeep. I'd slid right off the road into a ditch. Charged me ten bucks, but it was better than sleeping there for nothing."

"Winter driving can get pretty dangerous, all right," I say. "I almost got stranded around here once, myself."

Last semester break a year ago. Dayo, Gaga, Robin, and I had gone skiing at Breckenridge. Robin was one of the cute young things I was going with at the time. The skiing hadn't been too good, because the sun never came out and snow kept falling intermittently all day. The wind gathered up the cold from the frozen snow and tried to blow it down our throats in order to freeze our lungs. We could make only one, maybe two runs before having to dash into the lodge for a hot buttered rum and sit by the fire to thaw out, before venturing out to try another run or two. We finally gave up around three o'clock and started back to Boulder, just as the snow began to fall harder. Gaga had gotten permission to use her mother's car, and Dayo was driving the cold convertible with the wind whipping through the top.

The highway stayed clear at first, a black, wet, shiny ribbon laid across the soft white expanse of mountains, and we thought we might be able to get home without any trouble. However, just before the darkness finally kicked aside the last patchy remnants of steel-gray daylight, the snow came down even harder and the road became slippier as the suicidal snow started sticking to the surface of the highway. Dayo knew what he was doing, though, and we continually passed other cars that were struggling wearily up the pass, spinning snow out behind their back tires in twin rooster tails, sometimes sliding off to the side. Other cars had given up the struggle and were stopped in the middle of the highway to let their drivers curse and put on snow chains.

"What do you think, Dayo?" I asked.

"Well, if it doesn't get too much worse, it'll stay about the same, unless it gets better. No, actually, it's not too bad yet, if you drive carefully. However, Loveland Pass is what we've got to worry about."

Then we came to a highway patrolman standing in the middle of the road like an animated snowman, signaling all the cars into a gas station at the side of the highway.

"I'll find out," I said, struggling out into the snowstorm, fighting my way through wet dunes of snow being formed around the gas station, millions of crystals being swept furiously across the highway by the storm's windy broom.

"Well, what's the story?" Dayo asked when I jumped back inside the car again. I realized how cold it was inside the convertible. Almost as cold as it was outside.

"Not good at all," I said, knocking my hands together to get some warmth back into them. "Loveland Pass is closed. They had a big snow slide there about an hour ago. It caught a car, they think. Anyway, the pass is closed and will be, he says, until at least tomorrow morning."

"Oh, no," Robin said. "What are we going to do? I have to register tomorrow."

"So do I," Gaga said. "And my mother will be worried to death about me if I don't come home tonight. With the car."

"Isn't there any other way to get back to Boulder?" Robin asked.

"Yeah. The cop said there's one way we can try. We can go back to Breckenridge and catch the road there that goes over Hoosier Pass. Then—."

"*Hoosier* Pass? I never heard of it," Dayo said.

"Me, neither, but the cop says it's there. He said we can get over Hoosier Pass—he doesn't think it's closed yet—and catch Highway 285, which will take us into Denver. It's a mought out of the way, and a bit extra longer, but that's about all we can do outside of spending the night around here someplace."

"Well," Dayo said, "I guess we might as well try it. Hoosier Pass, here we come."

"Why is it named Hoosier Pass, I wonder?" Robin said.

"There used to be a lot of Indians around here," Dayo said.

Eventually we found the road that took off to the south over Hoosier Pass. The snow was still falling heavily, and the driving was becoming more difficult.

"Oh, great!"

"What's the matter?" I asked.

"The road just ended," Dayo muttered.

"What? What do you mean, 'the road just ended'?"

"Well, the pavement just ended. Same thing, I guess. We're on a dirt road. No wonder I've never heard of Hoosier Pass. Hang on, Gang, this is going to be an experience worth remembering. If we survive it."

"Oh, I wish you hadn't said that," Gaga said.

Dayo was a bit nervous, himself, because he was driving someone else's car, and the driving really was getting difficult. I settled back with Robin in the back seat and decided to enjoy the ride.

Of course, in years to come, carefree college skiers won't have the same problem. The Eisenhower Memorial Tunnel will make Loveland Pass virtually obsolete, and whenever the pass is closed because of "inclement weather situations," the returning cars full of merry but weary skiers will be able to zip right underneath the mountains in sterile, dry comfort. Then, however, irony of ironies, occasionally the tunnel will be closed because of icy road conditions at the mouth of the tunnel and too many automobiles jamming the highway and too many accidents stopping the traffic, and sometimes the fastest way back to Boulder and Denver will be to go over Loveland Pass. Ironic, no?

Even though the tunnel will suit future generations too busy and too always in a hurry, Loveland Pass will stand silent, defiant, and melancholy, brooding as though accused of some mysterious, unforgivable sin in its past, unable to deny any legends of wildness, evil, and debauchery that might have grown up about its name. If the pass were a man, it would be a poet, much admired by women and involved in several intrigues before marriage and promiscuous even after marriage, even though he would be short as mountains go, somewhat stout, and extremely slow of foot. The heroes of his poems would be swashbuckling brigands who perform heroic feats, and his satires would answer his attackers, expressing his sardonic opinions of people and events. Byronic, yes?

"It's really beginning to come down hard, isn't it?" Gaga said.

Robin balanced on the edge of the seat with her hands on the back of the front seat, peering over Gaga's shoulder at the snowflakes hurling themselves to their death into the windshield. Dayo had to slow down to twenty miles an hour, and he had to keep the headlights dimmed, because the brights were reflected too much by the silent, furious flakes.

"Do you think we'll make it?" Robin asked.

"Oh, sure. Assuredly sure," Dayo said. "There's nothing to worry about. We'll just get home a little later than we had planned, that's all."

He started humming and then whistling an obscure, off-key tune in an attempt to reassure the girls that we had nothing to worry about, that we would just get home a little later than we had planned, that's all.

"You know, Dayo," I said, "I used to wish *I* could whistle. Now I wish *you* could. Hey," I said to Robin, "how about worrying about me a little bit?"

"Why?" she asked, turning to look at me.

"I'm lonely."

"Oh, Hud. How can you act that way at a time like this?"

"At a time like this? What's the matter? Haven't you ever been in a snowstorm before? We don't have a damn thing to worry about! All you have to do is drive carefully, make sure you keep a steady pace, watch out for the other idiots driving on the road . . . and then pray a lot, because everything is all a matter of chance, anyway."

"I wish we were home," Gaga said in a tiny voice. "Wouldn't it be just awful if we got stuck and had to spend the night out here?"

"Oh, I don't know," I said, looking at Robin, smiling, thinking about her, naked. "What about you, Dayo?"

"Don't bother me," he said in mock anger. "I'm driving."

The snow was coming down so thick now that Dayo really did have to give all his attention to driving. You couldn't see ten feet in front of the car, and the mocking snow had completely obliterated all marks of the highway. Dayo had to steer by what looked to be the general depression that was the road, trying to keep the correct distance between the pines on both sides. He had to be extremely careful not to go into a slide, because if we went off the road, we would never be able to get back on it again, even if we found it.

"Come on," I said to Robin gently, pulling her back toward me. "You can't help by watching. Forget it and enjoy the ride. Besides, this will take your mind off it."

"Oh, Hud, stop it. I never know when you're serious and when you're joking. How can you be so unconcerned? I'm simply a nervous wreck. Dayo must be, too."

"Yeah," I said. "Rivers are coming out of his armpits. Isn't that right, Dayo?"

"Don't bother me," he said. "I'm driving."

"And you really don't have to worry about a thing," I said to Robin. "I'm keeping my eye out for cabins to spend the night in if we get stuck."

"Oh, sure," she said. "That's a big help."

"I'm scared," Gaga said.

"Hey," Dayo said. "We're not alone. There's another car coming up behind us."

The darkness was complete now, and we could see the headlights of the car behind us making stabs of light through the snow. They gave us a relieved feeling, knowing we were not alone in this unpopulated, lonely area. The car began catching up with us.

Dayo watched them in the rearview mirror. "I don't see how they can be driving so fast. It's kind of dangerous, if you ask me."

We couldn't make out what kind of car it was, but it was obviously going to catch us soon. This was strange, because Dayo was no timid driver, and he was driving faster than the average driver would have dared under the same conditions.

"The stupid idiot's trying to pass us."

Dayo slowed down as much as he dared and pulled closer to the right of the road to let the car pass. It immediately picked up more speed and passed us on the left, fishtailing a bit as it went by, showing us three young men in it. As it pulled in front of us, we could make out the Texas license plates on the car, half covered by the snow.

"Stupid bastard Texans," I said. "Wouldn't you know they would be some touristy, loudmouthed Texans. They've probably never even *seen* snow before, much less driven in it. Don't know what the hell they're doing."

Although no one said anything, we all wanted to keep the other car in sight for the feeling of security it gave us. Dayo tried to keep up without endangering ourselves, but soon the other car's taillights winked around a curve, and when we reached that same curve we couldn't see them ahead of us anymore. The frightful feeling of cold aloneness settled over the car.

"I don't suppose we can get anything on the radio up here, can we?" Gaga asked.

"I doubt it," Dayo said. "Too high up and too many mountains. You might try, though."

Gaga spent the next few minutes fiddling with the radio dial, but all she could get was static. Once we heard the brief snatches of a song, but that subdued and faded away. Not even KOMA in Oklahoma City could come in on a night like this.

Robin finally settled back and allowed me to put my arm around her—but just to keep her warm. She was in no mood to snuggle, and after having my advances consistently resisted, I finally gave up and lost all the desire I had had before.

The snow continued to fall heavily, and the headlights tried to shine their way through the mass of flakes, which piled up on the windshield forming sides to the tunnels created by the wipers. Through the side windows, we couldn't see anything. Occasionally the headlights would reveal lonely frozen pines alongside the road, silently watching us struggle through their domain. But through the side windows all we could see was the black covering of night.

"Holy cow!" Dayo said.

"What?"

"Look up ahead."

The faint headlights of a car were glowing ahead of us. But they were stationary and pointed upwards toward the mountain, not in the direction they should have been.

"Those damn fool Texans have run off the road," I said. "Served the bastards right."

"Oh, no," Robin said. "Maybe they're hurt. We'll have to help them."

"Ha!" I laughed. "You're out of your mind. *I'm* not getting out of this car to help them. The way they were driving, they deserve to run off the road."

"Hud! How can you say that?"

"Watch my lips. It's easy. Besides, what difference does it make to you? *You* won't be getting out of the car. Drive on, Dayo."

"I don't know, Hud," he said. "Don't you think we should see if we can help?"

"Nope."

We could see the car now, and all three men were trying to push the car back onto the road. The driver had misjudged a curve and slid off. The dirt on the road behind the wheels showed they had tried to back onto the highway, but they had succeeded only in getting stucker. The driver had the door open and was trying to help by pushing on the frame and keeping his other hand on the steering wheel. They saw us and began to wave desperately.

"If you stop, Dayo, we may never get started again."

Robin pushed my arm away. "Hud, you are absolutely inhumane."

"I think we'd better give them a hand," Dayo said.

I clapped, but nobody except me appreciated the joke. Dayo slowed the car carefully, gently pumping the brakes, but even so we slid about one foot sideways for every five feet we went forward. Eventually we came to a stop about ten feet past the other car. Dayo and I got out, I reluctantly.

The wind immediately whipped the breath out of me, and the snowflakes stung into my face. The hood of my parka wouldn't stay over my head, because the wind kept ripping it off. We plowed back through the ankle-high snow to the three guys.

"Sure glad you came along," one of them said. "If you can just give us a little help, we can get this out right away."

"Yeah, sure," I muttered.

With the five of us pushing, we managed to get the car back on the road in the right direction. All of us were completely, wetly, and frozenly covered in snow, I had also slipped, and my right leg had gone into the ditch up to my crotch. After saying goodbye goodbye and you're welcome (motherfuckers), Dayo and I raced back to the car like rampaging snowplows and jumped in.

"Jesus Christ on a crutch!" I yelled. "It's colder than a witch's tit on the dark side of the moon out there! And twice as windy! And I had to fall in a damn ditch and get myself all wet. And all for a bunch of damn stupid loud-mouthed, fast-driving Texans."

"Brothers and sisters," Dayo said, "let us all get the flock out of here and get home to some hot coffee and warm beds."

"Here! Here!" I said, and I added, "I take it, you mean to our own separate, but equal, beds?"

"Are there any other kinds?" Dayo grinned, looking back at me.

"I'm beginning to wonder," Gaga said, in mock disgust.

With careful nudging, Dayo managed to get us moving again without sliding off the road, ourselves. The car slowly picked up speed and we all settled back somewhat. I was beginning to thaw and dry out and was even thinking of trying to sleep, if Robin would hold my head in her lap.

"What's the matter with those guys?" Dayo said.

I looked out the back window, which was now almost completely covered with snow. But I could make out the headlights of the Texans' car, and from the way they were acting, I could tell that the driver was trying to gather up enough speed to pass us again.

"What's the matter?" Gaga asked.

"Those damn bastards won't ever give up," I said.

Dayo slowed down and edged over toward the right again. The Texans came slipping and sliding past, their wheels skidding and throwing up snow as the driver tried to gun the car past us. The maneuver was dangerous and stupid, because their car could easily slide sideways into ours and knock us both off the road.

No one breathed as we watched them slowly gain ahead of us in the darkness. The Texans all waved merrily at us as they passed—including the driver—and I gave them the finger as they managed to get ahead of us and then eventually pulled in front.

"Look," I said. "I don't give a damn if they crack up and they're all broken and bleeding and dying inside. I'll be damned if I'm going to get out of this car again to help them get back on the road out of some ditch. I wouldn't even do it if they paid me. That does it and that's final."

"Well, they do seem a little foolhardy," Robin said.

"Crazy idiots," I muttered, as we watched the car disappear in front of us.

No one said anything else after that all the way to Highway 285. We never saw the car from Texas again. I hoped that they had gone off a cliff somewhere and we had missed them.

We were all relieved to enter whatever town was at the junction of Highway 285, and from there on we had paved highways all the way into Denver. The roads were still bad, but more cars were on them, and we weren't in any danger of being stranded. Just outside Denver, the roads cleared up—snow wasn't even falling hard there. We got back to Boulder forty-five minutes after that.

SIX

*Robin never forgave me for the way she said
I had acted*

Robin never forgave me for the way she said I had acted during that episode, and she wouldn't go out with me anymore after that. That was okay by me, because she wouldn't go down for me, either, and I was tired of taking her out, anyway. Perhaps I was getting tired of everything, because everything seemed to be the same old same old thing every other day. Nothing was new; nothing was different. Powerful word, that: nothing.

Except for the spring vacation right after that episode, when Theo and a new girl, Patti, and I spent two nights in Denver in a fleabag hotel on Larimer Street.

Everyone else was going somewhere for spring vacation. T.K. was going home to Colorado Springs; Gaga was visiting a sister in San Francisco; Dayo was going to the Bahamas; Rape was going to Mexico.

Everyone was going someplace except for Theo and Patti and me. We were too broke to go anywhere exotic, and we didn't want to go home. So, we decided that we would bum it for the week—I mean, *really* bum it. We got some old clothes from the Salvation Army store, we didn't take any baths, and we let our hair grow as long as it could in the two weeks of preparation. Theo and I didn't shave, and Patti even stopped shaving her legs and underarms, which was a disappointment to Theo and me, because we were kind of looking forward to seeing how a woman actually did that. Everyone thought we were crazy, especially when we refused to explain our strange, new, natural, no-additives-whatsoever appearances.

When the day of the big adventure came, we took Theo's car to Denver and parked it where it would be safe. Then we just wandered around Larimer and Market Streets, scrounging meals, sampling homemade wine, digging through trash cans, and having a grand old time "living off the land."

Theo and I wanted to try sleeping out on the sidewalks at night, but Patti wouldn't have anything to do with that, and she refused to stay in a flophouse all by herself. So, we would stay up as late as we could "being cool" and then finally crash and spend the night in a fleabag hotel for fifty cents apiece. We talked the crippled old desk clerk into letting Patti stay in the same room with us, because, as we told the decrepit old codger, she would go crazy and throw a fit when she couldn't be near us, and he certainly didn't want the police to be called, did he? Patti then rolled her eyes and drooled a bit for the effect. The old guy was leery of—and at—her, but he finally let her stay with us. What the hell did he care, anyway?

In a few short years to come, this kind of talk will sound ridiculous, because who will care who stays with whom and what sex who is and who has with whom and who used to be and is going to be. But in those days people still cared and thought they had morality and thought it was their duty to make sure that men and women were married when they stayed together in a hotel, motel, or do-tell, especially when they were as young as we were, and what was going on here with two guys and a girl anyway, even if this was Larimer Street.

And, then, in a few short years after that, everything new will be old again, and the disturbing thing will not be that a guy and a girl want to spend the night together, but that two guys do. That old devil Mr. Morality will raise his ugly head again and think it is not only his Business but also his bounding Duty to make sure that everything he comes in contact with is on the same up-and-up strict smooth-pants, praise God, thank-you Jesus level of secret-smirking hypocritical, do-what-I-say not see-what-I-do ugliness. Our so-called "respectable" religious leaders will get caught with their pants down and their hands in the nookie jar. What goes around comes around, but if it just came around sooner and more often, maybe we could recognize it for what it really is, rise above it, and lead more decent, sensible, forgiving lives.

The bed was a riot, lumpy and sagging in the middle, and we had to sleep in it sideways so we could all fit. Even so, we still tended to roll toward the middle, which happened to be Patti. She objected at first, mainly, I think, because she was supposed to be going with me. But after I assured her that I really didn't mind and the idea even excited me, she got excited, too, and she agreed to do it, and Theo and I took turns, while the other one tickled her nose and her ass, and a pretty little ass it was. Then when we all got tired and Theo and I couldn't do it anymore, we went to sleep in everybody's arms, and from then on Theo and I always agreed, next to a beautiful woman, sleep is the most wonderful thing in the world.

The funny thing is, however, that after only two days of our carefree, irresponsible, free-love, slogan-filled, unwashed noble experiment, we started to smell, we longed for some real food, we wanted people to look at us with respect and without prejudice for a change, and we wanted to stop the embarrassment of having to ask for spare change. We had had enough, and we returned to the real world of Boulder, baths, and store-bought beer.

So when the others came back to school with their stories of vacation, we also had a story to tell, and in most cases, our story outdid their tales of San Francisco, the Bahamas, and everywhere else someone had gone, especially after we embellished ours a bit and extended it beyond the embarrassing, barely bearable two days. They all thought it was great, and they were all envious.

"I don't believe you," Rape said.

I looked back at him across the table.

"For Christ's sake, Rape, do you think we would make this all up?"

"Yes, I think you would. I think the three of you got together and cooked up the whole damn story."

We were all crowded around a table at the Gondolier, the first time after spring break that all of us had been able to get together and compare vacations, also the first time that Theo, Patti, and I had gotten together after getting clean and haircuts.

Patti looked at him with those big blue eyes of hers, tilted her head just so, and said, "Rape, you don't think I would lie to you, do you?"

What could he do? He looked down into his coffee and muttered, "Well, it just sounds too far out. It sounds crazy and it sounds great, but it just sounds too far out to be true. I wish I could have been with you guys. You must have had a blast."

Rape's real name wasn't Rape. It was either Edmund, or Edgar, or some other ugly E-name, no one knew for sure what, nor cared. Sometimes Rape himself seemed as if he had to stop and remember what his real name was, but that was just for effect, because he liked the name Rape. He considered himself a symbol—a living finger shoved up into the face of the world—letting everyone know just what he thought of the whole damn mess called Life.

That's Life.
What's Life?
A magazine.

How much does it cost?
A dime.
I've only got a nickle.
That's life.

Rape's mother had never been married. When she was eighteen or nineteen, she had been attacked by a gang of hoodlums right out of *The Wild One*, she was embarrassed and scared to have the child, but more embarrassed and terrified to even think of having an abortion even if she had known how to go about getting one, and she had always referred to him as "my little rape," and the name somehow stuck. Librarians' eyebrows always shot up like rockets whenever he checked out a book.

The awful thing that happened to Rape in his senior year was that he got drafted. If any one thing could kill Rape—and it did—it was the Army. Rape was an individual, in fact, the most individual individual in the crowd. He was the one who most nearly approached being the leader of the group. He was the one we went to for advice when we had problems, who never worried about anything, who was never concerned, never at a loss, never blew his cool. He was a kind of hero, and then afterwards, naturally, a kind of martyr.

We all stayed with him that last day and wandered around Denver with him trying to cheer him up, and then we saw him off at the train station that night. He had to go with a group of twenty others leaving from Denver. They were all going to basic training at Fort Leonard Wood, in Missouri. All the others in that sorry group of inductees looked forlorn—except for the ones who had gotten drunk for the occasion and those few others who had actually volunteered and were—can you believe it—actually looking forward to some lost years of taking orders, mindless duty, and maybe even get to go to Viet Nam and kill a few gooks—but none of them looked forlorner than Rape.

That was the only time I had ever seen him sad, and I felt sorry for him. I felt as if I were watching something I shouldn't be allowed to even think about, much less see.

"What the hell am I going to do?" he asked me as we waited at the station. "Hud, what the hell am I going to do?"

"Look," I said with false cheeriness, "you've got only two years. Two short years and then you're finished. And we all know that only volunteers are going to that place called Viet Nam, so you've got nothing to worry about in that category. Hell, we'll all probably still be here in school when you get back. You can make it, Rape, old buddy. You can do it standing on your head."

"I don't want to do it standing on my head, Hud. I don't want to do it at all. This has all got to be a dream, I keep telling myself. A big, fat crazy nightmare, that's what this has got to be. Hud, they're going to take away two years of my life. They're going to take away two years of my life and try to make me into something I don't want to be, just to suit their own perverted purposes. That's not right, Hud. Nobody should have the power to do that. I don't want to fight their stupid war for them, hot, cold, or in-between. Nobody should be able to wipe out two years of my life, except me. Only I should have that power."

"It'll be okay," T.K. said. "Look, I've got it all figured out. Now, we all know that they try to destroy your personality in the Army, so they can give you a new one. So, all you have to do is acquire an entirely different personality before you get there! Let them destroy *that* one, instead of the real 'you.' So, take my personality, Rape. I don't need it, anyway. Take my personality and let them destroy the hell out of it and leave yours alone. Besides, I'd kind of like to see if I can survive in the Army, anyway."

That cheered him up a bit. "Thanks, T.K.," he said.

"Anyway," T.K. added, "write us all about it, so we'll know all the shortcuts to take and what to do if *we* have to go in . . . . Anyway, if you write us, and we write you, it'll make the time go faster."

"Yeah, sure," Rape said. He was the loneliest looking soul I ever did see.

We all said goodbye and shook hands, and Diane and Gaga kissed him. The girls had made some cookies for Rape to take on the train, and they gave them to him in a shoe box. Somehow, the cookies didn't seem right, but they didn't know what else to do.

I got the first letter from Rape six days later.

> *The very last part of the trip was the hardest. It was at night, and we were outside this dinky little hick town which is right outside of Fort Leonard Wood. We went the last leg of the trip into Wood in a little old bus with hard wooden seats, and I couldn't get the song "500 Miles" out of my mind. I was practically crying.*
>
> *After issuing us our bedding, and giving us some kind of lecture, and taking away all our "pornography" magazines and comic books (yes, some of the guys had comic books—I couldn't believe it) and switchblades and blackjacks and everything, they finally let us get to bed about 11:30.*
>
> *That night I had the worst dream I've ever had. I dreamed I had been drafted and I was in a barracks in a top bunk and that it was 4:00 in the morning and some stupid bastard sergeant came in, turned on the lights, and yelled, "All right, everybody up!"*

And then the lights hit me in the face, someone yelled, "All right, everybody up!" and I woke up, and I saw that it was no dream, and I felt bad, Hud. I felt real bad.

Since they only work a half day on Saturday around here, they couldn't do much in the way of processing us. I'm in what they call the reception center. They'll give us shots and tests and clothing and everything, and then send us on to our basic training companies in about four or five days—if we're lucky, they tell us. Can you believe it? They actually turn SOME people down! Who can't be good enough for the fucking Army?

Anyway, those of us who came in last night didn't get our Army clothing today. This afternoon I had a chance to go to a movie, and I jumped at it. I figured that I could escape reality for two hours, no matter what the movie was.

"Well, they grouped us all up, and they marched us to the movie. Then they made us all sit together in the back, as if we had the plague or something and they didn't want us to contaminate the "regular" people. I really forgot during the movie, Hud, but when the lights came on, and I saw myself sitting around in my civilian clothes in the middle of a bunch of bald guys all looking exactly alike in their little green "unies," I realized what all I have ahead of me, and how long it's going to take, and I just don't know if I can do it.

I don't know if I can take it, Hud.

I passed his letter around to everyone, and we really felt sorry for him. We all made a point to write Rape as often as we could, to try to cheer him up, and Gaga and Diane sent him fresh cookies whenever they could.

We will look back at this time in the early Sixties and wonder how we could have been so naive at the beginning of such an important era. Later, we will wonder how we could have been so naive at the height of what we thought was such an important era, but at the beginning we will all go "back to our roots." We will start eating natural foods. We will start wearing comfortable, casual clothes. We will start singing "songs of the folk" and worshiping unwashed, single-minded, surly singers with angelic and gruff voices.

And we will all stand idly by while our boys make lonely trips in the night to military outposts where they will learn the ways of war. Oh, some of us will try to stand in front of the troop train and make it stop, but one person can't stop a train, no matter how slow it's going, and not enough people will be brave enough to stand or lie down in front of the nation's wheels of progress.

If you go against the will of the majority, you're likely to get your head bashed in and thrown in jail. I hate it when people hate people.

We will watch our TVs and sing our folk songs and become outraged at our Government. We will speak out for what we believe is right and for what we believe is necessary to change our way of life and our society.

And we will be crushed in body and spirit by the collective forces that are always stronger than individual efforts. We will watch our boys die in foreign jungles while we sit in our living rooms eating popcorn watching the nightly news as we enjoy and then become shocked and then cry at our home movies of war and death. We will grow weary of simple tunes and simple words, and we will start listening to hard-rocking, convoluted, intricate and loud songs screaming at society and our elders.

And we will give up.

I got another letter from Rape written just before he left the reception center.

> *It's actually kind of amazing to see how the Army works. Right now I'm at the very lowest bottom. I mean, you can't get any bottomer than I am. So I receive it from everyone, since the Army sucks and works in channels. When someone catches hell from above, he gets it out of his system by kicking the guy below him. So that guy kicks the guy below him. Even the inductees here at the reception center have a pecking order. You reach one plateau when you get your head shaved. I got mine on Monday, but before that all the others who had been here for a day or two would jeer at us as we were marched from one place to another, and they would whip off their caps and point to their naked skulls and yell, "Yeah, yeah, you're going to get yours!" just like a bunch of little kids.*
>
> *It's the only way to try and keep your sanity around this place, having someone who hasn't been here as long as you have to pick on, I guess. So when we got our GI haircuts we joined the group. The peer pressure is unbelievable. Now we look just like every other God damn idiot running around here. And, Hud, it's the most I can do to keep myself from pulling my cap off and doing the same thing when I see any new guys.*
>
> *Hud, I think I'm going to go crazy.*

We discussed Rape and his letters whenever we ran into each other between classes and at parties. He was the only topic of conversation we had at the time, and somehow we felt a little guilty when we realized that we had been enjoying ourselves at Friday Afternoon Club or on a woodsie, suddenly realizing that Rape was in Missouri crawling around in the mud with a rifle and playing soldier.

We all made a point of writing him as often as we could, because that was about all we could do to help him. And somehow, I realized that we all had the feeling he was suffering for us. He was representing each one of us there, sort of like a Christ. Except, of course, Rape didn't choose to be there, and he would have snorted at any ridiculous comparison between himself and "The Big J.C."

> You just can't imagine how much mail call means. After we've been out at the firing ranges all day, or slopping through the mud learning how to crawl under barbed wire, and we march back (we march everywhere; even when we're just walking to the PX we can't help keeping in step) and eat chow. I've been trying my darndest to keep from using Army jargon, like chow, and latrine, etc., but I think it's a losing battle. Also, you couldn't believe the language here. I'm no Puritan, you know, but after a while you just get fed up with it. Even the sergeants can't speak four words without one of them being an obscenity . . . . In fact, obscenity is so rife around here that it ceases to be obscenity. The words are just stuck in as a normal part of the language. The most common expression with the sergeants is "Wake the fuck up." And if you can tell me what part of speech "fuck" is in that sentence, I'll be eternally grateful as long as I live—if I live that long.
>
> But anyway, as I was saying about mail call, it comes after chow (I mean DINNER!). We go back to our barracks and wait for the mail clerk. Eventually he comes around and stands up on a porch and we all crowd around him. He'll yell out a name, and the guy will say, "Here, Sergeant!" and then the sergeant will throw the letter at him. I mean throw the letter at him. Or if it's a package, he'll say, "I sure hope there's nothing breakable in here," and then throw the package at the guy. He doesn't care what's in it. And you have to say, "Here, Sergeant." Once a guy forgot and said, "Yeah, man!" and the sergeant made him stay in the front-leaning rest position (that's a pushup without going down to the ground) while he called out the rest of the mail. You know, there's something degrading about having a letter from your mother thrown at you.

> "But the worst feeling in the world is not to get any mail. "Is that all?" you ask, and the sergeant says, "Yeah, knucklehead, that's all." And everyone else is sitting around reading their letters and smiling and chuckling, and you have to go up to your bunk and lie down and try to forget that you're alive.
>
> But thanks to you guys I don't have to experience that very often. I want to thank you all for writing so much to try and cheer me up. I say "try" because I'm not very cheerful. I haven't made any friends; I don't even attempt to. I don't want any. I just want to be left alone.
>
> I just want them to leave me alone, Hud.

"Fuck," T.K. said, "let's write our Congressman, or something. Does anyone know who he is?"

"I doubt if that would do any good," Theo said. "This has been going on ever since Washington stood around at Valley Forge calling his troops 'knuckleheads.' I don't think it's ever going to be changed as long as we have an army made up of people. When they can get machines to do all the fighting for them, then there won't be people like Rape being broken down by moronic bullies."

"Yeah," T.K. said, "but you'd think there would be *something* we could do."

"All we can do," I said, "is to hope."

"What do you mean by that?" T.K. asked.

"I don't know," I said. "I don't think I really know."

Fuck. One of the most interesting, useful, colorful, emotional, and emotionless words in the English language. It is a magical word, and just by changing its sound you can describe pleasure, pain, love, and hate. Just by using it, you can manipulate the emotions in others, cause others to become blind to reason, forget their argument, be filled with rage, simply because you have used the "F" word. Some linguists believe that it may have come from a Scandinavian language and can even be traced back to the Greek word for "fist." (I can picture Homer getting into a literary argument with a critic and then snapping his left palm onto the inside of his right arm as he thrust his right fist into the air at the other guy, and then punctuating it all by jerking his middle finger even higher into the air.)

Fuck. The word falls into many grammatical categories. It can be used as a transitive verb (John fucked Mary.) and as an intransitive verb (Mary fucks.). It can be an active verb (John fucks Mary and he really gives a fuck.) or a passive verb (Mary is fucked by John and she really doesn't give a fuck.). It can be used as an adverb (John is fucking interested in Mary.) and as a noun (Mary is a fine fuck.). It can even be used as an adjective (Look at that fucking Mary.). The versatility of "fuck" is fucking endless, and it grows on you, because it is so dangerous.

Fuck. I remember one morning during my freshman year as I was shaving in the bathroom in the dorm, morningdreaming as I wiped the razor across my chin. I absentmindedly thought about something and realized I had used "fuck" in my thinking. "Wow," I then thought as I realized I was becoming smuttymouthed, "I'd better watch my fucking language."

Fuck. In addition to its sexual connotations, the word can be used to describe a whole range of situations with great accuracy and precision:

Fraud: I got fucked by an investment shyster.
Unhappiness: I've been fucking unhappy lately.
Confusion: What the fuck?
Kindness: I really fucking like you.
Yearning: I really fucking want you.
Optimism: I'm going to get fucked tonight!
Ugliness: Have you ever seen anyone so fucking ugly?

Fuck. Even with random thoughts and musings, the word adds music to the language:

Fickleness: I don't know who I'm fucking interested in.
Dismay: Oh, fuck it!
Trouble: I guess I'm really fucked now.
Aggression: Fuck you!
Passion: Fuck me!
Indecision: Anybody want to fuck?
Ignorance: I don't fucking understand!
Despair: Oh, well, fucked again.
Existentialism: This is the fucking end!
Incompetence: He's a real fuck-up.
Laziness: He's a real fuck-off.
Displeasure: What the fuck's going on?
Insubordination: Fuck you, Boss!

It can be used to describe anatomy: He's a fucking asshole.
It can be used to tell time: It's five-fucking-thirty.
It can be used in business: How can I get that fucking job?

It can be a prediction: Well, I'll be fucked.
It can be maternal: You motherfucker!
It can be paternal: You motherfucker!
It can be soldierly: Fuck the Army. (Also known as FTA.)
It can be nautical: Fuck the Admiral. (Also known as FTA.)
It can be political: Fuck the President. (Also known as "Fucking-A!")
It can open the door to a wonderful relationship: Let's fuck.
It can even be used to enhance the meaning of another word, such as "beauti-fucking-ful" and "out-fucking-standing."

However, as with anything else, if used too often, it loses its meaning, as well as its impact. But, because of its versatility and endless variations, because it can be used to mean anything you want it to mean, and because if used intelligently it can get you practically anything you want, why should anyone be offended by the word? That's the beauty of it: It means everything and it means nothing, and it's so fucking powerful. As T.K. said, "What's in a word?"

The last letter I received from Rape was the worst.

> *All of a sudden it came to me what the whole fucking mess was. I figured out the whole reasoning—if you can call it that—behind basic training. T.K. really didn't know how close to the truth he was. The idea is to tear you down completely—*
>
> *I mean COMPLETELY—but at the same time trying not to let you know what they're doing. They are trying to mold us into mindless fighting men, even though very few of us will be in the infantry when we get out of here, and in order to do that they have to wipe out everything we have ever been. Those few of us who have been to college find it better to keep that fact quiet around here. The sergeants look at us and treat us as if we were potential troublemakers, and they give us all the shitty details, and they even make us do their typing for them.*
>
> *But the purpose is to destroy every bit of intelligence, every bit of creativity that we possess, in order to make us do nothing other than what they tell us to do, with no questions asked. When they say "Jump!" we jump. When they say "Kill!" we kill.*
>
> *The whole thing is so much like a fraternity Hell Week that it's almost funny. My platoon sergeant and another platoon sergeant even gave their platoons a spot "full field inspection" the other night.*

We had to spend all evening cleaning our equipment and laying it out on the bunks. And then they came in drunk to inspect, said it was terrible—which it was—because not everyone was finished (We have to get our GI haircuts every Monday night and with only three barbers trying to cut a whole company's hair, some didn't have enough time with their equipment.). So we had to have another inspection at 4:00 o'clock the next morning. Half the guys slept on the floor rather than mess up their display. I said the hell with it, threw all my stuff on the floor, and tried to get some sleep. I see so many comparisons to a fraternity Hell Week that sometimes I can even guess what's coming next. Ha! I could even give them some ideas—like tying a string around some guy's balls and leaving it hanging out his shirt collar so the actives can pull on it in public and really cause some pain. Remember that one? After the coeds found out what the string was tied to, they really enjoyed pulling it, too. Ha!

But it gets worse, Hud. It gets so bad that sometimes the only thing I can do is lie in my bunk and brood. I don't even go to the movies anymore. The only time when we got passes over a weekend to get out of the post, I didn't even take it. There's no place to go, actually, except Waynesville, that hick town I told you about, and I have no desire to get drunk and lay an ugly Negro whore, especially at five bucks a shot. So I just stayed in my bunk and thought and brooded and wrote letters and read. (Can you imagine? They confiscate all your books when you get here. I had to turn over The Natural History of Nonsense, American Folksongs of Protest, and How to Win at Poker, which caused some excitement among the sergeants, and they told me I'll probably never see THAT book again. So I bought a book at the PX and keep it hidden in my foot locker. They tell us, "If you have time to read, then read the Army Manual.") The only, the ONLY thing I can do that is in the least bit creative around here is to write a letter. It is the only way I can do any creative thinking. The other favorite expression of the sergeants is, "Don't think! We'll do your thinking for you." How true that is.

Sometimes I find myself just rambling on in a letter because I'm so afraid to stop writing. In fact, I find that I actually CAN'T stop writing. The pen just refuses to stop and I write on and on for pages and pages, and don't even have anything to say, or else it doesn't make sense. Sometimes I tear these letters up and start over again, but I usually find that the same thing happens.

I don't know if I can take it anymore, Hud.

I keep getting into trouble with the sergeants, too, because I can see through them. Because I'm more intelligent than they are, they know it, and they have it in for me. They enjoy making me do a little extra more than the other trainees. Once, the senior drill instructor made us run in and out of the barracks in full field gear, pack and rifle, after we had marched back eight or nine miles from the rifle ranges, because he didn't think I had fallen out fast enough, or showed enough spirit, or something. So he made us run into the barracks and he would blow his whistle and we'd run out and stand at attention, and he'd yell "Fall out!" and we'd run back in again, hating him with every weary step we took. The other guys in the company were hating me too because it was I who had made them have to do it in the first place. I had been too slow, the sergeant had said, since I had walked and not run when we were dismissed the first time, and he was going to stand out there all night until we got it right, he said, and he would blow his whistle and off we would go again, the sweat pouring down from underneath our steel pots.

I don't know if I can take it anymore, Hud.

I didn't receive any more letters from Rape after that, even though I continued writing him, and no one else received any letters, either. We were afraid that he hadn't been able to put up with it any longer and had gone AWOL. We didn't want to write to his mother, in case he really was AWOL and she didn't know about it, and the only thing we could do was to keep writing to him, hoping.

We were shocked to learn that Rape was dead.

His commanding officer had written to Rape's mother, and she had sent the letter on to us, because she knew how much we had loved him and how much we meant to him and how much we had tried to cheer him up. She just sent me the commanding officer's letter with a short note saying, "I know you'll be interested in finding out what happened to my lovely, little Rape. Please tell all his friends for me how much I appreciate all they did for him. God bless you all."

The letter from the Army went on to say how Rape had been killed on the infiltration course through an accident somehow. He had been crawling through the course at night with the rest of his basic-training company, underneath the barbed wire and the machine-gun fire. When the flare had lit up the course at the end, when they had thought everyone was finished, they saw him lying alone out in the middle in the flarelight. He had taken a round in the back. It must have been a bad charge in one of the machine guns, he said. The commanding officer was very sorry.

Gaga and Diane both cried when I told them.

SEVEN

We discussed Rape's death for some time after that

We discussed Rape's death for some time after that, but we couldn't reach a decision as to what we thought had really happened. Maybe the Army was right. Maybe a bad charge had caused it, and Rape had been shot accidentally rather than intentionally. After all, a national institution like the U.S. Army wouldn't lie to us, would it? That would be unthinkable. After all, We the People pay their salaries. (Well, those of us who pay taxes, that is.) And if you can't believe the Army, who can't you believe next? The FBI? Big Business? The President?

However, I tended to believe that Rape had been shot on purpose, that he simply could not take any more shit and with tracer bullets flying all about him had stood up in the mud in the middle of the rain-swept field on that dark and lonely, God-forsaken night to meet the machine-gun fire. Perhaps he had even turned his back in defiance, perhaps to make it look like an accident, perhaps throwing his right arm straight up in the air with an extended middle finger thrust up in one final act of hopeless anger. At any rate, we hoped that his death had been sudden and poor Rape hadn't had to suffer any more.

T.K. kept insisting this as we drove over to pick up Bido one Sunday afternoon.

"I hope the poor bastard didn't even know what hit him," he said. "I just hope the poor bastard didn't feel a thing."

We had decided, Dayo, T.K., Murphy, Bido, and I, that this was one Sunday when we were going to get some serious studying done, and we decided that we would get some beer and some blankets and take advantage of the beautiful day and drive up to the mountains. Without the girls. Find a nice quiet grassy meadow high up somewhere, not even take a radio, and just lie back and get some serious studying done.

"Jesus, I hope the poor bastard didn't suffer. Can you imagine what it would have been like if he hadn't been killed right off, and he was lying there in the cold and the dark and the rain, and the machine guns blasting away right over his head, and he's been hit and the blood's oozing out, and guys are crawling around him in the dark, ignoring him, and he can't even cry out for help?"

"Jesus Christ, T.K., will you shut your goddam mouth?" Murphy said. Dayo was driving A-Frame, and we were on our way to Bido's to pick him up and head for the mountains—in Bido's car, of course, since Dayo's could never make it around all those mountain curves.

"Well, Jesus," T.K. said, "I just hope the poor bastard didn't even know what hit him."

A-Frame jerked to a stop in front of Bido's apartment house and we all stumbled out. Bido lived in an old house near the campus that had been converted into apartments, and he shared the top-floor apartment with another guy. They took turns every other night as to which one of them got to bring his date back to the apartment. Once Bido had had to pay his roommate five dollars to let him use his roommate's night, because Bido had a real good date that night, and he really thought he was going to score.

"I had all the angles covered," he told me afterwards. "I mean, I had everything all arranged. I paid Ted the five bucks to go someplace else that night, because I had come home the night before, and it wasn't supposed to be my turn again until the next night. But I really believed that this was going to be my Bingo Bango Night with this girl. I mean, I had been working on her for a week, solid. She's really a cold bitch, but, Man, is she beautiful. And what a body! Ooh, ooh!"

Bido tended to get carried away with emotion whenever he talked about his girls.

"Anyway, she had been sort of warming up lately, and I had this date with her, and I really thought that if I tried hard enough, I could score. So I had everything planned. I would ply her with drinks, which I would fix in the kitchen. And in hers I would add an extra shot of grain alcohol to help her along a little faster and without her knowing what was hitting her. Then she would warm up, and bingo! Bango! Score! I even had rubbers stashed all over the apartment, in the bedroom, under the cushions of the couch, in the kitchen, bathroom, everywhere, so that nothing possible would detract from the mood. I mean, I had everything planned. Wherever it occurred, whenever she was ready, I was ready. There was nothing in the world that could mess it up. I even had 'Bolero' ready on the record player. It's a great psychological helper, you know, the way it builds up to a climax at the end, even though it only gives you fourteen minutes and thirty-two seconds with which to work."

In years to come, Hollywood will make fun of this lovemaking music helper in a popular film, but the writers and producers will not steal the idea from Bido, who was making out and humping to "Bolero" in 1962 when Bo Derek was only six years old. Independent inventions do work sometimes, even though the mad inventors may be crackpotted and palmed off. Anthropologists know this, too.

"So, what happened?" I asked.

"I fed her too much grain," he said. "She got sick and threw up all over the goddam bathroom. She won't even speak to me any more."

So much for independent inventions.

Bido's apartment doesn't have a front door, because the narrow stairs that lead to it from the floor below his just come out right in the middle of his living room. So we yelled up at him as we climbed the stairs.

"Open up, you bastard! This is the police! Open up or we'll tear down your goddam door!"

We emerged into the living room like a band of banditos and saw Bido in the kitchen sitting on a chair in front of the open window. He had a pair of binoculars and was staring intently out the window.

We all crowded around him and looked out the window.

"Jee-zuz H. Christ," T.K. said slowly.

We stood there and watched and licked our lips, mentally, figuratively, and literally. Bido was observing the back of a women's boarding house. From the height of his apartment, he could look right smack dab down onto the sundeck at the back of the boarding house, on top of the flat roof of the first floor. And busily, lazily sunning herself, unseen from below and everywhere else except for the five of us in Bido's kitchen, was a nice little coed in a red two-piece bathing suit—without the top.

"Gimme the glasses!"

A brief struggle erupted over the binoculars, and Bido finally, reluctantly gave them up to be passed around.

"I've been watching her for a full goddam thirty minutes," he said, "and she hasn't moved an inch. Ooh! Ooh! Except when she wiggled her fanny once."

The girl was lying on her stomach, her head on a towel, apparently asleep. Two unopened books were lying beside her head. Another girl was sitting with her back to the side of the house, reading, but she had all her pieces in the appropriate places, and besides that, she wasn't even good looking. Sometimes, you can be fooled into thinking a girl is beautiful when she's not, especially when she has nice hair and her back is turned to you and she has a nice figure, and you might follow her for a couple of blocks, building up your excitement and anticipation, only to be disappointed when she finally turns around, but in the case of this other girl, we could tell right away that the sleeping one was the one for us.

"What do you think we should do?" Murphy asked.

"Does anyone know who she is?" Dayo asked.

No one did.

"Well, then, what do you think we should do?" Murphy asked again.

"I think we should forget the whole thing and go study," T.K. said without taking his eyes off her.

After we finished throwing jelly jars and canned corn and stolen silverware at him, we resumed our vigil by the window. One of Bido's spoons had accidentally flown through the window, and Bido was going to have to climb out and retrieve it from the gutter when he eventually ran out of clean ones.

"Hey, she's moving!"

"By god, you're right!"

The girl slowly raised her head and looked around, then glanced up at the sun. She turned to the other girl and said something, and the other girl said something back.

"Get up, Baby. Get up, get up, get up!"

Bido was practically crawling out the window. But the girl just reached over, took one of the books, opened it, and started reading, all without once shifting her body so that anything could be seen. The top of her bathing suit was protecting her nipples from the hot roof where she had untied it and let it drop down.

After she had read without stirring for a minute, we decided that something else would have to be done.

"I've got it, I've got it, I've got it," I said.

"What, what, what?" T.K. asked.

"Look, I said, "it's so simple, it's almost ridiculous."

"Coming from you," Dayo said, "it's got to be simply ridiculous." He even made a Groucho movement with his right hand, as if he were wiggling a cigar.

"Quiet, quiet!" Bido said, waving his arms. "What is it?"

"All we have to do is call the boarding house and ask to speak to her. Then she'll have to get up to go to the phone."

"Yeah, sure," Murphy said, "but we don't even know her name. How can we ask for her when we don't know her name?"

"We don't have to ask for her by name. All we have to do is ask to speak to the girl on the roof in the red bathing suit."

"It won't work," T.K. said.

"Why not?"

"I don't know. I just don't think it'll work."

"Okay, okay," Bido exclaimed. "Let's stop talking and try it. Give me my binoculars and somebody go call."

"Now, wait a minute," T.K. said. "I've got the binoculars."

"But, they're my goddam binoculars!"

"Well, I've got them now! Go call, Murphy."

"Are you crazy? What would I say to her?"

"For Christ's sake, you don't have to *talk* to the girl! Just ask for her and hang up or something. All we want to do is see her titties, not talk to her."

"Wait a minute. Wait a minute," I said. "Everybody settle down. Now, let's go about this cooly and calmly. First of all, let's draw cards to see who gets to use the binoculars. I think that's only fair."

"Fair?" Bido yelled. "Fair? They're my goddam binoculars!"

"I've got the cards," T.K. said, running in from the living room. "Has she done anything yet?"

We drew cards, all the time Bido yelling, "But they're my goddam binoculars!" T.K. and Murphy both drew kings, so they had to draw again. T.K. won and got to keep the binoculars.

"You see?" he said. "There is a God."

"But they're my goddam binoculars," Bido muttered.

"Next," I said, "somebody's got to call the boarding house."

"You call," Dayo said. "It's your idea."

"Okay, I'll do the calling. I can run back in here after I ask for her and get back in time to see her titties. So I'll do the calling. Are we forgetting anything?"

"Yeah," Dayo said. "What's the name of the boarding house?"

None of us knew. Bido thought he had an idea, but when we looked it up in the phone book, the one he thought it was was on another street entirely.

"Wait a minute, wait a minute," Dayo said. "Here it is. This is it."

I got the phone book, my finger marking the place, took one last glance at the girl to make sure she hadn't done anything or looked as if she were about to do something, and I went into the living room to phone. The telephone rang just as I was about to pick it up and scared the shit out of me. I snatched it off the hook and said, "Get off the line! This phone's busy!" and hung it up again.

"Who was it?" Bido yelled from the kitchen.

"Wrong number. Has she done anything yet?"

"No. Hurry up and call. It's starting to get cloudy."

I dialed the number and waited.

"It's ringing," I yelled. "Can you see anything?"

"Yeah," Murphy yelled back. "The other girl's going inside to answer the phone, I think. Hang on."

Someone picked up the phone at the boarding house, and a girl's voice said sweetly, "Hello-o."

"Hello-o," I answered, trying to sound just as sweet and disguise the fact that I had smutty intentions. "I'd like to speak to the girl on the roof in the red bathing suit, please."

Short pause.

"What?" she said.

"I said, 'I'd like to speak to the girl on the roof in the red bathing suit, please.'"

She didn't say anything, and then she said, "Just a minute, please."

I dropped the receiver on the couch and dashed back into the kitchen. They were all grouped around the window, and I had to force my head in between T.K. and Dayo's armpit.

"She's getting her," I said.

Just then the other girl stuck her head out the window through which the girls had to go in and out to get on the roof. She said something to the girl in red. The girl in red said something back, obviously puzzled. The other girl said something back to her, just as obviously puzzled, maybe more so.

"Oh, boy. Ooh! Oh, boy. Ooh!" Bido said.

And the girl in the red bathing suit glanced over toward us, smiled, flipped her top up around her, fastened it, stood up, and walked toward the window, all in one smooth effortless motion. We didn't see a thing.

I walked back into the living room leaving all the disappointed groans and moans behind me. T.K. gave Bido's binoculars back to him.

I picked up the phone and heard the girl saying, "Hello? Hello?"

"Beat it, bitch," I said and hung up.

Why couldn't all the problems involved with the female sex be solved with those three simple, effortless little words, "Beat it, bitch"? No explanation needed, no feelings hurt, no desperate hangings on. Just short and sweet and simple. Beat it, bitch.

Well, the problem is that the word "bitch" is loaded with almost as much thinkingless emotion as "fuck" is, even though it has other, emotionless meanings. Even if you intend a meaning that is only an innocent synonym for a person of the female persuasion, your listener might think you intended a flame-filled meaning and take immediate offense. Even if you might say "Bitch, bitch, bitch" to a woman when you mean only "Complain, complain, complain," she can very easily and wrongly think that you are calling her "Whore, whore, whore." Language sure is a funny thing, T.K. And a very powerful tool but a very dangerous weapon.

A very powerful tool and a very dangerous weapon was published in the United States about this time: Henry Miller's *Tropic of Cancer*. Man! Was this a real eye-opener to us sweet little naive innocent college kids from Anytown, U.S.A. Jesus! The fucking words were printed right there on the goddam page! You didn't even have to whisper them! Hell! You didn't even have to read the whole goddam book! "Hey! Have you bought *Tropic of Cancer* yet?" "Yeah." "Have you read page 5 yet?" "Yeah." T.K. even tried to make a little extra money by publishing his own version of Cliff Notes, which was just a one-page listing of the page numbers of the best pages to read from the book. He had dreams of even expanding into other books, such as *Lady Chatterley's Lover* and *Lolita*, until we reminded him that he was going to have to read all those books himself all the way through, and, besides, even though he was now the so-called expert on dirty words, what he thought was dirty might not be what other people thought was dirty.

"Yeah, I guess you're right," he said. "Fuck 'em. Let 'em find their own goddam pages."

And this was during the time when a *dictionary* could be banned, for Christ's sake! Think about that. If you can't go to a dictionary to determine the meaning of the dirty word that offends you, then how can you be sure that the novel, or fairy tale, or song that offends you really means what you believe it to mean?

In years to come, the blue-nose stupidity of "Banned in Boston" will evolve into the brain-dead asininity of public bookburnings in a futile attempt to eliminate someone else's thinking and replace it with your own, or else to simply draw attention to your own ninnified, piss-poor way of thinking: "If everyone else thinks the way I do, then I must be right, right? Am I right, or am I right?"

"Evolve"? Yeah, right. Hitler tried that misguided step toward public acceptance of one's personal point of view and look where it got him.

In more years to come, "political correctness" will become a catchphrase of the day, and it won't have anything to do with politics and it won't have anything to do with being correct. It won't have anything to do with being right and it won't have anything to do with being left. It will be just one more futile attempt in a long line of futile attempts that stretches back to the pre-Dawn of Time in which poor thinkers try to persuade others to share their beliefs by using thoughtless arguments that ignore thinking. The invention of paper just made it easier. Before that, you had to smash the books. Thank God for the invention of fire.

I think about all the bitches I have met and known—most of them briefly—in my life, as the traveling salesman of blue jeans drives down the main street of Grand Junction, leaving me standing on the curb. He would be in town for a few days, he said, and I wanted to get the hell out of Colorado and the hell into Utah.

Diane perhaps affected me more than any other girl I had known. I went with her—in the sense of going with someone—longer than I had gone with any other girl. In all fairness, I guess I should say that *she* went with *me* longer than anyone else had. She put up with me longer than any other girl did would be an even better way of saying it. But then, even Diane couldn't go on forever without getting what she wanted in return. Even she had to give up eventually. We all have to give up, eventually, when our desperate needs aren't met. It's foolish not to do so.

I go into a cafe to get something to eat and run into a guy driving all the way out to the West Coast. He offers to drive me to California in exchange for a little gas money, some pleasant conversation, and a few turns at driving.

I don't know why, but I am reluctant to get there that fast.

"No, thanks. Sure, I want to get to California, but I'm in no hurry right now. I'd sort of like to take my time, you know? See the country along the way. Take in the sights."

"Take in the sights? In Utah?"

"Yeah, even in Utah. I've never been in Utah before. You can't really say nothing's there, because *something's* there, even if it's just wide-open spaces. Even if it's just desert and mountains. Even if it's just the 'there' missing from Gertrude Stein's Oakland."

"What?"

"Nothing. Private joke. Look, I just think if Utah's going to go to all that trouble of being there, the least I can do is look at it."

He looks at me closely and then slowly shakes his head.

"I think you're crazy, kid, but I'll be glad to give you a ride as far as you want. How far do you want to go?"

I look down into my coffee cup and think for a minute, trying to discover some coffee grounds that might give me a clue. How far do I want to go? Do I want to go that far? How far *can* I go?

Maybe I *am* crazy.

"I want to see a little town in Utah. Just let me ride along with you, and you can drop me off in some little town in Utah."

"You don't have any town in mind? You don't even care *which* little town in Utah?"

"No, I'll just pick one out as we come to it. Anything that suits my fancy." *And a pretty little fancy it is!* I smile to myself as I think of Dayo wiggling his invisible cigar.

"You sure you want to go to California?"

"Sure, I'm sure. But I don't want to go too fast, see? I want to take an easy trip. I want to take my time. It's my time, isn't it?"

Did you know that "sugar" is the only word in the English language that begins with "S-U" and is pronounced "sh-h—"?

Sure.

"Kid, you are crazy."

"So what? Maybe so, maybe no. But, my sanity is my problem, not yours. Will you take me?"

"It's mine, too, if you're going to be riding along in my car. But, yeah, I'll take you. Drink up and let's go."

EIGHT

T.K. wondered about his sanity the time he went with the Catholic girl

T.K. wondered about his sanity the time he went with the Catholic girl. The problem wasn't that she was just a Catholic. She was a *staunch* Catholic, whereas T.K. wasn't a staunch anything, unless you could call him staunch areligious. He didn't have anything against or, for that matter, for religion. He just found that he could have a happier and calmer life by simply leaving it alone as long as religion left him alone. He didn't mind religious people, either, as long as they didn't try to convert him to something he already wasn't or try to lord a "holier than thou, you *scum*" attitude over him.

"The way I see it," he said, "you're either religious or you're not. I'm not. And that's that deal. So, don't waste your time. Don't waste my time. And don't waste God's time, either."

Then he met the Catholic girl. T.K. always wondered why he started going out with her in the first place.

"I know just exactly why I started going out with her," he said in the Sink. "I thought I could get in."

The occasion was a typical F.A.C., and T.K. and I were crammed into a corner booth with two bottles of beer. We were drinking quarts, because they lasted longer, and fighting our way back up to the front for refills was too hazardous, so we could put that dangerous journey off for as long as possible and for as long as our thirsts would allow.

"I assume that you didn't," I said.

"Didn't what?"

"Get in," I said, almost yelling. Being heard above the thunder of the conversations around us and the roaring of the jukebox in the crowded room was difficult.

"Are you kidding? That would be like digging through the Great Wall of China with a plastic spoon."

"Well, then, why did you think you could get in in the first place?"

"She has this look about her, you know? Girls that do it, they have this look about them that I can spot a mile off. Most people can't, thank goodness, but I can. Bido taught it to me, and you can see how well it's worked for him. Ha, ha. Anyway, after he taught me what to look for, I checked out a few girls with all my fabulous, newly acquired knowledge. She passed the test with flying colors."

"You must have been wrong, then, huh?"

"Hell, no, I wasn't wrong! In fact, since she was the first one I was able to find who fit *all* the symptoms, I even had Bido check her out for me. He agreed with me. 'She does it,' he said, 'abso-fucking-tootly. What's her name?' 'Lay off, Man,' I told him. 'I saw her first. Besides, I'm your pupil and you're supposed to have a sense of teacher-pupil pride and client confidentiality. At least, give me a chance to show you what I've learned.' He reluctantly agreed."

"Well, now, wait a minute. How could both you and Bido be wrong about her? Especially Bido?"

"Yeah, I know. He doesn't miss a trick, does he? Ho, ho. Well, after I had gone out with her, I discovered that in her case what we had both taken for the signs of putting out had been nothing more than her naivity, with a little stupidity thrown in."

"*Naivity?*"

"Yeah, naivity."

"You mean, she was dumb?"

"Well, I don't know about that. Maybe not by their standards. But, my god! She was really out of it."

"Get the story well in your mind," I said, sliding out of the wooden bench, "while I go get us some fresh quarts. Wish me luck."

"Yeah, but if you're not back in an hour, I'll know you've gone and absconded with my money."

I pushed and wiggled my way through the mass of human bodies to get to the front. Somewhat of an open space was in front of the jukebox where two couples were dancing, one of the couples being composed of two guys. Everyone was standing around and cheering, and one of the guys started to do a strip. I got the beer and slowly shoved and plowed my way back to T.K. The stripper had his shirt off and was starting on his pants.

"So, anyway," I said, sliding back into the booth, "you found out that she was naive."

"Naive? Man, she couldn't have been any naiver!"

"*Naiver?*"

"Yeah, naiver. We used to get into all sorts of arguments about religion while I still thought she was capable of doing it. So, once I asked her, 'Look, don't you ever have any doubts about your religion? I mean, don't you ever have any doubts at all, that just possibly it might not be exactly what they tell you it is?'"

"And what did she say?"

"She paused, and then she said, 'Well, sometimes it *is* a little hard for me to believe that the wafer really turns into Christ's body.'"

"You're kidding."

"No, no! I'm not. I swear to god, it's the truth. The blessed truth. And you can put any god in there you want to. Did you know that I found out she was going to confession every Saturday and telling the priest what all we had done Friday night?"

"But, you told me you didn't do anything."

"Look, with this kid, even French kissing is a sin. Playing 'stink finger' is probably a mortal sin. Honest. She would confess that we had been French kissing. She believed that only married people should French kiss. I had to practically French-kiss rape her, for god's sake. Sometimes, she would be caught up in passion and she would suddenly realize what she was doing and almost bite my tongue off. Damn, that hurts!"

"T.K., you're impossible. I don't believe a word of it."

"It's the honest-to-god truth, and you can put any god in there you want to. I probably would've had to wear a rubber over my tongue, except they don't believe in prophylactics."

"I don't believe you."

"Well. . . ."

"So, then, you finally broke up with her, huh?"

"Yeah, I finally decided that 'Bido's Formula' had somehow screwed up in this case. Hee, hee."

We sat in relative silence for a while to sop up our suds and stare at the human wall around us. Mad cheering was coming from over near the jukebox, and we could see female clothes being tossed into the air.

"You know, those Catholics are sure funny," T.K. said.

"How's that?"

"They've got a name for every day."

"You mean, like Sunday, Monday, Tuesday—?"

"No, no. Well, I don't know if they have a name for *every* day, but I remember that around Easter she was calling the days by funny names. Like for in-un-stance, the Thursday before Easter is Monday-Thursday.... Or is it the Monday before is Thursday-Monday?"

"I think it's Maundy Thursday."

"Yeah, and then comes Good Friday. And then next is Holy Saturday."

"What's Sunday?"

"Happy Easter."

"T.K., why don't you go home?"

T.K. had that quality about him that made you never quite sure whether he was telling the truth or simply telling a story he had made up on the spot. If he was telling the truth, you had to give him credit for telling a truthful story in an entertaining way. But, on the other hand, the reverse is also true. If he was making up a story, you had to give him credit for having a strong imagination, even if he was putting you on.

At any rate, he told a good story, and he always had plenty of credit.

Theo could never tell a story. His problem wasn't exactly that he told a bad story, but he just got so absorbed in how he was going about telling it that he sometimes forgot what his point had been and what he was telling. This had a dulling effect on his listeners, who weren't all that excited in anticipation about his stories in the first place.

One night he came home and had a story to tell. He had been dating a freshman girl for some reason, perhaps for a change of pace, and he had had a date with her that evening. He had just returned from tucking her into her freshman-girls' dorm.

"Hey, guess what happened," he said, strolling into the study. I was sitting in the easy chair, trying to study.

"Oh, you had a flat tire," I suggested.

Dayo walked in from the bedroom, saw a story was about to unravel, and sat down on his work stool.

"No, no," Theo said. "This funny thing happened when I took Barbara back to the dorms."

"You lost your way," Dayo said.

"You went to the wrong dorm," I offered.

"I've got it, I've got it! You forgot Barbara and left her at the movies."

"Come on, you guys, do you want to hear what happened or not?"

"This time we have a choice, Dayo."

"Let's go to the Gondolier," Dayo said.

"All right, I won't tell you," Theo said. He turned and slowly started out of the room with his hang-doggie look, but Dayo and I just sat there. Theo got to the door and stopped. We waited. He turned. Dayo was grinning from here to here.

"Oh, all right," I said.

"Hey, what happened tonight, Theo?" Dayo asked, in all seeming innocence and naiveté.

Theo walked back in, forgiving us hesitatingly.

"Well, as we were walking through the lobby, there were these two freshman girls talking to each other."

"Do I know them?" I asked.

"No. Well, I don't know. Look, what difference does it make?"

"I might know them," Dayo said. "Was one of them chewing orange bubble gum?"

"Anyway, these two freshmen girls were talking, and one of them was very Jewish looking. I mean *very* Jewish looking. She had the black kinky hair, kind of dark skin, the big hook nose—."

"He's getting kind of personal, isn't he?" Dayo asked me.

"You think we ought to report him to the Jewish fraternities?"

"So, anyway," Theo continued, "as we walked by these two girls, the very Jewish girl was saying to the other girl, she said, 'You know, you're lucky. At least you don't *look* Catholic.'"

Dayo and I sat in silence, looking expectantly at Theo. Theo stood there and looked from Dayo to me, his smile slowly fading down his face. Even though this scene happened many times, it was still hilarious to Dayo and me.

"Let's go to the Gondolier," Dayo said finally.

"Can't," I said. "Murphy's coming over to copy a book report."

Theo walked back into the bedroom, weeping silently to himself, and probably once again swearing never to tell us another story.

"Hey, Theo!" Dayo called out. "How does a Catholic girl look, anyway?"

"Go to hell!" Theo yelled from the bedroom.

"Ask Murphy," I told Dayo. "He's Catholic."

"Funny," he said. "He doesn't look Catholic."

In years to come, getting upset over matters xenophiliaphobic will become even more ridiculous than it was in the preadolescent Sixties. The same year that Theo took his date back to her dorm, the C.U. regents approved renaming the men's dorm next to hers from Fleming Hall to Nichols Hall, after Capt.

David Nichols, the man credited as being the legislator who brought the University of Colorado to Boulder. Twenty-two years later, however, Nichols' name will be stripped from the men's dormitory after students and campus administrators will raise a stink about the fact that Capt. Nichols also took part in the Sand Creek Massacre in 1864, in which about 200 men, women, and children of the Native American Indian persuasion were slaughtered by men of the Immigrant American White persuasion. In the months following the stripping, the regents will establish a naming policy to avoid future such embarrassments, and eventually they will settle on renaming the renamed dormitory Cheyenne Arapaho Hall, after the two Indian tribes that engaged in intense fighting with the whites in Colorado in the 1860s. How long before a group of incensed whites object to the name after they discover that one or so of *their* ancestors were killed—perhaps even scalped!—by a Cheyenne or Arapaho Indian, and therefore they (the Indians) should not be honored with their name on a decaying dormitory?

As further evidence of the ridiculosity of these name games, at the same time as the C.U. regents pat themselves on their collective backs for removing the honor of Legislator Nichols and anointing Cheyenne and Arapaho descendents with undishonor at Capt. Nichols' expense by putting their names on a public building, the Minnesota Civil Liberties Union will take steps to *remove* Indian names from public institutions, namely the nicknames and logos of high-school athletic teams, on the grounds that such symbols are discriminatory and demeaning. Union leaders will even argue that the names violate the equal-protection clause of the 14th Amendment. What is even sillier, a number of the high schools under attack will be in northern Minnesota, where most of the state's Indian reservations are located, and many of the students will be Indians who don't object to being called "Warriors" or "Indians" or "Braves."

And the mascot name game gets even sillier-er. In many more years to come, Native American groups will object to the time-honored and -worn names of professional baseball and football teams, claiming the argument that such names are offensive and derogatory. What would they like the teams to call themselves? The Washington Black and White Boys? The Atlanta Knuckleheads? What people seem to forget is that these mascot names are chosen for their anthropological totemism, not their condescending tokenism. The names were chosen in order to strike fear in their opponents' hearts, not laughter and chuckles in their throats. Nobody ever chose the name Englewood Idiots, Detroit Drunkies, or Washington Wimps as a mascot name. No. They wanted a name that would instill pride in their teams. And that's why no team ever called themselves "White Boys."

How long before future incensed Coloradans learn in a history class that in 1914 in Trinidad, Colorado, a number of innocent white women and children were killed in a battle between striking coal miners and the state militia after long-simmering labor-management conflicts, and therefore students and campus administrators successfully lobby to change the name of Cheyenne Arapaho Hall to Coal Miner and Dependents Hall?

Labels are silly and dangerous to yourself. They allow you to stop thinking and let your brain atrophy. One of my best friends in high school was Jewish, and I didn't even know it until he joined a Jewish fraternity in college. When I found out, I thought, 'Oh, that's interesting. I never knew that.' A popular girl in my high-school class was Jewish, too, and I never found out until she went to college. In high school she dated a good friend of mine, but he went to college back East somewhere, and I always wanted to take her out, but I felt too guilty, like I would be betraying a friendship. Hell! I didn't care that she was Jewish! She was a good-looking, smart, interesting babe—and she might do it!

Anyway, if you let yourself fall victim to the label game, you're going to miss out on a lot of good friendships and rewarding experiences. Would Jesus have had any disciples if everyone had been prejudiced against Jews? Would Washington have been our first President if everyone had been prejudiced against people with false teeth? Would we even have a society if half of everyone was prejudiced against women and the other half prejudiced against men?

I think we should face up to the fact that differences exist, thank god, and some of us are better at some things than others, but for Christ's sake that doesn't mean we can ridicule, scorn, and kill those people whose skin can't reflect as much light as ours, whose god isn't as hairy and stern as ours, and whose population simply isn't as numerous as ours. Might doesn't make right, and when it comes right down to it, if there is a god, god is on *everybody's* side, animal, vegetable, and mineral.

Sure, there is something to be said for "survival of the fittest," but those beings and ducklings who don't make the cut shouldn't be scorned. They should be pitied.

The biggest problem facing the world, as I see it, is that we're running out of space and resources, and I sure don't mean metal and oil and money. I mean trees and water and air. We're all going to die someday, but it kind of adds meaning to our own lives if the race can last a little longer than our own lifetime, or the lifetime of our kids, or the lifetime of our kids' kids, or go on for a few more generations. And I mean the *human race*. Can't we extend the "ugly duckling" syndrome to encompass all human beings against . . . oh, for the time being, against *dead people*. Yeah, that ought to be safe enough. Let's not hate anybody at all. Let's try to meld all human beings and races and religions together. Let's try to get back on the right racetrack of a few ugly ducklings huddled together in a cave for warmth, terrified of the imagined danger out in the night, and dreaming up myths and stories and religion for comfort. Only, this time let's include every human being, regardless of race, color, creed, or sex. Hell, some of my best friends are *everybody*.

The early Chinese and North American Indians had it right. We all live better lives if we live a life of *balance* in the world. Treat everybody and everything with compassion and respect, even the wood you have to burn, the food you have to eat, and the air you have to breathe, but especially the people you have to live with. Remember: The fish probably think they are God's chosen, even the insects probably think they are the most intelligent beings on earth, and for all we know, the trees just might be thinking on wavelengths we haven't discovered yet. Remember where the word "natural" comes from.

I think we will be a lot better off, especially in the long run, if we try to live by destroying as little of our natural surroundings as possible. If we destroy our surroundings, we end up only destroying ourselves. Existential suicide never helped anybody.

Comic existentialism is much mo' better, as Stanley would have said. Even though life can be a despairing, despondent bitch, one can always find something to laugh at—smile, if you're timid—to try to take away some of the bitterness. "Laugh, I thought I'd die," as T.K. always said. "I thought my pants would *never* dry."

In years to come, many artificial, *national* boundaries will come down that in the Sixties we never imagined in our wildest dreams would ever happen, especially not in our lifetimes, even though we might have fought for them to happen. Well, it seems to me that it is in our human interests to bring down *all* artificial boundaries, every god damn last one of them. The only boundary we should concern ourselves with is a *natural* one, and for the time being that boundary should be the Earth itself.

In addition to not looking Catholic, Murphy was also crazy. He actually went crazy every time he happened to get caught in a crowd. Some people have claustrophobia and can't stand to be in small places. But all they have usually is an uneasy feeling, a little nervousness, or a hot flash of panic. Murphy is the same way in crowds, only worse. He kicks and screams.

He starts screaming and yelling and waving his arms all around, his eyes closed so tight that tears start running down his cheeks. This usually causes him to get dizzy, and he falls on the ground, still yelling and screaming and trying to wave his arms.

"Something just kind of goes snap," he tried to explain to me one time.

We never could figure out Murphy's problem, and those of us who had taken psychology couldn't remember studying anything at all like it, unless perhaps he was somehow afraid of anybody who outnumbered him. T.K. suggested that he must have been born in the middle of a subway rush hour, because that would be enough to scare anybody. Murphy said he couldn't remember, but he was born in Dubuque, anyway, which doesn't have a subway, and he couldn't even take psychology, because the lectures are in large rooms with over two hundred people in them.

Murphy couldn't go to F.A.C., either, unless he got drunk beforehand. So he would usually get himself a six-pack and sit in his room and drink beer and watch cartoons on television. The "Road Runner" was his favorite.

We had to watch him closely whenever we went someplace like the dog track, or a football game, or even the movies. Sometimes he even got nervous just sitting in a car with three other people.

"Jesus Christ, how many people does it take to make a crowd?" T.K. asked him.

"I don't know," Murphy answered. "Sometimes it takes a whole lot, and sometimes only a few. I just start feeling nervous and then something just kind of goes snap."

"Yeah, well, you ought to try and keep it down, you know," T.K. advised him, shaking his head. "Stuff like that can wind you up in the loony bin."

We thought we had found a solution to the problem when we all went to the Colorado-Oklahoma football game. Murphy wanted to go along, and he promised that he would try to behave. We had to go to the game two hours before kickoff to warrant a safe entry, and Murphy made us sit in the end-zone seats in order to reduce our chances of sitting in a crowd.

"For Christ's sake," T.K. said, "this is the Oklahoma game. The stands are going to be jammed."

"Maybe not this far back," Murphy said. "I think I'll be safe up here, and, anyway, I can kind of build up to it."

"Yeah, if an eagle doesn't fly by and take you off," Dayo said. "We're so high up I think I'm beginning to get a nose bleed."

"Very funny, *very* funny," Murphy said. "Pass the flask."

"That's *one* way to keep from getting nervous."

Unfortunately for Murphy, the stands did get crowded, and a few minutes before kickoff even the seats around us were filling up. We all watched Murphy nervously, trying to be inconspicuous about watching him, to make sure that he wasn't getting uneasy. Except for T.K. He was staring Murphy right in the face.

"How do you feel, Murph?" he said. "Huh? How do you feel?"

"I don't feel so good," Murphy said.

"It's those damn drinks," Theo said. "You've been drinking too much."

Murphy was weaving a bit and glancing out of the sides of his eyes at the people still coming in. He was twisting and wringing his hands together and trying very hard to keep himself under control. He closed his eyes and moved his lips as he counted to ten—two or three times.

"Look," I whispered to Theo, "if he jumps up or anything, you grab his arms and I'll try to pop him one. That ought to keep him quiet."

Before Theo had a chance to answer, Murphy let out a ferocious scream and jumped straight up in the air. T.K. had his paper cup up to his lips to take a drink of juiced-up coke and bourbon and Murphy startled him so much that the drink went flying over the couple seated in front of us.

"Get him! Get him! Get him!" I kept yelling.

Murphy went up again, but this time T.K. grabbed his right leg, and Murphy flew up only two feet before he started twisting and then landed on his head. The people around us had quickly vacated their seats and were watching us. The two teams down on the field had even stopped their warm-up calisthenics and were watching the commotion. I felt as if the whole world was watching a few college kids trying to have a good time.

Murphy stood up again and Theo leaped onto his back. He had both his arms and legs wrapped around Murphy's.

"Murphy!" I yelled.

Murphy turned to look at me and I hit him square on the chin, severely bruising my hand and making it hurt like hell. Murphy's eyes rolled upwards under the lids and he fell over backwards, pinning Theo underneath him between the seats.

"*Hot damn you all I swear*," T.K. said, looking up from where he was lying on his back.

"Get the hell off me," Theo said.

"You're all under arrest," the policeman said.

They kicked us out of the stadium and we all went to Murphy's place and put him to bed. We sat down and drank up all his beer and listened to the game on the radio and Colorado won, 7-0, the first time they had done that in 48 years. Pity the Sooners.

NINE

My ride lets me out in a little Utah town

My ride lets me out in a little Utah town that looks as if it had been tossed out alongside the highway as someone drove by during the night. I like the looks of it squatting there in the desert twilight as we drive over the hill toward it, and I have the guy stop there and leave me behind. He still thinks I'm crazy, but I don't want to bother doing anything to try to convince him otherwise. I don't care what he thinks; all I wanted was the ride.

I find a combination cafe-drugstore that is open and decide to get something to eat and worry about where I am going to spend the night. The dilapidated front part of the store holds up a conglomeration of assorted drugs, general goods, hardware, and a warped wooden lunch counter. Three old men are hunched over at the end of the counter talking to the man behind it. Two of the old men are sipping ice-cream sodas and the third is eating a banana split.

The banana-split eater wiggles his seat every so often, twisting back and forth on the high, backless stool, which causes it to pierce and moan, and they all laugh at a joke told by a man in the small television set behind the counter, turned so that the man behind the counter and the three customers can all see it.

The counterman wears a filthy, once-white apron over his skinny old frame and a little stoop on his shoulders, worn down from the weight of his many hard-working and small-thanking years.

"What'll you have?" he asks me, as I settle into the depressions in the top of one of the cracked red plastic stools.

"Hamburger and a cup of coffee," I say. "And maybe a piece of apple pie afterwards." I try smiling to show him that I am friendly, but I can't keep up the facade, my face tires, and I give up. The other men all look at me suspiciously, warily, wondering if I am going to cause any trouble. I am younger than they are, a stranger in their town, and my hair is longer than theirs. I sit and stare at the faded and cracked signs on the wall advertising ham sandwiches and banana splits and then turn both bored eyes toward the TV set.

Counterman places a glass of bubbled water and a spoon and a knife in front of me and then the coffee in a cracked mug that slowly leaks onto the counter, and he starts sizzling the hamburger. The three old men at the end of the counter murmur and mumble, never offering a word to me, friendly or otherwise, the TV set drones on and on, and the hamburger meat sizzles on the grill.

And then all hell breaks loose.

"IT'S SATURDAY, BY GOD!" a voice yells from the door.

Counterman jumps and drops my hamburger in the process of transferring it from grill to bun. I start dabbing my napkin at the coffee I spilled all over me when the thunder first broke through the door. The three other customers readjust their existence from TV to reality and back again.

"YOU DAMN RIGHT IT IS," Counterman roars back, glaring past me and wiping his hands on his apron, which probably just made his hands dirtier. "JEDEDIAH!"

The back door bursts open and a large boy in his late teens comes charging through so suddenly he might have been waiting back there.

"Yes, Pa!" he cries.

By this time the first man through the front door has been joined by two others, one as large as the first and the other just a little over half his size. They are all dressed in much-faded denim jeans and jackets, which are filthy and greasy. The two large men have day's-growth beards, and the three of them stand shoulder to shoulder to head, smoldering, glowering fiercely at Counterman, who has now come out from behind the counter and is standing next to his boy, Jedediah. The three old men at the end of the counter get up silently and edge along the side of the store toward the front door, leaving their sodas and banana split behind. They exchange hurried glances and nods with the three new men and quickly exit behind them into the night. The TV set laughter sounds out of place.

"It's Saturday, by God," the spokesman bellows again, although not as loudly as the first time, "and we just thought we'd come in to pay our little bill, Morgan."

"Yeah, well, now just you look a-here, George," replies Morgan, holding out his warning finger to the three. "Me and Jedediah don't want any trouble, you hear? And neither does the sheriff. You've been behind in your bill-paying now for two months, and I can't run a business on I.O.U.s."

"You can't run a business, period. Jonas and Bill and I just thought we'd come in and see you while we was in town, ain't that right, Boys?" he asks his companions.

Jonas and Bill smile in a leering sort of way, moving out from the big fellow to opposite sides of the room. Jedediah and Morgan keep their eyes on them, looking nervously from one to the other.

"Don't you go messing anything, now, George," Morgan says. "I got the sheriff behind me. So don't you go messing anything or there'll be trouble to pay, too. Now, if you want to pay your bill, you go right ahead and pay. If you don't, then just go right ahead and go."

"Now, that ain't being very friendly. Is it, Jonas?" George says to the littlest one. "Especially when he done give me that ul-tee-matum."

"No, it ain't," Jonas replies, moving away from the door, grinning. "What do you think we ought to do about it, Pa?"

Pa George slowly scratches his beard and surveys the room, finally bringing his eyes to rest on Morgan and his son standing in the middle of the aisle, surrounded by toys and soaps and toothbrushes.

"I think we ought to show old Morgan here that we don't need to do no business in his store. Ain't that right, Bill?"

Bill doesn't say anything. He is the drunkest of the three, and he is weaving in on the two men. I suddenly realize, sitting stupidly on my stool, that I am not in a very advantageous place, but I also realize that two men are outnumbered by three, and a fight definitely looks as if it is going to break out, in which case I should get the hell out of here. The three newcomers are all drunk, but that only makes their sizes look the more distressing—except for Jonas. However, right now Jonas looks as if he thinks he can lick anyone in the place.

I try to look inconspicuous on my stool, but the fact is, I am seated between the two opposing groups. I don't want to break the spell that has fallen over the store, because both groups are merely standing, staring at each other, waiting for someone else to make the first move, and I don't want it to be me—I. What the hell: me.

"Now, you look a-here," Morgan says, making the first move. "You've been drinking, George, and you don't know what you're doing."

"I know perfectly well what I'm doing," George says sweetly.

"All's we want to do is pay you a little friendly visit. What could be more neighborly than that? You said we was to come see you by Saturday. Well, it's Saturday, by God, and here we are."

"Yeah," says Jonas, "what could be more neighborly than that? And here we are." Jonas is moving in on Jedediah's left side, and Jedediah has turned to face him. Morgan is still eyeing George. Bill never says a word; he just weaves back and forth trying to focus on somebody . . . anybody. I have the fearful suspicion he is trying to focus on me.

"You said we was to pay you by Saturday," George says again. "Well . . . IT'S SATURDAY, BY GOD!"

He leaps forward and grabs Morgan around the chest in a bone-crushing bear hug. At the same time Jonas vaults toward Jedediah, only, instead, the little guy meets Jedediah's fist in his nose. He twists back and grabs at a display counter as he goes down. Most of the display, shaving creams and toothpaste, comes crashing down to join him on the floor.

Jedediah turns to help his father, who is struggling up in the air in the arms of George and is turning purple.

"Hey!" I say, and Bill slugs me on the side of my jaw, loosening a few teeth. I tumble off the stool, cracking my head against the next one as I go down, and Bill starts looking down for me.

"Hey, for Christ's sake," I yell. "I'm neutral! Watch the hell what you're doing!"

Jedediah is slugging George on the back of his head with a toy wooden baseball bat, until finally George loosens his hold on Morgan. Morgan drops straight to the floor on his rear, about two feet away from me.

"Hey," I say to him from under the stool, "what the hell's going on here?" But Morgan doesn't answer anything. He just sits there shaking his head and gasping for air.

Then Bill finds me, grabs my foot, and starts dragging me out from under my stool. I try to kick him, but he is weaving too much for me to get off a well-placed shot. Jonas is recovering from the display counter, and he jumps on top of Morgan, who is just beginning to get up again. Jedediah breaks the baseball bat on top of George's head, and George's legs start to fold.

I grab hold of the stool leg as Bill keeps tugging. "Hey," I yell, "for Christ's sake, I'm neutral! I don't belong to the store. Cut it out, will you?"

Jonas and Morgan both get up, square off, and swing at each other. Jonas throws a haymaker that misses, turning him partway around. Morgan counters with an uppercut that misses. Jonas turns back around to Morgan and gets caught with a wayward left that smashes him into the display counter again, and this time he finishes the job. The rest of the counter collapses.

Morgan sits down on a stool as Jedediah rushes up to pull Bill off me. Bill won't let go, so Jedediah kicks him twice in the ribs to encourage him.

Bill lets go. He then jumps up and catches Jedediah on the chin with the top of his head, and they both go down.

I get up warily, wearily from under the stool just as Jonas decides the time has come to try me. He has tried and failed with everyone else in the opposition, so he stalks me slowly in a crouch, with a half smile on his face.

"Look," I say, backing away and putting up my hands in front of me. "I really hate to spoil the party, but I don't belong here, remember? I was just having a burger when you came in, remember? I don't even know the owner. ISN'T THAT RIGHT!" I yell to Morgan. But Morgan sits pooped on the stool and doesn't pay any attention to us. Jedediah and Bill are stirring on the floor. George is just on the floor, the broken bat beside him.

Jonas backs me up against the lunch counter. "Look," I say, "I can take only so much. If you push me any further, I'm going to have to do something about it, okay?"

Jonas's smile turns into a fierce scowl, as much as a little man can scowl. I put my hands back behind me on the counter. Jonas grunts and lunges toward me, and I hold my right arm stiff out in front of me, fist closed, catching him full in the face while he is still in the air. He flips over backwards, lands with a crunch on his back, and my right arm vibrates all the way up to my teeth. My fingers go numb.

The place looks like a battleground. Two display cases are in shambles, their wares scattered all over the floor. George is out at the end of the lunch counter, snoring loudly. Morgan is seated on a stool, his head in his hands on the counter, not looking too well. Jedediah and Bill are still on the floor, but Jedediah is on the point of getting up. He keeps shaking his head to clear it. Bill lies on the floor moving his legs, trying to get up, but nothing will function right. Jonas looks as if he is dead, and I am afraid he is.

I am the only one standing, and I am neutral.

The front door opens, and a big man in a western hat walks in. "Jesus H. Christ," he says, looking around. "What the hell happened here?"

"It's Saturday, by god," I say.

"I'm the sheriff," he glares at me.

"I'm neutral," I gulp, trying to look innocent.

"You're under arrest," he says. Then he looks around. "All of you," he says. "The whole damn lot of you. Who can stand up on his own feet?"

Morgan is up; Jedediah gets up; and we manage to get Bill on his feet with a little trouble. But George and Jonas are something else again. George can't be brought to with a sledge hammer, and Jonas is still alive, but just barely.

"Okay," the sheriff directs. "You two, you take George. Morgan, you and Bill carry Jonas. We're all going to the pokey."

"Look," I say meekly, "you're making a little mistake. I didn't have anything to do with this. I was just sitting there waiting for my burger when—."

"You guys ready? Let's go, then."

I heft George by the shoulders, and Jedediah takes his feet. We get him through the front door and follow the sheriff to the pokey. Morgan and Bill bring up the behind with Jonas. A few natives of the white persuasion stand around and watch us march to the sheriff's office.

Where were you when I needed you?

"I think the best thing for all of you drunks," the sheriff says once we are inside, "would be a good night's stay in the pokey. What do you think?"

Those of us still conscious begin talking at once, each protesting his innocence and trying to give his side of the story.

"Hold it. Hold it! HOLD IT!"

The sheriff looks up at us from behind his desk, where he has started to fill out the paperwork.

"Now, some of you had to have done something. You aren't going to try and tell me that poor old George and his son Jonas stood there and beat each other's brains out while you all just sat around and watched with your thumbs up your asses, are you? There was a lot of damage done in there, Morgan. Now, surely some of you did a little bit of that fighting. Huh? Now, come on. Jedediah? You fought, didn't you?"

"Well, I . . . I had to protect Pa. That's all I did. I had to protect Pa."

"Morgan?"

"They all come in a-looking for a fight, Bob. We had to protect ourselves."

"Bill?"

"My head hurts."

Those are the first words I've heard him say all night.

"And who are you?"

I jump.

"I'm just an innocent bystander. All I was doing was waiting for a hamburger. These three guys came in and looked like they wanted to start something. Then, wham, bam, the fight starts, and I had a hell of a time trying to stay out of it. Jonas on the floor there kept coming after me after he had struck out with those two."

"And who knocked Jonas out?"

I look around trying to find someone.

"He kind of ran into my hand," I say, meekly.

"What?"

"He kind of ran into my hand."

In five short years to come a larger confrontation will take place in Chicago during the Democratic Party convention. People will come into town looking for trouble, other people will see that they find it, and other innocent bystanders will get involved and suffer the truth and consequences. The whole country will practice for the war in Vietnam on television and become outraged at what they see on TV, and the young people looking for trouble will discover how they can use television to help their cause, and people will go to jail, and Chicago will get a black eye, and young people will get bloody heads, and the whole nation will wonder what the hell has become of us. Except for those who knew all along that we had all gone to hell in a handbasket.

In even more years to come, television will change again, from innocent bystander oblivious to the action to innocent bystander observing the action to interested bystander causing the action. A television program will be created that consists of a TV crew following south Florida police around as they make drug busts and stop domestic squabbles. Television: Entertainer, documentarian, social shaper.

"Well, I'm going to kind of run you all in a cell," the sheriff says. "I've got enough on my hands without this whole damn town being turned into a bawdy-house brawl. It will do the three drunks here some good to sleep it off. Morgan, you and Jedediah better stay here, too. I hate to do it, but you *were* disturbing my peace, even though you may not have wanted to and it was in your own place. I'll call up the Mrs. and tell her what's happened to you. And you, Son. I don't know who you are, and I don't care. But a night in the pokey probably wouldn't do you any harm, neither. You just traveling through town? You looking for a place to stay?"

"Yes, sir. I'll be leaving tomorrow. Uh, that is, if it's all right."

"Sure," the sheriff chuckles. "Maybe I can even get you that burger."

"It's Saturday, by God." George stirs on the floor, rolls over, and starts snoring again.

TEN

*I am kind of interested in how the jail looks,
having never been in one before*

I am kind of interested in how the jail looks, having never been in one before, and in how the people feel who are locked up in it. But we are the only ones here. I had heard stories about how Utah is a pretty dull place to live, even if you could have more than one wife, sort of like a perpetual Life in the Fifties.

The cells are worse than I expected them to be, colder, harder, not at all like the one Andy puts Otis in every weekend on "The Andy Griffith Show." The sheriff puts George, Bill, and Jonas in one cell and Morgan, Jedediah, and me in the adjoining one. Bill and Jonas in the other cell go to sleep immediately, joining George, who is still snoring loudly. Morgan is tired and exhausted, and he's extremely worried about what his wife (which one, I wonder) is going to do to him the next morning, but Jedediah puts him at ease, and soon they too are snoring in the dark.

I lie back on the slab and stare up at the ceiling. The darkness settles over us like a cold blanket—the sheriff left us alone—and the quiet is broken only by the occasional snorts and rasps of the sleepers. George turns over and gives one final "It's Saturday, by God" as if to place the cap on one pretty darn good successful day.

I have come a long way in one day. I have virtually left my former life entirely behind me. I have completely and successfully severed all connections with the existence I had led before. Even though I saw some of them only yesterday, my friends from school are already fading from my mind. In time, I will probably go back to them. But now I want to be apart from them. I want to forget.

Or is it something else?
Perhaps I am simply running away.
Running away from what?
Okay, then, perhaps I am running toward something.
Yes, I am. I am running toward the ocean. I am running toward the sea. I want to see the sea. I want to see the water wash the shore. I want to smell the air, feel the sand beneath my bare feet, wash the past from my mind.

Some months ago I was in a philosophy class, taking notes and trying to keep from falling asleep while the instructor droned on and on about logic. I would start to write a sentence and then doze off for a few seconds, then suddenly snap back to reality and see where my pen point had dribbled down the page from the last word of my conscious notes, sometimes right in the middle of a word. After one of these peaceful dozings, when you half-hear the professor's words buzzing around in your brain, seeming to make sense, but not really, I came back to reality with a phrase in my mind. I knew the professor hadn't said it; it had bubbled up from the depths of my own subconsciousness, perhaps stirred up by the professor's droning, perhaps stirred up by my own dreaming.

But the sea can't be me.

What is the logic of that, I had thought, silently repeating the phrase. *But the sea can't be me.* Why not? I even wrote it at the top of my page of notes.

But the sea can't be me.

How true. Nothing else and nobody else but me can be me. But, when I was a kid, I wanted to be Plastic Man.

Plastic Man had always been one of my favorite comic-book characters when I was growing up. And, what was his sidekick's name? Iggy? It doesn't matter. Sidekicks get laughs, but they don't get respect.

Plastic Man was dressed in a neat, colorful costume, and he could change and stretch his shape and arms to fight the evildoers of the day. I always wanted to be like Plastic Man, to be able to change my shape to fit whatever situation, to have a cocky sense of humor and laugh in the face of anything, to lead an exciting life of crime-fighting, to be a hero.

I didn't much care for the costume or running around with Iggy, but I sure liked the part about being different from everybody else and being able to get out of any difficult situation whatsoever just by adapting to it, just by changing.

Plastic Man could stretch his arm fifty feet long to catch that crook. Plastic Man could squeeze his body into the shape of a snake to slither through a keyhole. Plastic Man could expand into a whole house if he wanted to, and the unsuspecting bad guys would blindly walk inside him, thinking they had found the perfect hideout.

Plastic Man was my hero. Plastic Man could do anything.

Years later, long after I had given up believing in heroes, I came across a new Plastic Man comic book, and I was curious to see how my childhood hero was getting along. Plastic Man and Iggy had changed. Plastic Man now seemed to be almost evil, cruel somehow, and mean to people. The craftsmanship didn't seem to be as good as I remembered it, either. The drawing seemed to be cruder, the lines not as professional looking.

Plastic Man! What happened to you? Why did you change?

But the sea can't be me.

From that time onward, I knew that eventually I would have to go to the coast to find out if the sea can't be me, and if so, why. And when events happened as they did at school, I knew that I had to seize the opportunity . . . .

Besides, I was fed up, exhausted, bitter.

I needed a vacation.

No.

No, something else was the reason.

I think about Diane.

Poor Diane, why could we never see eye to eye? Why could we never see eye to poodle-eye?

I called her "Poodle-eye," sometimes, when we had been sitting quietly together in the evening, sharing the silence and holding on to each other and our little dreams. I could stare into her eyes and see the poodle in the right one. Her right eye had a black spot in the iris—which was brown—that was in the shape of the head of a poodle. She got mad at me the first time I mentioned it, when I kept telling her she had a poodle in her eye.

"Are you trying to tell me I'm a dog?" she said, half jokingly.

No, no, I said. And I explained to her, and then she had to pull out her mirror and see for herself. She had never noticed it before.

Well, I said, not many people stare at their own eyes in the mirror. Mostly they're looking for pimples, or wrinkles to smooth out, or hair to smooth down, when people look in the mirror. Most people really don't spend much time looking at their eyes. And yet that's where you can tell what a person is. The essence of a person is always right there in the eyes.

But then, she said, most people already know what they are. They already know who they are, so why should they look into their own eyes? They're more interested in their face.

Yes, I replied, they're more interested in their face, because that's what they show to other people. They believe they must always keep a pretty face forward. But too many people are interested only in how they look to others. Aren't people interested in how they look to themselves anymore?

What are you talking about, she said.

Don't people care what their eyes look like?

Hud, I can never understand you, she said, and she turned away, hurt.

Diane was always trying to understand me, or if she wasn't trying to understand me, then she was trying to reach me. Like the time she, Theo, and I went on a picnic above Chautauqua Park. It had been just another boring Saturday morning; Diane was at my place, and suddenly she and I decided to go on a picnic, and Theo came home and we invited him along. We went to the delicatessen and picked up some bread, Swiss cheese, sliced turkey, and a bottle of Chianti.

We parked Theo's car along the dirt road next to the park and walked the rest of the way up to the top of the grassy, flower-bedecked hill. Diane put down the blanket from the car and began spreading out the food.

"Well," I said, "I think we can have a cocktail before dining. What do you think, Theo?"

"Yes, I think that would be very nice. What do you have?"

"Well, let me see here. I've got some very nice things. I can give you some very nice *Vino Rosa,* uh, *California nineteen-ought-ought.*"

"Oh, that would be very nice. Yes, I believe I'll have some of that, please and thank you."

I poured him some of the wine into a paper cup.

"And you, *Madame?*"

"I'll have some of the *California nineteen-ought-ought,*" she said, holding her nose in the air.

"Very good choice, *Madame.* Excellent choice, I might add. May I pour?"

"You may."

"There."

"Oh, thank you so very much."

"You're so very welcome, I'm sure. Now, how about a goddam sandwich?"

Diane fixed the sandwiches, and Theo and I lay back to enjoy the sun and the view and to sip our wine. From up here we could see most of Boulder stretched out before us. We could even just barely make out the house that Theo, Dayo, and I were renting. The air was warm, and the day was gentle. The only sounds were those that we made and those of a few stray birds.

"From up here," Theo said, "it reminds me of flying, looking down on Boulder like this."

"Yes," I said. "Have you ever dreamed you were flying?"

"Yes! Have you?"

"Sure, quite a number of times. In fact, the last time I dreamed I was flying was about two weeks ago."

"Are you serious?" Diane asked, looking up from making a sandwich. "Do you really dream you're flying?"

"Sure," I answered. "Haven't you?"

"No. No, I'm sure I haven't. Is it fun? I mean, I'm sure it is, but how is it? Describe it."

"Oh, it's great," Theo said. "There you are, just floating around in the air with nothing else around you."

"It sounds exciting."

"A lot of times," I said, "I dream I fly sort of like I have wires attached to me. You know, I'll be sitting down and all of a sudden I just lift straight up into the air and then float over to some other place and sit down again. Whatever position I'm in doesn't matter. I can be sitting or standing. I'm usually watching myself do it in my dream then, you know, like I'm somebody else watching me."

"Yes," Theo said, "that's how it is with me."

"But about two weeks ago I had the best flying dream yet. When the dream started I was already up in the air, *really* up, like a thousand feet or so. And I was flying like you normally think of flying, you know, with your arms stretched out like an airplane. I wasn't flapping them like a bird; I was more like floating. Only I wasn't watching myself like in the other dreams. This time I was inside my body; I was actually observing everything with my own eyes. And I was high up in the air, and then I started doing loops. I just spread my arms out and tilted my head back, and started doing loops. I looked up and saw the sky reach out in front of me, and then slowly the horizon came into my view, only upside down. And then the whole earth started rotating from the top of my vision down, as I completed the loop. I don't remember how many I did."

Diane was just sitting still, fascinated, listening.

"Oh, darn. I wish I could dream about flying. Do you think if I thought really really hard about it before going to sleep that I would dream about flying?"

"It's possible," Theo said.

"I don't think so," I objected. "I don't think it's something you can will to happen. I think it has to be a part of you already. It has to be inside you to begin with. You've got to have a flying soul."

"And I don't have one," Diane pouted. "Is that what you mean?"

"Now, I didn't say that," I said. "Come on, give me a goddam sandwich."

"Yeah," Theo said, "and have some more wine. That's the closest we'll come to flying today."

"It's the only way to fly. Okay, okay! I'm sorry I said it."

Poor Diane. Perhaps she is flying now. Who knows. Her nose knows, perhaps. P'raps not.

I enjoyed the times when I first started taking her out the best of all, those wonderful moments when two people become aware of each other—really become aware of one another for the first, best, and only time. Something happens to your body, and your thoughts are constantly about her. We first met each other at Dayo's swimming party at his folks' house in Fort Collins. I called her the very next day and asked her out, but she already had a date. So, I asked her out for the following night—a very crass thing to do. But, then, I've never minded being crass to achieve an objective. I'll do anything for a joke and practically anything to overcome my shyness in order to achieve an objective.

She accepted.

See?

Unfortunately, I already had a date with Robin that night, but I wanted to go out with Diane, instead, and I didn't want to take the chance of breaking my string of good luck with Diane, so I was going to have to break my date with Robin. But, because I always pride myself on my honesty, I didn't want to have to lie to Robin, and I also didn't want to tell her I was breaking our date because I had made a date with someone else I would rather go out with. So, I didn't tell Robin anything. I just didn't show up that night.

Also unfortunately, the date was for a Sunday night, and the only thing to do was to go to a movie. And the only movie in town worth seeing was one that she had already seen. But we didn't have anything else to do, and I hadn't seen it, and she assured me that it was a good movie and she wouldn't mind at all seeing it again. So, she saw it again.

I'm sure she got bored seeing it for the second time, because I got bored seeing it for the first time. I borrowed a fraternity brother's car for the date, and after the movie we went to a drive-in for a snack. After that I drove out of town to a spot on a hill which overlooks the lake behind the Public Service building. Not much to talk about, but it was pretty at night, and besides, it was closer than the top of Flagstaff Mountain, a rather notorious place for sex, not really a mountain but with a prettier view, and no place I wanted to take Diane on our first date. I'm not *that* crass.

She told me later that she didn't know what to think when I took her there above the Public Service lake on our first date. And I could tell that she turned cool toward me, and she sat on the other side of the car and stared out at the water and the lights of Boulder and the Public Service building reflected on the lake. But all I honestly wanted to do was talk, to get acquainted. Normally I don't like to bother with a lot of preliminary, get-acquainted-type chitchat, but with Diane I felt different. All I wanted to do that night after our boring first-date movie was just get acquainted.

And try to impress her a little bit.

After a few abortive starts on my part, we managed to get a conversation going, and she warmed up a little when she realized that I wasn't after her body. The evening turned out to be pleasant after all.

So, after that I started meeting her during the week at night and we would study together. Sometimes we would go to the library, and afterwards we would go up on the Hill for a cup of coffee before I took her back to her sorority house. Sometimes we would study in Hellems Annex, in the classrooms that were left open for that purpose, the same building where T.K. had done his graffiti research. Once when we went to Hellems Annex to study, all the rooms except for a large lecture room were occupied by someone else, and because we liked to be alone together, we used that one. A piano was in the room, and I amused Diane by composing a song to her, right there on the spot.

I never told her that I had composed that same song many times before, only changing the name to fit the girl. But, actually, that didn't make much difference. It had her name in it. That made it her song.

I also think about during that magic period of our getting acquainted how I would take her back to her sorority house at closing and kiss her good night, and then walk back to my place. I would go to bed then and lie back and think about her, and put my hand over my nose so I could smell the perfume—her perfume—that still lingered on my fingers where I had held her hand.

I would lie in the darkness and smell my perfumed hand that had held hers through the movie or on the way home, and I would smell my hand and think about her and hope that I would dream about her and then I would go to sleep.

Sandman, Sandman, show me your wares. Here, Sir, here, Sir, here are my wares. Now we're getting some wares.

But you can't will yourself to dream about something.

ELEVEN

The sheriff stands on one foot leaning against his desk

The sheriff stands on one foot leaning against his desk and gives his lecture before releasing us. We all stand in a semicircle around him, and *canyoubelieveit* we all have our heads down in a sort of hangdoggie fashion. We look like little boys getting bawled out for biting sister Susie or stealing her cookie or something. I guess this is what the whole law system is built upon. After all, grown-up society is just a reflection of childhood society, and punishment for doing wrong is just an extreme extension of the forms of punishments that are carried out on us when we are very young and go around biting sister Susie or stealing her cookie or something.

"Now, I want you boys to remember this little episode, and I don't want it to ever happen again, or else I'm going to have to do something harsher. Now, you, George, you ought to be real ashamed of yourself. First, for going out and getting real drunk like that in the first place, and then for going into Morgan's store and starting a fight."

George mumbles something into the floor.

"What did you say?" the sheriff asks.

"I said, 'And then not even getting to enjoy the fight.'"

"Well, that's good enough for you. I understand you still owe Morgan that money. Now, you know this trouble wouldn't have happened in the first place if you'd just plain pay him what you owe him. Then you could all be friends again like you used to be, and then you wouldn't be making my Saturday nights one hell of a mess."

"Yes, Sheriff. I know. And I'm real sorry about that. Morgan, you know I wouldn't hurt you for the world. I'm real sorry about what happened. And Bill and Jonas are real sorry, too. Aren't you, Boys?"

"Yeah. Yeah, Morgan, I'm real sorry about what happened."

"Me, too, Morgan. Jedediah. Real sorry."

"I'm sorry, too," Morgan says. "And so is Jedediah. Aren't you, Jedediah?"

"Yes. Yes, of course. I'm real sorry about what happened."

"All right," says the sheriff. "Now that you're all sorry about it, you'd better *do* something about it. You boys caused some more damage to Morgan's store last night, you know, so you'll have to add that on to your bill."

"Oh, yes," George replies, "we won't forget that. We won't forget that, Morgan, and we'll pay it just as soon as we can. We'll pay it all just as soon as we can. And we're real sorry about what happened. Aren't we, Boys?"

"Yes. Oh, yes."

"Yeah, real sorry."

"Well," Morgan says, "don't worry about it. I know you'll pay it just as soon as you can. You're all good fellows, and we're all friends here. And I'm real sorry about what happened, too."

This is beginning to turn into a real sorry state of affairs, and then the sheriff turns to me.

"There's no reason why you can't go trotting along, young man. Sorry about all the inconvenience caused you, but at least you got a free bed out of the deal, right?"

"Right. Thanks, Sheriff."

George comes up to me and starts pumping my hand.

"I'm real sorry that we drug you into this mess. I wouldn't have had it happen for the world. I'm real sorry."

"Yes, me, too," Jonas says, grabbing my left hand and starting on it. "I'm real sorry I flattened you like I did, and I hope you'll see it in your heart to forgive me."

"Yeah. Sure. That's okay. You know? Yeah, sure. Look, everything's really all right. So, I'll just be shoving along now, and thanks for everything, Sheriff. Goodbye. Goodbye."

I manage to break away from them, and as I close the front door behind me, I hear George say to Morgan, "I'm real sorry this all had to happen. The Lord knows I never meant to cause you any harm."

Those guys just never give up.

I stand outside the door for a second and catch my breath before it darts around the corner and we can take off again. I am glad to get away from that sorry bunch inside. I start walking down the dusty road toward the highway, where I can pick up a ride going west. Actually, considering the location, I will have to go more south than west. Not too many highways and byways—and probably not too much traffic, either—goes this way across Nevada. And Nevada would be one hell of a place in which to get stranded. I figure my best bet is to head south to Las Vegas and then cut across the desert to Los Angeles from there.

As I walk out to the highway and prepare to set up shop, I start thinking once again about the group I shared the night with. I am amused and, yet, somehow repulsed by the way they were carrying on when I left them. I have an intense aversion to small talk.

Hi. How's it going?
Great. Just great. How about you?
Oh, pretty good. Can't complain.

Words that are just meaningless sounds. Words that go on and on and on and on and don't mean anything. Well, actually, all words mean *something*. No, what I mean is words that don't actually contain the speakers' intended meaning in them once you examine them. Trouble is, no one cares *or* examines them.

Well, that's the way it goes.
Yeah, I guess you can't win them all.
Yep, that's the way the old cookie crumbles.
You said it.

Words that do nothing but fill up empty spaces in conversations because the speakers are too lazy to think before they open their mouths. Small-talk words that have lost their original meanings. They have been used so often that they just fall into a pattern that fits easily into the grooves along people's tongues. People no longer have to consider a choice between two words. All they need do is mentally flip the switch to fit the occasion, and the patter comes out. Hello. Good to see you. Is that so? You don't mean it. Isn't that nice. Yes, that's really something. Catch you later. Goodbye.

How do you get down off an elephant?
I don't know. How do you get down off an elephant?
You don't get down off an elephant! You get down off a duck!

Words are fun to play with. However, for some people with no other outlet for creativity or for some people who just don't have a good sense of humor that is appreciated by anyone else, wordplay just turns into another way for them to be obnoxious.

An awful lot of the words we use every day don't mean much. In some cases they have lost their meanings altogether. In other cases they have acquired new meanings that no one could guess. Two people can be rambling on and on and not mean at all what they are actually saying, and yet the two people know what the other one means. At least, they *think* they know what the other one means. In actuality, the speakers, to the listeners, mean what the listeners think the speakers mean. But the speakers think they mean not what the listeners think they mean, but what they themselves think they mean. Or something like that. The words themselves are only tools for a lot of hoped-for understanding. See you later, Alligator. After 'while, Crocodile.

A philosophy professor of mine once discussed how to put an end to an argument one Saturday afternoon when he was playing faculty supervisor at a fraternity woodsie. He said, once you perceive that an argument is not going to be resolved to your satisfaction, interrupt the other guy and ask for a definition of a term that's being used, like, "What is the meaning of 'saippuakivikauppias'?" Then, once you've got that definition, ask for the meaning of another word that's being used. Finally, once you've got a side discussion going on about the meaning of words that are being used, bring the whole discussion to a crashing stop by asking, "What is the meaning of 'meaning'?"

No two people have the same meaning for a word. Every word means something just a little bit different to everyone else. So, in order to make yourself understood, you have to keep making stabs at a word, hitting around all possible definitions of it like darts thrown at a bull's-eye, constantly explaining, defining, refining, until finally your listener understands just exactly what you intended. Or, at least has a pretty darn good understanding of what you thought you meant. However, that takes a lot of time, and most times your listener will leave you standing all alone with a handful of darts.

In years to come, the inane patter of public communication will reach resounding depths. Someone will think up a clever way to signify the end of an encounter and say, "Have a nice day." We will keep hearing "Have a nice day" and seeing little circular yellow Happy Faces so much that we will soon afterwards get sick of them both. Some people will abstract the abstraction two steps further and substitute "Have a good one" for "Have a nice day." Other people will think they have thought up a cleverer encounter-ending and start saying, "Have a good rest of your life." At least one obnoxious wordplayer with no outlet for creativity will think the ultimate clever encounter-ending has been conceived when he will walk away and say, "Have a good eternity." Few people will consider the irony that some of the original meanings of "nice" were "foolish," "wanton," and "ignorant."

"Have a good eternity."

Screw you, Charley! Where do you come off playing God by directing how the rest of my eternity is going to be, how the rest of my life is going to be, or even how the remaining portion of my day is going to be?

Okay, okay. Surely, they will all *really* mean "(I hope you h)(H)ave a nice day," and they will not consciously or subconsciously take on any Deitic responsibilities. On the other hand, how will I really know what they will really mean? What is the meaning of "Have"? What is the meaning of "really"? What is the meaning of "meaning"?

In years to come, I will also become annoyed in restaurants when the waiters and waitresses and waitpersons and waitperdaughters will set my plate before me and say, "Enjoy your meal." What audacity! Don't tell *me* what to do with food I haven't even seen prepared! Okay, okay. Surely, they will all really mean, "(I hope you e)(E)njoy your meal." But maybe not. Maybe they don't even care. Maybe they are not even realizing that they are uttering anything. Maybe they are just flipping a switch and out it comes. At any rate, as often as I can, whenever this inane, meaningless meal encounter-ending is tossed over the waitsomething's shoulder, I will counter with, "I will, if it's any good."

And don't call me "Shirley."

Communication is a funny thing. In many instances it has deteriorated into nothing but a ritual that people go through when they see each other. The standard greeting, for example. People don't really mean "How are you?" They usually don't even care. And they certainly don't want to have to stand there while you go through a list of how you are feeling and what your latest health status is. What they undoubtedly mean is "Hello. I see you and I acknowledge that I see you, and that's all." And you know that this is all they mean, so you don't answer the actual question by telling them how you really are. In other words, you ignore their question, because it doesn't mean anything. You tell them you're just fine and then ask them how they are, knowing full well that they aren't going to answer your question and tell you, either. I wonder why the thing that human beings do best—communicate—has deteriorated into the thing we do worst.

I got tired of the old "How are you?" "Fine, how are you?" ritual so much once that I couldn't fulfill my part anymore. When people who didn't really care how I was asked me in passing "How are you?" I just couldn't say "Fine. How are you?" and keep on walking. I couldn't go through with it, even though I *was* fine. So, instead of answering "Fine" as expected, I used to say "Terrible" and make a face. That's all. Just simply "Terrible."

The result was catastrophic. The people I met would suddenly stop and turn and watch me walking away, and they would laugh nervously to themselves, their gears all shot. They couldn't cope with it, because I hadn't followed the ritual. I hadn't completed the pattern. You could actually see them struggling to try to explain to themselves what had just happened. They acted as if they had been derailed suddenly and they had to force themselves back onto the track after having lost their train of thought. Woo! Woo!

Diane finally made me stop doing it. She said my answer was really disconcerting to people, and it caused a lot of unnecessary trouble, and it was upsetting, and why couldn't I just make things a lot easier by answering "Fine" like everybody else?

So, I started answering "Fine" like everybody else, but I didn't like it. I didn't want to be like everybody else. However, everyone else liked it, and people didn't suddenly stop to watch me walk away as they used to do, standing there trying to get their brains functioning right again. Every once in a while I would forget, though, especially if I were surprised by someone and had to make a fast answer. If I could see encounters coming, I usually responded with the oh-so-proper answer, Fine. Just fine. How are you.

Usually, if I could see them coming, though, I tried to avoid them altogether. I would rather pretend I didn't see people than have to go through with the ritual. If they were across the street, I would look off to the right, or watch a passing car, or anything else to avoid coming into contact with their eyes. Sometimes they would speak, anyway, and I would have to act surprised.

Oh! Hi! Fine. How's it going?

Of course, this was only people with whom I had only a passing acquaintance. With my friends, with T.K. and Dayo and Bido, a chance meeting on the street was no problem. We had no ritual that had to be followed, unless it was an intentional ritual of *no* ritual. With friends, you don't even need to say anything, and you can carry on very intelligent, silent conversations. With friends, silent communication is very satisfactory at times and sometimes it's even best; no words at all are needed. It's easier on the ears, too.

No, I would pretend not to see only people to whom, say, I had been introduced at a party or something, but whom I didn't know very well. They would recognize me as being that person to whom they had been introduced at that party or something and to whom they thought they ought to say something. But what do you say to someone you don't know very well?

Hi. How are you?

Oh, fine. Just fine. And you?
Fine. Just fine.
That's fine.

I'd rather look the other way and pretend I didn't see them.

But eventually that gets you a reputation of being stuck up, aloof, egotistical, cocky, and self-centered. And an anti-social s.o.b., besides.

But, then, nobody's perfect, They sometimes say. On the other hand, the reverse is also true. What do They know? And just who are these "They," anyway?

So, I stand alongside the highway and start thumbing. For hours my thumbing is to no avail, and I'd like to know what the hell *that* means. Something is always to *no* avail. Just *once* I'd like for something to be to an avail, and I don't even know what the hell an "avail" is!

The few cars that are out on the road are apparently just on a Sunday outing and don't want to pick up any hitchhikers. Actually, it's the drivers of the cars who don't want to pick up any hitchhikers, but you know what I mean. I mean, you know what I meant to mean. I have to wait until the afternoon before a car stops to pick me up. I mean—. No, forget it. I don't know how far I have walked down the highway backwards with my thumb in the air until a car stops, but I have not gone through any other towns. I am seeing some real slow backwards scenery, though.

The driver is a man, about forty, wearing a suit with his shirt collar open and his tie pulled down. He reaches across the seat and rolls down the window.

"Where you heading?"

"Las Vegas. On the way out to California."

"That's where I'm going. Vegas. But I'm in a hurry. You mind sharing the driving and going all night straight through?"

"Heck, no. that would be fine with me. I've seen enough of Utah already."

"Good. Then, climb in and let's go."

I barely get seated before he roars off.

"My name's Parker," offering his hand without taking his eyes off the road. "Got to get to Vegas by tomorrow morning. Business deal. Can't wait. Then spend the rest of the week on a little vacation. You know, gambling, girls . . . . Heh, heh, know what I mean?"

He doesn't give me a chance to say anything, which I like, because I don't like talking to strangers, anyway, and all I can do is nod my head once in a while and say "Oh?" and "Yes." and "Is that right?" That is all he wants me to do, anyway. Rest of the ritual. Part of the pattern.

"Been living in Utah for the last ten years. Hate it. Hate it like crazy with a passion. Wouldn't live here if you paid me, except I had to. And I have to. Business keeps me here. So, I guess you *can* say they pay me to live here. Heh, heh. Except now I might be able to get out. That's why I'm going to Vegas. Might be able to pick up a little business there. Store owner. Liquor store, you know? Yeah, I'd like that. Lots of action in Vegas, know what I mean? I'm not married. No, was once, but I don't like to be tied down. Some people just can't be tied down to one woman for the rest of their lives. Against their nature. They belong out in the wilds, out in nature. That's where life is, you know? Free spirit. Give me the free life any time. You married? No, of course not. Take my advice, if the notion ever gets you, check her out pretty carefully, know what I mean? Heh, heh, make sure you know what you're getting into. Ha! Ha! Get it? Yeah, heh, well, I didn't know what I was getting into when I got married. She wanted all the dainty little things some women like, you know, knickknacks, or whatever the hell they are. Doilies, dainties . . . God, enough to drive a man wild. And it did me, too. Couldn't take it any longer. Got to going out on long hunting trips, camping trips, you name it, because she wouldn't go. Hated it, couldn't stand it. Couldn't see why I enjoyed it so much. I didn't, actually, but it was just a chance for me to get out of the house and get away from her. She didn't see that, couldn't see it, thank God. Couldn't stand Vegas, either. Didn't like it, the fast action, bright lights, wild life. Now, there's a town! Hope I can swing this deal and settle there. I'd really like that. You ever been to Vegas?"

I am exhausted and I haven't said a word. I practice taking breaths with him just to see if I can keep up with him. I can, but with difficulty. He never takes his eyes off the road, and he drives carefully, using only one hand to talk with, but he is a terror with the speeches. If he drove the way he talks, we would have either been dead by now or already in Las Vegas.

"No," I answer. "No, as a matter of fact, I've never been to Las Vegas before. In fact, I've never been to Nev—."

"Yeah, well, you'll like it, let me tell you. If you like bright lights, places that never sleep—except around nine o'clock in the morning, heh, heh. People dressed up—I mean, *really* dressed up. Of course, you've always got your hick tourists, too, you know what I mean? Mom and dad and kiddies on a vacation all dressed up in their fake Western garb. You know, from out in Kansas or Iowa or some place, and think they're really going to dress the part and get garbed up in all sorts of corny outfits and walk around the streets like everybody owes them something with their little cameras hanging around their necks like little saddlebags and their awful shirts and shorts and their constant looking to see a movie star or somebody famous getting married or getting a divorce. God, are they awful! But I'm talking about the dressed-up upperclass people, you know? Nothing like the night life there, nothing like it anywhere! Of course, I haven't been everywhere, and I'll be the first to admit that, but I'm sure that Vegas night life compares favorably to that anywhere, you name it. New York, Paris, uh, anywhere! Where you from?"

"Huh? Oh, uh, Colorado. I go to school there."

"Yeah? Vacation or something like that for you?"

"Yes, something like that. Sort of a leave of absence."

"Yeah? That's interesting. Pretty desolate country around here, huh? Yeah, desolate's the word for it. Even worse in other parts around here. Blah! You can have it. Course, there's desert around Vegas, too, but it's a different kind of desert. The people make up for it there, you know? Not like the religious crackpotted nuts around here. Say! I've got a riddle for you. You ready? When is a Jew a Gentile? Huh? When is a Jew a Gentile?"

I play the game. When is a Jew a Gentile?

"You mean, like the fact that Jesus, the father of the Christians, was a Jew?"

"He was? Nope. Nope, but that's a pretty good answer. No, when is a Jew a Gentile? You give up? When he's not a Mormon. Heh, heh."

My god, I think, I've latched onto a raving maniac here, a real loony. I smile and chuckle knowingly, even though he isn't looking at me, and shake my head in the polite way Diane taught me.

"You don't get it, do you? Well, not knowing much about Utah, I guess you wouldn't. No, it's like this. A Mormon calls everyone who isn't a Mormon a Gentile. So, a Jew isn't a Mormon, right? So, to a Mormon, a Jew is a Gentile. Right? Ha! How about that? Religion sure is a funny thing."

Yes, I have to agree with him there, all right. He goes right on into another suppository expository, and I half listen to him just enough to know when I have to make some answer to let him know I am listening, but his comment about religion being a funny thing starts me thinking about Xeno.

Xeno the Philosopher. "Xeno" was short for Xenocrates, an actual ancient Greek philosopher, and once you knew the modern guy, you could see how easily Xeno had picked up the name—even if he did give it to himself. He was a sort of pseudo-beatnik, but in the sense that he wasn't as pseudo as most pseudo-beatniks. I think sometimes he really believed himself. He was sincere, whereas most of the other pseudos I knew just acted that way for a kick, to shock people, to rebel against somebody or something, or just to rebel for the sake of rebelling. But Xeno was an honest-to-god pseudo-beatnik.

He had been around C.U. for some time—forever, some people said. At least, he was well established when I got there, and he didn't seem to be in any hurry to leave, either. Perhaps he was just another professional student. His major was philosophy, and he could usually be seen in the student-union cafeteria sitting at a table with a bunch of other philosophy students and pseudo-beatniks expounding on some sort of thing or other. He wrote way-out articles for the school paper, too. He was always on a religion kick, always studying some exotic religion. Just as soon as you thought he was going to be a practicing Buddhist, he switched on you and the next time you saw him he was a Muslem, or maybe a Sufi.

Like the pseudo-pseudo-beatniks, Xeno wore outlandish garb, I guess you would call the clothes he wore. His constant outfit, summer or winter, was sandals, cut-off jeans, and a Mexican vest. No, actually I'm kidding. He didn't always wear this outfit, but he wore it often enough to make you think he did. No, actually I'm kidding again. I don't think he meant to make you think anything. No, actually I'm not trying to "kid" you; I'm just trying to get through this paragraph.

He had dark black hair and a full beard—a really good-looking beard, as a matter of fact. He kept his beard much neater—well trimmed—than most other bearded beatniks.

He also had a look about him that caused people—even straight students—who didn't know him well to refer to him as "Dopester." Xeno always had an energy in his body that these straights interpreted as the influence of drugs, and he always talked in an energetic, hyper fashion that reminded some people of being high on dope. I never knew Xeno to take any drugs. I believe that was just the way he was: high on life.

But most people who didn't know Xeno always judged him by his appearance, and they either sneered at him or made fun of him. Once, as Xeno was leaving a movie at the campus theater, some guy behind him was making fun of Xeno to the guy's date, cracking jokes about look what the cat drug in, as they followed Xeno up the aisle. Xeno turned around to the guy, gave him his best "holier-than-thou" look, and said, "It is unfortunate, Sirrah, that the only thing we have in common is humanity."

That put the joker down.

"Hud," Xeno said to me once, "what is your goal in life?"

"My goal? My point? You mean, what do I want out of life? I don't know. Just to be happy, I guess."

"Yes," he said knowingly, slowly nodding his head up and down and pursing his lips. "Some form of hedonism. But which kind, Hud?"

"Which kind? What do you mean?" I said, walleting my mouth.

"Well, explain your philosophy further. What form of hedonism do you practice?"

"I don't know what you're talking about. I'm not trying to practice any form of hedonism. I'm practicing happiness—at least, I try to. I don't know nothin' 'bout no birthin'! I don't even know anything about any hedonism. Can't I just be happy without being some kind of hedon?"

Xeno leaned back as best he could on the backless stool. We were in a place that catered to the pseudo-beatnik clientele, a kind of hip coffee shop down in the basement of a drugstore, called The Place. Even though the beat movement seems to have been beaten down by now. The tables were high and small, and the stools were just as high and smaller. I was having a cup of hot cinnamon cider, but I'll be damned if I knew what Xeno was drinking. I had never seen such foul-looking sludge before.

In years to come, the Beats will be totally beaten out by another wasted, idealistic, unrealistic, optimistic but ultimately worthwhile-to-society movement, the hippies, the Flower Children, the Love Generation, the "Oh, wow, everything is beautiful" kids. Black turtlenecks and tights will be replaced by tie-dyed T-shirts, granny skirts, and glasses; bongo drums and poetry readings will be replaced by sitars and acid rock; and Kerouac will be replaced by Leary. "Tune in, turn on, and drop out" will become a catch phrase, and long dirty hair will become the norm. "Never trust anyone over 30" will become another catch phrase, "freaks" will become an admirable label, and "pigs" will attain an additional, pejorative meaning, whatever that means. Haight-Ashbury will become a Mecca in San Francisco, free love will become freer, and LSD and "trips," both bad and good, will enter the straight lexicon. In fact, "beatniks" will become old-fashioned, hippies will become tiresome, and the times they will a-change some more.

Well, society needs an innocent, safe shot in the arm, a bust in the butt, a chop to the chops now and then. Of course, the ruling generation will never get it, can never see the worth of the younger, revolting generation at the time—only many years later when the ruling generation has been phased out, passed by, and passed over and now becomes the passé generation, and then the revolting generation becomes the ohmygodcanyoubelieveit establishment. Then we can look back at the long hair and the unwashed bodies and the casual sex and the freely used drugs and the chemical and spiritual mind benders and the kids leaving home for San Francisco being sure to wear some flowers in their hair, and then we can see that maybe, after all, those beatniks and those hippies did some good. Either that or else they were just one big embarrassment from the Embarrassing Sixties. At the time, however, the straights just don't know what the hell the bents are talking about. All we need is love.

"What are we, Hud?"

"Huh? What?"

"What are we, Hud?" Xeno leaned forward peering into my face. He was serious.

"What do you mean, 'What are we?'? I don't know about you, Xeno, but I'm a boy, and I can get the girls to prove it."

"No, no, no, Hud. I'm not talking about sex. I'm not talking about gender. I'm talking about humanity. What are we, Hud, if we're not people?"

I took a sip of cider.

"You've got me there," I had to admit.

"We're people, aren't we, Hud?"

"Yes," I agreed. "Yes, we're people, all right, by gosh and by golly."

"Know thyself."

"What?"

"Know thyself, Hud. Do you know who you are?"

"Look, Xeno, are you sure this conversation is going anywhere? I've got a class in about fifteen minutes."

"Hud, this may come as a shock to you, but you do not know who you are."

"Xeno, this may come as a shock to *you*, but I know exactly who I am. I'm Hud Holyoke. Who the hell are you? And what the hell are you talking about?"

"You don't understand, Hud Holyoke. You don't know who you are."

"Okay, okay, I don't know who I am. Who am I?"

"You're a people, Hud. You are a humanity. And we all must know who we are, not just singularly, but collectively, as well. In fact, we would all be better off if we all owned a globe of the Earth and every day looked at it just to remind ourselves how little we are, how little we know, how little we mean to the world, but how much we *Earthlings* depend on each other in order to keep on keeping on. In point of fact, we should know more about ourselves collectively than singularly. And how do we get to know about humanity? What are you doing in school, Hud?"

"I don't know, Xeno." I finished my cider. "What am I doing?" I had figured out how to move the conversation along more briskly.

"You are studying, Hud. At least, you should be. So, I study humanity, Hud. And what is it that all humanity have in common?"

"Uhhh . . . don't tell me. Sex?"

"Religion, Hud. All humanity has some form of religion. Even the Russians, Hud, only they don't know it. They call it by a different name, or else they keep it hidden from the authorities. So, if all humanity have religion in common, then doesn't it follow that in order to understand humanity, one must understand religion?"

In years to come, keeping a globe of the Earth to remind us of how much we Earthlings depended on each other would be frustrating, because the colors and boundaries in Africa will change now and then. In many more years to come, a better idea will be to have a globe with no national boundaries at all. Who would have thought back in the Sixties that a nation such as the U.S.S.R. would ever break up and have to be recolored? Who could have imagined that a country such as Czechoslovakia would have to become bi-colored?

I don't know if I was just anxious not to miss my class or if I actually caught a few gleanings from his logic, but somehow he started to make sense and I just had to agree with him.

"I have to agree with you, Xeno."

"And that is what I've been doing all this time, Hud. I have been studying religions in order to study humanity. Before I know who I am, before I know who humanity are—. Is? Humanity is? Humanity are?"

"I don't know, either, but go on."

"Before I know who we are collectively, I have to know all the different religions. When I know them all, then I can settle on one—if there *is* one true religion—and then I will know who I am. And then I will know who *we* are. And then I will be satisfied."

"Well, yes. Yes, I see your point now. So, that's why one day you're a Jew and the next day you're a Mormon."

"Well, I don't change quite that quickly. But, yes, that is why I seem to practice many different religions. Not only do I find it educational, but I also find it satisfying. Have you tried Zen?"

"No, uh, I can't say that I have. Not lately. Why? Is it nice? Look, I've really got to get to class."

"This will only take a moment. You know, part of Zen is the mental problems. When you know the answers to the problems, then you reach the soul-satisfying state and you are at one with yourself and the universe. Tell me, you know the sound of two hands clapping. What is the sound of one hand clapping?"

"Xeno, what is the sound of one fist in one face? Mine in yours?"

"Ha! Ha! Well said, my friend. Okay, then, how trained is your mind? If I say 'Do *not* think of a white elephant,' can you do it?"

"What?"

"'Do *not* think of a white elephant.' Most people can't. If you tell them 'Do *not* think of a white elephant,' they immediately start thinking about a white elephant. Some, even, with Dumbo ears. When you have mastered your mind, then you have mastered the ability not to think about white elephants. Come, let's go to class."

We slid down off the stools and started to climb our way back out into the sunshine once again.

"Aren't you going to finish your . . . uh, coffee, Xeno?"

"That? No. Frankly, I can't stand the stuff."

TWELVE

"So I figured, what the hell, you know?"

"So I figured, what the hell, you know? I had some cash that was just lying around doing nothing, so why not invest it in a little business? Especially if the other guy was going to do all the managing and all I had to do was take in my share of the profits, you know?"

I nod my head and say "Yeah" again for the somethingth time and vaguely watch the rolling landscape roll by. The afternoon is late, and my ears are getting tired, even though I have been using only half of both of them. I have long ago given up keeping an interested look on my face, because he never bothers to look at me, anyway, but just keeps his eyes on the road ahead and his mouth moving south.

"So I'm heading down there now to see if I can finish this deal and get things rolling along, singing a song. Say, how's about us pulling into that place up ahead there and breaking a bean together?"

And before I can even get my "Yeah" in, he drives up in front of the roadside diner and parks. We get out and go inside. Stretching my legs feels good, and so does resting my ears while he chews his cheeseburger.

He insists on paying for my meal, because I am going to do most of the driving from now on, and not only for that reason I have to agree with him. Only to myself, of course. Naturally I have to make some modicum of social protest, but also naturally he won't hear any of it. Save it to shoot at the tables when we get to Vegas, he says.

"Now, look," he says as he climbs into the back seat of the car. "I want you to wake me up around midnight or so, you hear? No sense in you driving any longer than that. Wake me up around midnight, and I'll take her on in from there. I've been up since four o'clock this morning, and I'm just a wee bit pooped, you know? But if you start getting sleepy before then, then think nothing of waking me up, and I'll take over, okay? If you start nodding, or catch your mind drifting, then pull over to the side of the road and wake me up. I can stay awake for days on end and don't mind it, but you're probably not used to it. Also, watch the steering wheel. It's pretty bad and there's a lot of play in it, so be careful. These roads we're going to go on are pretty winding and treacherous, and it's going to be darker than a witch's cunt, so be careful about the play in the steering wheel. We're not in so big a hurry that we want to go flying off the road, so just take it kind of easy until you get used to the car. Got any questions?"

Yes. When are you going to shut up?

"No, I don't think so. I can't think of any."

"You've got the highway numbers all straight in your mind? You won't be getting us lost, now, will you?"

"Nope. I'm okay there."

"There's money in the ashtray if you need gas, and I think you will. Keep an eye on the gauge and don't let it get too low. We don't want to run out in the middle of nowhere, so it might be wise to stop at the first convenient one. Around these parts at night everybody just closes up at sundown and goes inside to screw and beat off."

"Right."

"Well, if there's any problem, just pull over to the side and wake me up. And wake me up around midnight anyway, okay?"

"Right toe."

My god, will he never shut up and go to sleep and leave me alone?

"Well, I guess that's about all I can think of to do. You ought to be all right. Just keep a cool head and a steady grip and keep your eye on the road, and don't let your mind wander. You start letting your mind wander and next thing you know you wake up in the bottom of a ravine."

Yes, Dad.

"Right. Right."

"Well, good night."

"Good night . . . . And don't worry about a thing."

Oops. I am afraid that my closing comment might start him off again, but luckily it doesn't.

He lies down in the back seat with his knees sticking up in the air, and I start the car off and bump back onto the highway. I am nervous as hell, as if this were the first time I'd ever driven and my dad had just finished with all his preliminary, but unnecessary, instructions, the same way he did when he nervously tried to inform me about sex. However, not too much later I hear regular breathing and an occasional snore from the back, and so I relax and settle down to do some serious driving. The sky is dark now, and the night is going to be a long lonely one of monotonous driving. Not many cars are on the highway to keep me company.

The darkness pulls itself in around me and soon the only illumination comes from our car's headlights. The moon is nowhere to be seen to light up the surrounding countryside. I can tell from the curves in the highway that we have moved into some mountainous terrain, but I can't tell how mountainous, because of the dark. Every once in a while the headlights catch some critter's eyes scurrying along the side of the highway.

Xeno used to say in his more despondent moments that we were all God's critters scurrying along the highway of life, stopping every so often to stare into the illumination of the speeding headlights of knowledge speeding toward us and, then, WHAM!

No one knew exactly what he meant, but I believe that's not only what Xeno wanted, but also the best way to accept whatever he had to say. Let his listeners and disciples make of it what they will. Let it mean what they want it to mean to themselves. Gee, isn't that how religion is supposed to be? Assuming there is any reason behind anything, that is.

Xeno didn't get despondent too often; he was comparatively one of your "more happier" beatniks, as Xeno himself used to say, ungrammatically, just to bug people. But when he did get despondent, he really went all the way. Like the night of the party at his place that Dayo and I went to. We usually didn't fraternize with Xeno and his crowd too often on a social basis, because they tended to be a bit too far out for us. But this particular time, Dayo and I had run into Xeno at F.A.C. at the Sink, and he told us he was having a party—rather, a party was going to be happening at his place—and he urged us to come on by. Xeno and his roommates didn't *have* parties in the sense of, say, "Say, why don't we have a party this weekend?" "Good idea! Who'll we invite?" He said that somehow a party just happened to happen at his house every other Friday night. Along about seven o'clock people started showing up at the door with their liquor and their dates and their appetites, looking for fun, and the party just grew like that little Topsy girl everybody hears about but nobody knows the trouble she's seen anything about. Some cats would show up at the door saying they were from Denver and So-And-So said a swinging party was happening at this address. Xeno or one of his roommates would just open the door wider and tell them to come on in, the party's fine. Except for off Fridays. Then they would tell the visitors to come back next week.

Sometimes, Xeno said, he would have a paper to do or a test coming up, and he would just trot off to the library and the party would get along just as well without him. In some cases neither he nor any of his roommates stayed at the party, and apparently everybody still had a good swinging time. Xeno didn't mind, as long as nothing was broken or stolen, and sometimes not even if something was broken. Or stolen. Everyone brought extra liquor and many times music, so what did he care? Life was too short to care.

This particular Friday night, nothing else was happening, and Dayo and I didn't have anything else to do, so we decided that we might as well go and see what Xeno's parties were like. We figured we could always leave if we didn't like it.

"The way I figure it," Dayo said as he slid in behind the wheel of A-Frame, "is we can always leave if we don't like it."

"Dayo," I said, "sometimes your profound analyses of the obvious simply astound me. Even the dullest of minds is champion of the obvious, you know."

"Eat it," he smiled.

"Tich, tich. Such talk. Hump it and let's go. We gotta get the beer first."

"Eas-y! Eas-y! A-Frame isn't a machine to say 'Go' and 'Stop' to. She has to be handled gently. She has to be stroked. She has to be warmed up first, just like any woman."

"Yeah, well, just goose her and let's go, huh? We don't have all night, as the well-worn saying wears well, and we have to get the beer first and I'm afraid old A-Frame just might poop out on us before we get there if we don't hurry."

"He didn't mean it, A-Frame, Honey. Honest, he didn't."

"How come this piece of junkyard reject is left-handed, anyhoo?"

"Because most interesting people are left-handed," Dayo snapped back in mock anger. "Or maybe she's just declaring her politics literally to keep all the yahoos away."

"Yeah, well, her politics gets damned inconvenient sometimes," I mock-berated.

"Yeah, well, some regular people can be damned inconvenient, too, at times," he mock-rejoindered.

"What the hell do you mean by that?"

"I don't know," he smiled. "It just sounded good."

A-Frame caught, kicked, roared, and sputtered.

"We're off! We're off!" I yelled.

"We're all off!" Dayo yelled back.

"Now we're getting some off!" we both yelled in unison.

We bought a six-pack of beer for each of us at the closest, outside-of-city-limits liquor store and started winding and wending our way to Xeno's house via left-hand turns.

"I still think we should have gotten some dates," Dayo said.

"What? Is this my friend Dayo speaking? 'Dates'? 'Dates,' you say? Dayo saying we should have 'dates'? 'Dates'? We'd better turn back. You're too sick for a party. You're obviously not well."

"Well, look, I date every once in a while. Besides, Gaga would have gone with me to this party."

"Gaga would go with you if you were leaving on the Titanic's maiden voyage. Gaga would go with you if you were flying on the Hindenberg. Gaga would go with you if—."

"Okay, okay, already. I get your point!"

"—you cut off your dick."

"What?"

"Besides, when you go to one of Xeno's parties, he told me once, you really shouldn't bring a date. You just arrive, look over the crop, and choose what you like. He said that that way, the evening is more exciting."

"Yeah, but what if you don't happen to like any of this year's crop? Then what do you do?"

"Drop back ten and punt . . . . I don't know what you do! If you don't like any of them, then screw it. Sit in a corner and drink your beer all night."

"I liked your first suggestion better."

"Which one?"

"Screw it."

A-Frame, Dayo, and I finally got to the house. Xeno lived with three other fellows in a small house on a corner lot not too far from the Hill. The house actually looked as if it had been constructed from materials left over from a larger house—not so much as to looks, but as to size. Why would anyone building a house on such a large lot go to all that trouble for such a small place? The lot was big enough to hold four more houses of the same size and have enough left over for a double garage apiece.

The entire one floor contained a kitchen, a bedroom, a living room (which also served their purposes as a study room and library), and another room that joined the living room. The house also had a basement, but I never got down there to see how large it was or what it contained. Xeno told me once, however, that one of his roommates made his own beer down there.

For such a small house, it had plenty of entrances (or exits, depending on which way you were going). It had three doors to the outside (or inside, etc.). One door led outside from the bedroom, and one led from the living room, of course, in addition to the back door in the kitchen. The interesting thing about all the doors was that they had been painted, one of the current inhabitants being a self-taught dabbler in the arts. But they weren't painted like a house painted; they were painted like a picture painted. And abstract, at that.

In years to come, art will go downhill—assuming it was ever on top of the hill to begin with. People calling themselves artists will believe that all they have to do is represent their own emotion to achieve art. They won't even bother with craftsmanship, won't even understand the basics of whatever field they are in, but instead will simply hack and saw at, with, and around the tools they are using, stop when they get tired, or inspired, or perspired, and call the result art. They will give Art and Artists a bad name, and Art never liked his name to begin with, anyway.

Dayo and I chose to enter through the living-room door, which was a nice creationistic endeavor of swoops and swirls in basic reds, blues, and yellows. Art had gotten pretty tired or inspired or perspired pretty early, if you asked me. Xeno met us at the door.

"Come in! Come in! Glad to see you could make it. Now, maybe I'll know someone here."

"You're kidding," I said, as we felt our way inside.

"Yes, I'm kidding, of course, but it's a typical party. I think I know maybe one-fourth of the people here. Of course, my roommates may have invited some I'm not familiar with. But what better way to get to know people than to drink with them, right? Right."

Sometimes, Xeno just cut through the Socratic bullcrap and answered his own questions.

The room was dim, but not dark enough yet to be absolutely black. I think about ten people were in the room, a few sitting on the floor, talking and listening to the soft, mesmerizing John Coltrane jazz coming from the record player. Two of the couples were Negroes. Both partners. Opposite sexes.

"It would be awfully silly if I tried to introduce everybody every time somebody comes in," Xeno apologized. "And, besides, I don't even know everybody, myself. So, you can all just wave 'Hi' right now and introduce yourselves to those whom you want later on, or *to* whom to, as the case or mood may be."

"Part of speech."

"Object of the preposition!"

"Hi."

"Hi!"

"Hi."

"You and Dayo have never been here before, have you?" Xeno asked rhetorically.

"No, this is our first trip," Dayo replied drolly before Xeno could answer.

"Then let's head for the kitchen where you can stash your beer, and I'll take you on a tour of the palace, or place, as the case may be."

"Nominative case!"

"Object of the preposition!"

"Subjunctive mood!"

"You can see for yourself it's going to be a rather long, tedious, dry tour, so I suggest you gas up before we take off."

We stumbled on through the living room, and the guests didn't even look up as we climbed over their bodies on the floor. A quick glance assured me that no member of the opposite sex there grabbed my attention hard enough yet to slow me down and make me want to introduce myself. We walked into the kitchen, which was about the same size as the living room, and were greeted by another dozen party comers.

"Hi!"

"Hi."

"Hi!"

Xeno opened the refrigerator and shoved some food around. Some six-packs were already inside, along with a plastic bag of ice. Some brown and beige bottles of liquor were on the small table in the center of the room, interspersed with the clear bottles of requisite gin, vodka, tequila, and grain alcohol.

"Just put your beer in here, dear, "Xeno said. "It will probably get mixed up during the evening, but by then no one will care, anyway. Just contribute to the pool, I always say. I always say that."

Dayo and I each took a can and put the rest in, while the kitchen crowd watched closely. They were more attentive than the living-room crowd, but that was probably because the kitchen had more light and they could see us better. About half of these people were Negroes, or Blacks, or Afro-Americans, and I realized that this could be a very interesting party. I could never keep straight what they wanted themselves called these days, and so, usually, I didn't call them.

As we walked out to continue our tour, I turned to the kitchen crowd and said, "Bye."

They all looked at me puzzledly.

"Bye, Hud," Dayo said.

"Thanks, Dayo."

We followed Xeno past the bathroom door into the bedroom. The bedroom was larger than the other two rooms we had seen, and actually at one time, I imagine, it could have been the living room. However, Xeno and his roommates had moved in two sets of bunk beds, which gave them an awfully spacious bedroom. Only six people were in here.

"This is the bedroom," Xeno said.

"Don't tell me! Don't tell me! Uh, this is the bedroom," said Dayo.

"Hi," I said.

"Hi," they answered, except for two guys who were engrossed in discussion.

"No, I swear to you. You can make $100 a day working up there moving the cemetery. My roommate's brother knows somebody who knows somebody else who knows all about it. They pay so much, because it's so dangerous. A lot of people died from some disease, like the plague, I think, and you might catch it. Also, they've got to hurry to move all the bones and graves before that new dam floods the old cemetery."

"Well, hell, I could use a hundred bucks to buy that Corvette I heard about. Some cat died in his brand new Corvette up in the mountains someplace, but they didn't find him until weeks later, and his death smell is all throughout the car. My girlfriend said she heard about it from some sorority sisters."

"Wow, that would be cool, wouldn't it? Maybe you could cover up the smell with perfume, or aftershave, or something."

We followed Xeno out of the bedroom and back into the living room, pausing to glance in at the bathroom and scaring hell out of a girl who had forgotten to lock the door. Over twenty people were now in the living room, and more were coming in the front door. The color ratio was fast approaching the halfway mark.

"That leaves us with the most interesting room of all on the main floor," Xeno instructed us. "The meditation room."

"Oh?" Dayo said. "Who's sick?"

"No, Dayo," I groaned. "You're thinking of *medication*. This is the room decorated in Italian Renaissance."

"No," Dayo groaned. "You're thinking of *Mediterrarium*. That's the room where they keep all their plants."

Dayo and I followed Xeno through the doorway and were struck dumb, but not deaf once inside the meditation room, the room where you sat silently thinking that your thoughts were significant. Xeno and his roommates had hung a parachute from the ceiling, fastening the sides to the four walls. Red light bulbs had been placed in the fixtures, giving the room a warm—and yet at the same time, a chilling—effect. The windows had been blackened, so no outside light could come in. In one corner, behind the silk of the parachute, was a kind of altar, with its own red lights played behind it, and a small statuette and incense burners. The statuette looked like a small Buddha of some kind, or maybe it was Hotei. I could never keep those guys straight, either.

The room had no furniture, only four large beanbags strewn about on which to sit. They were all occupied at the moment by various people who all had their attention focused on the guy in the center of the room, who was beating softly on a conga drum. He had the beard and the long hair associated with the beatniks, along with the uncared-for clothes. He looked up as we entered and raised his hand toward us, fingers together, palm forward, without saying a word. Xeno answered in the same sign, and unconsciously so did Dayo and I, although I couldn't resist wiggling my fingers just a bit at him.

He then went back to playing, beating out a slow, sensuous rhythm. No one said anything, because the atmosphere gave the feeling that any noise other than the drum would be a sacrilege. Only the beating of the conga was permitted in this, the meditation room.

In years to come, silent hand-and-finger signals will take on more significance, and powerful meaning will be communicated, depending on the position, placement, and pairing of our pointers. The middle finger, of course, thrust defiantly upward, will serve only to make us feel better, piss off the other guy, and sometimes get us into a heap of trouble. Held sideways, that symbol will come to mean jokingly "And the horse you rode in on!" Two fingers held up in Winston Churchill's famous "V" symbol, palm forward, will come to mean "Peace" and will be both a demanding sign and a hoping sign, although some wags will try to spread the rumor that Churchill had just been signaling that he wanted another cigar, which will gain popularity by the signal to challenge another driver next to you to see who can peel out from the stoplight first: "Wanna drag?" All fingers held up with the third and fourth separated, palm forward, will come to mean that you watch and admire a popular television show and are passing on the wish to Live Long and Prosper. And all fingers clenched tightly in a fist, palm forward, will come to mean power, black power, white power, people power, depending on your color, or politics, or both, and will even cause a nation to be embarrassed and angered at a future summer Olympics. Palm toward you with a clenched fist means "Wanna fight?" either seriously, or literally, or figuratively, or virtually, or just as a parting shot as you get the hell out of there.

Of course, the Peaceniks will never realize the fine line between their peace symbol and the trick you do to someone standing with you when you are getting your picture taken together, the one when you stick your fingers behind the guy's head to make him look like he has finger feathers. Or she. Mostly shes.

And again, of course, one dichotic President, who will be prone to overdo everything, will become semi-famous for his pose of both arms outstretched stiffly with both hands forming his personal victory signs and will immensely please half the people and disgust half the others. Some of the people all of the time and all the people some of the time. And those are very good odds, as Maverick used to say his pappy used to say on his Sunday TV show.

We tippy-toed back into the living room and suddenly got blasted with loud noise. Big noise. The conversation and the music were reaching a high party-pitch, and the number of people had increased even more.

"Well," I said to Xeno, "how many people do you recognize now?"

"Oh, I guess I know about ten or fifteen in here right now. Of course, that doesn't mean that I've ever spoken to them," he laughed. "I've just seen them before. Maybe so. Maybe no."

"Look, I've got to make a phone call. Where's your phone?"

Xeno pointed over to the bookcase against the wall by the bedroom door.

"It's on the top shelf. It's got a fifteen-foot extension cord, so just take it into the bedroom if you want some quiet."

"Fifteen feet?" Dayo asked.

"Yes, you can even take it into the bathroom with you and talk while you're sitting on the can."

"Yeah," I said. "Great conversation piece. 'Hey, Baby! Guess where I am!'"

In years to come, a long extension cord will no longer be a status symbol, just another example of conspicuous consumption. We will zip right through the CB fad when Good Buddy truckers and other aspiring rednecks will talk up a storm on the highways, blithering and blathering away as they create new language for unnecessary thoughts. We will also invent, develop, and use cordless phones, so we will no longer need to be tethered by fifteen-foot cords or even thirty-foot cords. Dick Tracy, here we come!

And we will create cellular phones to carry in our cars so we can act important in our yuppie suspenders as we wait to drag the fellow next to us at the stoplight, only discreetly, without the symbol challenge, acting nonchalantly as we hold our foot just above the gas pedal, prepared to casually and mentally speed-shift through the gears. We will even create phoney cellular phones that don't even work, but are to be used only for impressings' sake as we drive and stop and wait. Image is all, some people will believe. And to hell with craftsmanship. But some people can always tell a phoney. But not much.

I found the phone and took it into the bedroom with me. The people who had been there during our tour had since joined the party in the rest of the house, except for one couple who were getting it on early. I looked the other way and called Diane at her sorority house. I had to let the phone ring twenty-three times before someone answered, and then I had to wait about five minutes more before whoever answered it found Diane and she finally came to the phone.

"Hi," I said. "Congratulations. You set a record."

"What do you mean?"

"The phone rang twenty-three times."

"Oh. Say, what's going on? Where are you? What's all that noise?"

"Oh, that? I'm calling from the Sink. You know how it is on Fridays. Say, how would you like to go out formally next Saturday night? The fraternity's having a party after the football game."

"I'd love to. That sounds like fun."

"Yes, well, it's going to be a beatnik party. You know, everybody comes dressed up as beatniks—fake beards, black turtlenecks and tights, the whole intellectual rebellion bit."

"Okay. Fine. I'll have to think of something to wear."

"Good. I'll call you later on in the week and give you the times and everything. I'll probably see you sometime before then, anyway, okay?"

"Okay. That will be fine. Thank you, Hud."

"Yeah, sure. I'll see you, then. Bye."

"Goodbye."

I snagged another can of beer and strolled back into the living room to find Dayo. I finally saw him squeezed back into a corner talking to a large guy with a mass of red hair and a full red beard. He wore a thin jacket over a white T-shirt, khakis, and sandals, and I recognized him as the kind of freelance unpublished author and poet that he claimed to be. I joined them.

"Look," the poet was saying to Dayo, "if you can't enjoy *life*, then what *can* you enjoy?"

"Uh, death?" Dayo asked meekly.

"Man, are you trying to bug me?"

"No, no! Man. I'm just trying to understand you."

The would-be poet turned on his sandaled heels and stalked off. I had to jump out of his way, and I shook my head and rolled my eyes knowingly at him as if to say, "Can you *believe* this guy? *I* know what you're saying. Man."

"My God," Dayo wheezed, "do you think we really belong here, Hud?"

"Why not? I think it's fun. Besides, this'll give you background for the party next weekend. I just called Diane and she's going with me."

"Naturally . . . . I mean, that's nice."

"Who are you taking?"

"I haven't asked anyone yet."

"Gaga doesn't have a date."

"I *know*! I *know*! Get off my back, will you?"

"Just keeping you informed, good buddy. Drink up. Cheers."

"Good Buddy? Is that what you're drinking? I thought it was Old Buddy."

"No, you're thinking of Old Granddaddy."

"No, you're thinking of Old Jackie Daniels."

"No, you're thinking of Old Jackie Robinson."

"No, you're thinking of Old Jack and Jill."

"Now, you're doing some thinking."

The party had now risen to a subdued roar. The ratio was a good solid fifty-fifty black and white, with the Negroes—Blacks—Afro-Americans—people of the dark persuasion perhaps getting a slight edge. For the most part, they were handsome, dressed-up, very stud-looking dudes and dudettes. Most of the guys had on sport coats; many had ties. Half the girls had on heels and looked dusky and sexy and sleek. They made all us white folks and honkies look positively sloppy. Slow jazz was still playing on the record player, but you could barely hear it, and some couples were dancing slowly in the middle of the room, the girls pressed very close to their partners and grinding their groins al-l-l-l-l-l over their bodies.

Xeno came by, looking a bit distressed. He had a glass of whiskey in one hand and a can of beer in the other.

"Hey! Xeno!"

"Yeah? Oh, hi, Hud. How's the party?"

"Great. What's the matter? You looking for someone?"

He took a hefty sip from the glass and then finished off the beer can.

"You keep up like that," Dayo suggested, and you won't even be able to *see* to *look*."

"This stuff?" Xeno laughed. "Ha! I could drink it all night. See you around. Mix it up, hey? Have fun! Peace," he symboled, after tossing the empty beer can into a corner.

He functioned around, mixing and mingling with the crowd.

THIRTEEN

A really good-looking stud Negro walked into the house

A really good-looking stud Negro walked into the house, casually dressed, followed by five Negro girls. The first girl in the entourage behind him was carrying a stack of 45-rpm records.

"Hey, Man!" he said, announcing himself. "This party ain't swinging! This party need to swing!"

He was well known to almost everyone there, because they all got excited and agitated and started talking all at once.

"Hey, Man, Willis is here."

"This party going to swing now!"

"Hey, there, Willis!"

"How's it going, Baby?"

Someone grabbed the 45s, dashed to the record player, and substituted them for the fine sax solo currently playing, scraping the needle across the LP in his haste. Immediately the blast of electric guitars and beating drums filled the room and everyone crowded onto the designated dancing area and started shaking and gyrating. The room was so crowded you couldn't wiggle without hitting at least three people. Willis tagged one of his five girls and they started wiggling in the fashion of the latest dance sensation right in the center of the room, much to the envy of those of us less coordinated.

"Gee, I wish I could dance like that," Dayo said.

"Forget it. They've got natural rhythm from that extra bone in their feet. Oh, sorry," I said to a large buck standing nearby who started staring at me in stony silence. He stared me up and down once more and then went back to watching the dancing. I grabbed Dayo and we shoved ourselves over to another portion of the room. The walls seemed to be keeping time with the music.

In years to come, we will look back on the latest dance sensations with amusement, wondering what all the fuss could have been about. The Twist seemed to be the ultimate in easy-to-learn, sensual-to-watch, and ability-to-impress dancing, and even though you didn't get to touch your partner, you got to watch her twist and shake her body while you got to twist and shout your mouth as you sang along to the music. Of course, there was the East Coast Chubby Checker version and the West Coast less-sedate version of the Twist, and as you danced, you and your partner couldn't imagine a more raw, simplified dance.

And then came the U.T. In Colorado, we didn't know if the letters stood for the University of Tennessee or the University of Texas, where the mythology claimed the dance originated. This was simply the more raw, simplified dance we couldn't imagine. You stood on the dance floor and moved with the music and let your imagination and natural rhythm run wild without the imposed movement-and-step constraints of the Twist. You didn't even have to have a partner to dance the U.T., although boys were more inhibited than girls—as usual—and didn't dare get out on the dance floor alone or, heaven forbid, dance with someone of the same sex as much as girls were inclined to.

In those days of the Stormy Sixties, there were also many variations of essentially the same dance, each with their own name, each usually named because of its appearance to some activity that had nothing to do with dancing: the Swim, the Fish, the Mashed Potato, the Pony.

Once, at a party with Diane when I was particularly feeling my oats, I decided to test my dancing ability and took off in the Pony for the first time, prancing and preening, arms simulating pawing forelegs, and cantering around the dance floor trying to cover as much ground as possible. Diane followed me dutifully, as she was supposed to do, but obviously she was extremely self-conscious and embarrassed, trying to act like a mare while she followed a silly-looking stallion around the room.

Isn't the purpose of dancing to allow a man and a woman the opportunity to simulate sex in a public place, the chance to show off their bodies and physical prowess to each other, and the possibility to perform a preliminary mating mambo of love?

In even more years to come, the Lambada dance sensation will come and go so fast you could believe you merely dreamed it and it never happened, even though movies were made to document its reality and sensuousness and sexual simulations. However, I never answer a question that begins with a negative, because the form of the question itself tells me the answer the questioner is looking for, and I prefer to answer questions with my own opinion. Don't you agree?

Dayo and I stood near the doorway next to the meditation room and watched the locomotion commotion. The heavy beat of the music and the gyrations of the sleek girls in their tight skirts and their short skirts made me want to jump in and test the water. My body kept time with the walls. My eyes kept time with the girls, who hiked their tight skirts up to their thighs in order to give their legs freer movement.

"You see that girl over there?" I had to yell almost directly into Dayo's ear to make him hear me.

"Which one?" he yelled back into mine.

"The black girl in the white sweater by the bedroom."

"Yeah? What about her?"

"She's cool. She doesn't look like she's with anyone."

Dayo turned to me and gave me his quizzical look.

"So?"

"So, I'd like to dance with her. She's cool."

"She's also coon, to be crude, but alliterative."

"For Christ's sake," I said. "This is a mixed party. No one would care here."

"Do you see any of them dancing with any of us?"

"No . . . . But so what? I've seen it before."

"Sure, so have I. But if I were you, I'd just as soon not be the first one to try and start it here. Look around. There's plenty of nice selections in our own color."

I looked around.

"Yeah? Where?"

Dayo nodded toward the front door.

"That blonde sitting in the chair over there."

I hadn't noticed her before and she looked good. Her face was good, her legs were good, and her knockers were something else. She seemed to be alone.

"Oh, yeah," I leered.

"Easy steady, big fellow. I saw her first."

"Well, buddy, you'd better go grab her up quick like a bunny before I do something rash right here on the floor. This music's getting to me."

"Oh, I don't know. She might be with someone."

"She *will* be, if you don't hurry up. Go on. Asking won't hurt you. Hurry up. Go, god damn it!"

Dayo solemnly finished off his can of beer, handed it to me ceremoniously with an air of important nonchalance, gave a confident tug to the front of his shirt with both hands, and shyly went off to ask her to dance. She smiled up at him as he stopped in front of her with a casual air of "Oh, gee, I didn't notice you sitting here; well, as long as I'm here . . . ." I could see him stammer at her. She smiled wider, nodded yes, and got up to dance with him.

I glanced back to find the black girl I had seen, but she was now dancing with a big Negro halfback on the football team. Let him have her, I decided. Poor guy probably needs it worse than I do.

Suddenly a guy sitting on the couch jumped up, knocking a few people dancing on the floor into mass confusion. A mild riot followed and someone brought a glass of beer over. A cigarette had been dropped down between the cushions of the couch and was smoking. After two more cans of beer and a glass of water for a chaser, the temporary volunteer firemen decided it was out.

The guy who had jumped up turned the cushion over and sat right back down again. Seating space was at a premium at this party.

"Hey, buddy!" Xeno came slightly staggering up to me.

"How's it going, Xeno? Great party."

"Fine. Fine. What happened over here?"

"Uh, little accident, Xeno. A cigarette got dropped down in your couch. It started smoking a little, but no flames. They got it put out, but I think your couch is a bit damp."

"Pfah! No problem. I thought it was something serious."

I watched him chug from the glass and chase from the can. His right eye drooped somewhat, and a bit of the beer dribbled into his beard, but that was the only physical evidence that he was getting drunk.

"Hud, old buddy, I'm glad you could make it."

"Well, Xeno, old buddy, I'm glad I could make it, too."

"Hud, old buddy, I'm glad you're glad."

"Well, I'm glad you're glad I'm glad."

"Hud, old buddy, I'm glad you're glad I'm glad you're glad."

"Well, I'm glad you're glad I'm—forget it."

"Yes, sir, I'm glad you could make it. At least I've got someone here I know and someone I can talk to."

"What do you mean? You can talk to anybody here."

Xeno eyed the room suspiciously, his eyes darting about the people dancing and those sitting and standing around and talking. Then he looked back at me mysteriously and leaned closer.

"These bastards. I don't even know who they are."

"They're your friends, Xeno. They've come to have a good time on—. With you."

"Pfah! They're not my friends. They don't even know me. They've come to have a good time, all right. All they want is a place to have *their* party. I don't know them and they don't know me."

"Maybe your roommates invited them," I said, completely missing his point. "Maybe they know them."

"I don't even know my roommates."

Xeno giggled, and then tried to peer into the darkness of his empty beer can.

"Need some more beer, dear," he said. "Need another drink. Goodbye, Hud. Don't leave me."

"Sure, Xeno. Take it easy."

He shoved himself through the crowd on the dance floor and managed to get into the kitchen for more booze. I started to look for the good-looking black girl again, but before I could find her a sharply dressed Negro in coat and tie came walking up to me. His solid black tie was about an inch wide; his tapered gray slacks were tight across his calves. He was drinking beer out of a small eight-pack can, the top cut completely off so that the can made a glass.

"What's happening," he said.

"Hi."

He stood next to me and watched the crowd for a minute.

"You live here?" he asked.

"No. I know one of the guys who does. He just went into the kitchen for a beer. You want to see him?"

"No, no. I just thought you looked familiar."

He drained his beer, nodded, and walked off.

In years to come, we will look back at the clothing styles of the Sixties and find them ludicrous. Ties so narrow they were practically strings. Button-down collars so small they were mistaken for wrinkles. But best of all, miniskirts so skimpy the girls exposed themselves every time they crossed the street and stepped up onto the curb. Bell-bottom trousers. Paisley shirts. Platform shoes. Bleeding-madras shirts and shorts. Tie-dyed T-shirts. Nehru jackets. Hot pants. Topless bathing suits. Denim here, denim there, pre-washed denim everywhere.

And regardless of how silly and ludicrous the styles will be regarded in the future, regardless of how knowledgeable we will become about ephemeral fashion in fashions, we will still egotistically, but mistakenly, believe—at the time—that our generation is *different* from all other generations, that our fashions are *cool* and will remain cool forever, just like our haircuts and sideburns, that our voices and ideas will change the world forever for the better.

The more things change, the more they change. Or, to put it another way, what goes around comes around and then goes around again.

I tried to find the black chick again, but she didn't seem to be on the dance floor. I then became aware that someone was standing right behind my shoulder. It was the beatnik from the meditation room, the drummer. He was watching the action with a cool sardonic expression on his lips, nodding his head every so often. Then he looked at me.

"What a drag."

"Oh?" I smiled. "The place seems to be fairly rocking. I certainly wouldn't call it a drag."

He looked at me with that faint smile, explored my face, and then, apparently satisfied, shook his head slightly, almost to himself.

"What a drag."

I accepted his proclamation and dropped it. The smoke was thick now and the crowd thicker. The front door had been opened to allow some fresh air to try to penetrate the room. I saw Dayo and the blonde go outside. Dayo looked happy.

"What fools these mortals be."

"What?" I asked O Bearded One.

He looked at me, smiled crookedly, and said, "Bitchin'."

I nodded and gave him a crooked smile of my own.

"Crazy," I said.

He looked at me once more and then shook his head, sad faced.

"What a drag."

He pivoted and went back into the meditation room and his drum. I guessed at least that room wasn't crowded.

I then got bored with just standing, and I couldn't find anyone I was interested in dancing with. I decided I would check out what I had heard somebody talking about earlier, about a set of drums in the basement and a jam session that was going on. I had to go through the kitchen to get to the basement, so I stopped to get another beer.

"Come on, Gloria."

"No! I don't want to."

"Come on and dance with me."

"No! Leave me alone!"

I suddenly realized that a scene was going on before me. A small dark guy, who looked half-Negro and half-Mexican, was trying to get a white girl to dance with him. They were both drunk, but she simply didn't want to dance. Most of the people in the kitchen were just standing around watching, not saying anything, and most of them were Negroes. Gloria's temper was getting out of hand, and she stood with her feet apart, hands on hips, stretching her short skirt tight across her thighs, refusing to move, her breasts jutting defiantly forward in their tiny white halter top.

"Come on, Gloria, dance with me."

"Get away from me, Jasper! I don't want to dance with you!"

She shoved him away and started to walk out of the kitchen. Jasper's face lost his smile and turned into rage. He leaped at her, grabbed her bosom and swung her around, at the same time producing a switchblade which he held against her throat. No one said anything. No one moved. Time stopped.

"Listen to me, you red-headed slut. You don't treat me that way, you hear? Don't you ever talk to me like that."

Gloria was scared, afraid to move, her body rigid, her eyes wide. Jasper released her breast and started jabbing her gently with the point of the knife, just enough to cause a slight depression in her halter top, but not enough to cut. He touched her right breast, her left breast, her throat. Everyone else was too surprised to do anything—that and the fact that Jasper was drunk and had a knife.

"What's the matter, Gloria? You aren't doing much yelling now. Why don't you say something, Gloria? Huh? Why don't you tell me now why you don't want to dance with me? What's the matter, Gloria? Huh? Huh? Huh, Glo-ri-a?"

A body blurred at the side of my vision and hurled itself onto Jasper, striking him in the head and shoving him away from Gloria. She shrank back against the refrigerator and watched. I recognized her rescuer, having seen him around campus usually in the company of Gloria. He crouched, eyeing Jasper, who had now turned his attention to him, and he clenched his fists at Jasper.

"You dirty fucking nigger. You touch her again and I'll kill you."

I suddenly wished I weren't there. The crowd reacted as if a jolt of electricity had been shot through them. They moved in around him forming an almost solid wall. Their faces were hard and angry, and proud. They wanted revenge for scores of years of abuse, for centuries of slavery. But he didn't acknowledge their presence. He kept his eyes on Jasper.

"What did you call me?"

"I called you a dirty fucking nigger."

He certainly wasn't helping his cause any. But both would-be combatants were only about five-feet, six-or-seven-inches tall, and they looked incongruous, ready to fight each other while surrounded by towering six-foot-plus football players.

"You want to take that back now, or after I slit your throat?"

"Try it, motherfucker."

The crowd started murmuring and shifting weight. The dam was about ready to bust.

"Jim! Jim! Stop it!"

Gloria burst through the surrounding wall and stepped in front of him. She grabbed his arms and shook him.

"Stop it, Jim. There's no reason for this. I'm all right. Nothing's happened. Just a misunderstanding. Come on, Jim. Let's go."

Jim kept staring at Jasper and Jasper kept staring at him. They were playing the old staring-contest game when no more words can cause any effect, and you wait for the other one to make the first move. Jim quickly looked around him at the others, defiantly, and glanced back at Jasper. Then he nodded his head, once, to Gloria, and then took her arm. Jasper had won.

"You don't scare me, Jasper. Any time."

The parting shot. He guided Gloria through the hole in the crowd that opened for them, and they went into the front room. The Negroes stood in a hard knot, silent. Nothing had been decided, nothing had changed, no victory had been won. The ignorant hatred had only been brought out into the open once more, had been rubbed, irritated, and then left there to fester some more.

Why do we allow words to be so powerful? Why do we let silly symbols control our emotions? Isn't it because the symbols we choose also convey how we personally feel about the objects the symbols represent, as well as society's feelings at the moment, as well as the current fashions, current concerns, current fears?

Perhaps if we constantly exposed the slurs to open examination, we could see how silly the words, the thoughts, the ideas, the slurs actually are, just like staring at a word so long that it loses its meaning.

But, most of all, perhaps we could see how wrong we were in our thinking and how wrong we were for using words like boy, nigger, coon, jungle bunny, sambo, negroid, uncle tom, aunt jamima, bandanna head, jigaboo, darkie, monkey, ape, bush bunny, spear chucker, spick, wetback, greaser, pachuco, spic and span, bean eater, pepper belly, taco, low rider, wop, dago, spaghetti bender, polack, mick, potato eater, paddy, frog, chink, slanteye, slope, gook, slant, flathead, kraut, nazi, nip, jap, wog, limey, kike, jewboy, shylock, goyan, shiksa, whitey, honkey, ofay, carpetbagger, yankee, white trash, pig farmer, niggerlover, redneck, sod buster, cracker, gringo, male chauvinist pig, female chauvinist pig, slit, bird, bush, cunt, john, prick, pecker, beaver, broad, dame, doll, chick, skirt, twat, old maid, spinster, girl, cock, rooster, hooker, slut, crip, spastic, dummy, geek, fag, fairy, queen, fruit, queer, cocksucker, cuntfucker, swisher, flamer, dike, butch, lesbo, homo, gay, limp wrist, dogface, grunt, rube, nerd, wimp, square, turkey, chicken, four-eyes, dweeb, wuss, hophead, beatnik, hippie, freak, long-hair, bra-burner, libber, feminist, bimbo, bozo, preppie, yuppie.

And if you can't find yourself represented in there somewhere, then you're a better man than I am, Gunga Din.

Stick around long enough and what once was respectable becomes objectionable. What once was polite speech becomes fightin' words.

We are all open to criticism, because we are all criticized at some point in our lives, because nobody loves everybody hates somebody sometime and depending on how intelligent we aren't, we tend to expand that circle of hatred to include more than just the one person we happen to dislike at the time. And sometimes we discover that who we dislike the most is ourselves.

I lost interest in finding the jam session downstairs, grabbed a fresh can of beer, and headed back into the living room.

The music was just as loud, the crowd just as thick, and the dancers just as excited as before. No one appeared to have any idea of the scene that had just taken place in the kitchen. I didn't see Jim or Gloria. I grabbed a spot on the couch that suddenly became vacant and settled down to drink my beer and mind my own business. I had lost interest in trying to find the black girl. Maybe I could get drunk, I thought.

My eyes slowly focused on a beautiful girl leaning against the door frame of the bedroom. Her blond hair cascaded to her shoulders, and she was wearing black—black tights under a black skirt and a black turtleneck sweater. She had just a touch of makeup on her lips, or else I was becoming flushed with excitement.

I nudged the guy sitting next to me.

"Who . . . is that blonde . . . over there?"

He looked at me, looked at her, and then looked back at me, smiling.

"Forget it," he said. "I don't know her name, but she's married to the brother of one of the guys that lives here."

My thoughts of lust turned into extreme longing, unrequited love. Then they turned back to lust again.

"She's a dancer, you know, one of those modern creative ones? Sometimes, after the party's died down, she'll do a creative dance to a record for the people who are still here. Once, when she was feeling really good, she did a strip and danced around with nothing on but a towel. And a hand towel, at that."

My thoughts got dirty. I was trying to strip her in my imagination when Dayo appeared at the side of the couch.

"H'lo." he said.

"Well, well, well. If it isn't Loverboy. What happened to your girl?"

"What girl?"

He decided to play coy.

"The girl you took away from me. The girl you were practically screwing on the dance floor. The girl you went outside with. What do you mean, 'What girl?'"

"Oh. *That* girl."

"Yes. Oh, *that* girl."

"Well, everything was fine, up to a point."

"What do you mean? Up to what point? Come on. Tell. Tell."

"Well, I couldn't figure her out. When we were dancing, she really danced close. I mean, she was flat against me from the knees to the nose."

"Yes, I noticed. She's a real good dancer."

"Who can tell? Anyway, I seemed to be doing okay. I even nuzzled her a couple of times."

"No!" I said, in mock shock.

"Yeah," he grinned. "She really knows how to get a guy worked up. Ha ha. That's a joke, son. So, it was getting warm in here, and we decided to go outside to cool down for a while."

"You dog," I grinned. "Yes, I noticed that, too. What happened?"

"Nothing."

"Nothing?"

"Nothing."

"What do you mean, 'nothing'? *Something* happened. What? What what? Wha-a-a-at?"

"Well, we went out and sat on the grass for a while—."

"Yeah, that's a good start. Oh, sorry! Go on."

"Well, we were sitting out there, kind of close, like. And naturally I put my arm around her—."

"Naturally. Oh, sorry! Go on."

"And we moused it up a bit, you know. And then I asked her to go out with me next weekend."

Dayo paused. I waited patiently until I couldn't take the silence anymore.

"So? What did she say?"

"What did *who* say?"

"How would you like a punch in the mouth?"

"No, that's not what she said. Oh, sorry. She said she couldn't."

"Why not?"

Dayo smiled apologetically.

"She said her boyfriend wouldn't let her."

I had to stop everything to comprehend this statement. Her boyfriend wouldn't *let* her? Her boyfriend?

"Her *boyfriend*?"

"Yes, her boyfriend. Is there any more beer left?"

"Yeah, yeah—wait a minute! *Wait a minute*! Her boyfriend? She's got a boyfriend and she was acting like that with you? So what? Why didn't you say 'So what?'"

"I did, but she told me she was very attached to him. He's here at the party, as a matter of fact."

I was becoming inundated with the flood of each succeeding wave of staggering information. Whoosh, stagger. Blah, blah, blah.

"Wait a minute. I don't get it."

"I didn't get any, either."

"Ho, ho. Very funny. Now, wait just a minute. Her boyfriend is here at this party, she's very attached to him, and she was carrying on with you like that?"

"Yeah, I'm a real lady killer, aren't I?"

"Dayo, a lot of things you are. A lady killer you're not. I'm sorry to have to be the one to destroy your delusions like this, son, but when women are involved, you leave them cold. Usually, however, they leave you."

"Oh, *yeah*?" he grinned. "What about Gaga?"

"I said, '*women*,' son."

"Hold it. There she is now."

The girl Dayo had just spent so much time with came out of the kitchen on the arm of one of the large—one of the *very* large and very black—football players who had been in the kitchen for the episode with the knife. She clung to him tenderly and he had his arm about her, proud and defiant. As they walked in front of us, she smiled and waved affectionately to Dayo. Her boyfriend scowled at us and I could feel Dayo withering beside me. They left the party.

Dayo stood silently for a minute, just staring at the front door through which they had left. He wiped his mouth.

"I need a beer," he said and walked into the kitchen.

The shocking thing to Dayo wasn't that her boyfriend was black. That sort of thing occurred around campus, and people didn't stare as much as they used to when they saw mixed couples. The shocking thing to Dayo was the fact that she had carried on with him the way she had while her boyfriend was there at the party. The shocking thing to Dayo was the fact that if her boyfriend had seen them—especially when they left to go outside—the football-playing boyfriend just might have shocked Dayo into a few broken bones. Dayo is not very large, and like all of us intelligent people, he tends to be somewhat chicken. We would rather avoid a fight than get our brains beat out.

"What's the matter?"

"What happened?"

The dancers had stopped dancing at the sound of a loud crash from the bedroom. The music blared on, but no one paid attention to it. The crash had been appreciably louder than any ordinary party crash. We went over to the doorway just as a guy came out.

"Hey! Xeno's gone crazy! He just smashed a mirror with his fist."

Xeno was running around the bedroom, yelling, muttering, mumbling words and sounds to himself which we couldn't understand.

"Hey, Xeno! Hey, buddy! Slow down! What's the matter?"

He looked up and didn't even recognize me. His eyes were like flames, glaring and wild. He rushed past me and dashed into the bathroom, closed the door behind him, and locked it. The crowd grouped around the door. One of his roommates started knocking on the door.

"Xeno! Xeno! Let me in, Xeno. What's the matter?"

"What happened?"

"What's he doing?"

"What's the matter?"

"Get out!" Xeno yelled through the door. "Go away! Leave me alone! Get the hell out of here!"

"Xeno!" his roommate yelled. "It's me: Ralph. What's the matter?"

"Is he drunk?"

"What happened?"

"What's the matter with him?"

The sound or smashing glass came through the door. It sounded as if Xeno were smashing bottles and throwing things against the door.

"Go away!" he yelled. "Leave me alone! I want to be left alone."

"Xeno, it's Ralph. Let me in. What's the matter?"

"No! Get out! It's no good anymore. I'm going to kill myself! Do you hear? I'm going to kill myself. No! Don't listen! I take it back. I'm *not* going to kill myself. Go away. Just get out of here!"

"Kill himself?"

"What happened?"

"He's crazy."

"He's drunk."

"Xeno," Ralph said. "Don't be stupid. You're not going to kill yourself. Now, let me in."

Crash!

"No!" Xeno yelled.

Crash!

"No! Leave me alone! It's no good anymore, I tell you! It's all over! There's nothing left."

"What's he talking about?"

"He's drunk. Leave him alone."

"What happened?"

"Xeno, take it easy. Let me in, okay?"

The crashing stopped, and Xeno apparently settled down somewhat. His voice wasn't loud, but it was quiet, almost as if he weren't even speaking to us, as if he didn't care whether or not we heard him.

"It's no good. It's no use. I've studied them. All. I've studied them all and it's no good. There's none left. I've studied them all and there's none left. None. Nothing. Nothing, nothing, nothing. None."

Ralph beat on the door.

"Xeno! This is ridiculous. Now, if you don't let me in, you're going to hurt yourself. Let me in and we'll talk about it, okay? Xeno?"

"It's no use. It's over. I've studied them all and I've discovered nothing. They're no good. They're no use."

Then loud.

"*Do you hear that, Ralph*? Do you hear that out there? World? Do you hear that? I've discovered nothing. There's nothing there! Do you hear that?"

"What's he talking about?"

"Something about school."

"What happened?"

"Xeno," Ralph beat on the door. "It's okay. Let me in and we'll talk about it. Settle down. Okay? Xeno?"

"It's over and it's done and it's gone and there's nothing and it's over and it's gone. Nothing. All of them and not one damn one of them worth anything. Nothing! It's all as black and desolate as when I started. Nothing left. No reason in anything. Nothing. No thing. No meaning."

"Xeno. Come on. Open the door. Please?"

"It's over and done and nothing. There isn't anything! Do you hear out there? I'm telling you! There isn't *anything*! There . . . isn't . . . anything! So, go home!"

"What's he saying?"

"He wants us to go home. The party must be over."

"What happened?"

"Xeno, God damn it, if you don't open this door, we're going to beat it down. Do you hear me?"

No sound came from inside.

"Xeno? Xeno! Xeno, can you hear me?"

"Yes! But it's no use! It's over. There is no sense anymore. So, I'm going to save a lot of people a lot of trouble and I'm going to give up now. You hear? I'm giving up!"

Xeno wasn't talking to us anymore.

"Do you hear me? I'm giving up now. I've had it. Do you hear me up there, you fakes? I quit now. Don't wait any longer. *Ptui* on you!"

"What's he saying?"

"Who the hell knows? Come on. This is embarrassing."

"What happened?"

"Xeno, open the door. Okay? This is Ralph. Open the door."

The door suddenly clicked and swung open to Ralph's amazement. Xeno stood there, calmer than when he had run in. He stood and stared at us standing outside and staring at him. Then he slowly grinned. Bottles of shaving lotion and shampoo and deodorant were broken and scattered all over the tiles of the floor.

"You okay?" Ralph asked.

"No!" Xeno cried, and he leaped out, shoving and pushing people out of his way as he ran into the kitchen. He laughed and shouted meaningless obscenities. Some of us followed him into the kitchen. Some others collected their things and started leaving.

Xeno was throwing beer cans and bottles and glasses to the floor. The crashing mingled with his maniacal laughter, and he yelled and swore and danced around the table, smashing everything within reach.

"Death! Destruction! Die!"

Ralph stood in the door of the kitchen, helpless, at a loss as to what to do. The house was becoming emptier rapidly as more guests left. A few of us stayed on. The phonograph played, but no one danced.

Xeno kicked the kitchen table to the side of the room and the remaining bottles and glasses on it fell to the floor and most of them broke, scattering their liquid dreams across the linoleum.

"I'm going to save you. I'm going to save trouble."

Xeno stopped in the middle of the kitchen and looked around at the people observing him. We stood in the doorway and spilled into the kitchen. He looked at us hard, and then he smiled.

"Are you ready? Are you ready for the grand finale? *Are you ready?*"

He ran through the doorway pushing us aside, those who weren't quick enough to get out of his way.

"He's going back to the bathroom! Stop him!"

But we didn't have to, because in his absence a girl had already gone into the bathroom and was now using it. The door was locked and she was yelling, "Wait until I'm finished, Goddammit!"

Xeno banged on the door yelling, sobbing, "Let me in! Let me in! Don't lock me out *now*! Please don't lock me out!"

Then he stopped and looked at us.

"Damn! The bathroom is even closed to me." He laughed, but he had tears in his eyes.

He turned and ran into the bedroom. We all followed him and saw him spilling out the closets, throwing clothes onto the floor, turning over the chest of drawers. No one wanted to try to stop him. We just stood there silently and watched him destroy himself like a mad man.

He jumped and climbed onto one of the bunk beds, and stood up on the top bunk. His head touched the ceiling when he stood upright, and he began jumping up and down on the bed, pounding his head into the plaster at the top of every jump. He started singing "The Star-Spangled Banner" as loud as he could, punctuating it with his head against the ceiling on all the right beats.

Appropriately, at the end of the national anthem, the bed collapsed, and Xeno came crashing to the floor with all the rubble of the bed. He looked up weakly in the middle of slats, mattresses, and dirty sheets, and said, "I thank you," and he passed out.

Exactly seven people were left at the party, counting Xeno's roommate and Xeno, himself.

"Well, I guess Mary and I had better run along. Uh, thanks for the party."

"Yeah. Yeah, thanks a lot, okay?"

"I'll see you in class Monday."

I looked at Dayo. "About time we left, huh?"

Dayo looked down at Xeno, sleeping. "Oh, I don't know. The party was just beginning to get interesting."

"Dayo, you're not as dumb as you look," I mock scowled.

"I mean, you're dumber than you look. I mean . . . nobody likes a wise guy."

"Yeah," he said. "That's what I said. Let's go."

FOURTEEN

The Place, as I said, is a small cubbyhole cellar

The Place, as I said, is a small cubbyhole cellar underneath a drugstore on the Hill, a coffee shop of sorts. It calls itself a coffee shop, anyway, and most of the weirdo-beatnik set hang out there for their cider, bagels, philosophy, and chess. The ceiling is covered with egg cartons, opened and facing downward; the tables are circular, about three feet in diameter and four feet off the floor, so that the customers have to sit on high stools in order to reach the tables, and you don't feel so much like returning to the womb as you do returning to early childhood. The lighting is dim, or bad, depending on how you look at it, and the service is terrible. Occasionally on weekends the proprietor will have a guitar-playing, folk-song-singing misfit in to chant, rant, and rave and try to collect a few coins, but mostly the music is supplied by a phonograph in the back room playing classical music.

Xeno used to hang out at The Place quite a lot and had developed a following of sorts who were always anxious to hear him spout forth with his profound thinks. But that was all before Xeno's party. After that party, Xeno shaved his beard, moved into the dormitories, and became an engineering student. "Sold out" is how the other beatniks put it. They mourned their great loss from the ranks to the ranks, and they claimed they never got anyone else to replace him.

But before Xeno's party, he used to hang out at The Place quite a lot. He would gather his little group around him and lead the discussion on Life, Reality, Unreality, Sex, Unsex, God, god, un-God, and campus politics. One of the few times I happened to be at The Place on a Saturday night, Xeno was leading the discussion on the topic of Time. Apparently in one of his philosophy classes, he had just read St. Augustine's mental exercise on Time, from *Confessions*, Book XI, Chapters XII through XXXI.

Xeno and his entourage occupied one corner of the room, and they were quiet enough, but The Place is so small that everyone in the room was aware of the discussion and following the discourse. I nodded to Xeno as I entered, got a hot cider and cinnamon stick from the back counter, and pulled up a stool on the outskirts of the crowd.

"And St. Augustine says, 'For what is time? Who can easily and briefly explain it? Who even in thought can comprehend it, even to the pronouncing of a word concerning it?' He should have listened to his own words, because he then goes on to explain it, and he is neither easy nor brief."

Xeno took a sip from his cup and waited. He was waiting for further encouragement. A little blond freshman-type-looking girl with her hands clenched in her lap waited, nodding, and then said, "Yes? Well, what did he say?" She blushed and looked self-consciously around at the bearded ones sitting around her, afraid that her naivité was showing.

Xeno looked at her patronizingly and then at the rest of the group. He smiled ever so slightly when his eyes met mine.

"He said," he leaned toward her, "'What was God doing before He made heaven and earth?'"

"And . . . what *was* He doing?"

"Well, I'm afraid you'll have to ask Him that, yourself."

"Oh, you know what I mean. What does Augustine say?"

Xeno thought for a moment, apparently deciding whether or not he considered the topic worthy of his continuation. Apparently he did.

"Augie said that humans must have been the first creatures made, because no creatures could have been made before any creatures were made, and if more creatures were made, then where in the world are they?"

"Yes," came a voice from out of the dark, "where are the snows of yesterday-year?"

The girl was annoyed that anyone could take Xeno lightly, but Xeno, undismayed, lightly went on.

"Augustine's argument is this: God makes everything. Therefore, God makes time. Now, God didn't make time before He made heaven and earth, because It says that He refrained from working. Therefore, one can't ask what He did then, because there was no 'then' then. Not unlike Gertrude Stein's Oakland, which had no 'there' there."

Xeno looked at the blonde.

"Augustine didn't say that. I said that."

He took another sip from his cup to punctuate his statement. As if on cue, most of the followers seated around him also took sips. Aside from the blonde and one or two other coeds, they looked mostly like pseudo-beatniks, but apparently they didn't feel like joining in on the discussion. Or maybe they hadn't read their Augustine. Or maybe they had heard it before. Or maybe they didn't care. Or maybe they were all as confused as I was.

"Let's look at it this way:" Xeno continued. "There are three 'times,' as we call them: future, past, and present. Well, the future does not exist, because it has not happened yet, right? And I don't mean like Plato-talk with abstract things floating around up in the air being the only reality, the only existing things. All right, then, secondly . . . the past does not exist—except as memory—because it has already happened. It's over and done with. It's had its existence and shall have no more. So, the past does not exist. That leaves the present, and what is the present?"

"Must be the 'now' now," the voice in the dark said.

"The present is the only reality," the girl suggested solemnly, annoyed again.

"Ah, but wait. Just what is the present? How long does the present last? St. Augustine agrees that the present is but an instant. He says that one can't think of a year as being the present, or a day, or even an hour. Only a portion of time which cannot be divided into even the minutest particles of moments. But consider this:" Xeno said, putting his hand up to stay the wandering comments. "Is it not true that the present is actually only a dividing line, a mere means of division? Is it not true that the present is no time at all, that it is merely a separation between the future and the past? We're all sitting here. The future lies ahead. Here it comes. Here it comes . . . . Bam! There it went. It's now past. It was only present for . . . what else? Less than a moment? Not even that. There was an infinitely thin dividing line which separated the future from the past—that which can only be the present—and now it's past, gone, ceases to exist. In other words, my friends, if the future doesn't exist, and the past doesn't exist, and the present doesn't exist, then what else is there? There is nothing. Nothing exists."

We sat around in silence, finally broken by one bearded fellow who might have been "the voice" who said, "By God, I'll drink to that." And he did. We all did.

"But, wait a minute, Man," offered a beatnik from the other side of the shadows. "I exist. I know I exist. I'm sitting here and I *know* I'm sitting here, and therefore I know I exist."

He sounded like Xeno's straight man. The blonde slowly nodded her head, also, frowning, as if she suddenly realized that she knew she existed, too.

"Ah, but wait," said Xeno, "if you did *not* exist, you would not *know* that you did not exist, simply because you couldn't. But if you did exist, you could not be *positive* that you existed. And anyway, I have just shown you that you cannot exist. Because nothing exists. There is no such thing as time. There is no such thing as reality. There is no such thing as any thing. There is nothing. There is no thing."

"That's pretty despondent thinging," I said, unable to resist the pun, and bringing awareness to my own non-existing self. "If nothing exists, then it must follow that God also does not exist. Is that true?"

I knew Xeno and one or two others, but for the most part I was a stranger to the group. They all turned and looked at me as if I were a stranger in their midst.

"Yes," nodded Xeno, "it *is* pretty despondent thinking. But that is because this is a pretty despondent world. This is a pretty despondent life. At any rate, you tell us. Does God exist?"

"Well," I said, "I look at it this way," and I turned my head sharply to the left. Then I turned it back toward Xeno with a straight face. "If God exists, then He—or She—makes the rules. If God does not exist, then we make the rules. So, if God *does* exist, and I doubt His—or Her—existence, then that's all part of God's plan, and it doesn't matter. If God does *not* exist, then we make the rules, and arguing about the existence of God doesn't matter. In other words, nothing matters."

Xeno took another sip from his cup, and we all sipped, pondering the despondering life in which nothing existed and nothing mattered. Xeno kept his attention focused on me.

"Then, tell us, Hud, what is your philophy of life? What do you thing?" he said, throwing my pun back at me.

"Xeno," I said without too much pause, "my philosophy of life can be summed up in one simple statement."

"And what is that?"

"Desserts I desire not, so long no lost one rise distressed."

The silence of confusion fell over everyone as they tried to think about what I had just said. However, it's hard to think when nothing exists and nothing matters.

"What?" asked Xeno. "What?"

"Desserts I desire not, so long no lost one rise distressed," I repeated again, repeated I.

"What the hell is that?"

"'The hell is that' is my philosophy of life. It means nothing, and it reads the same backwards and forward. It means the same thing—nothing—whichever way you look at it."

I finished my cider and left, and they all ceased to exist some more.

In years to come we will become obsessed with what we want from this nonexistence on earth we call Life. In the Embarrassing and Stormy Sixties we will call it "doing my thing."

"What are you doing?"

"Oh, I'm just doing my thing."

And the meaning won't be physical masturbation. Mental, maybe—physical, no.

We will be "what's happening."

"This is where it's at."

"You know where I'm coming from."

These three statements will be the watchwords of the Sixties.

"What'd he say?"

"I don't know, but he must have said something, 'cause I saw his lips move."

"Well, I know what he *said*, but what did he *mean*?"

I don't know. What is the meaning of 'meaning'?"

Rather than talk about "philosophy of life," maybe we should just smooth the obsession down to "Primary Goal before We Die."

What is your Primary Goal? What do you want more than anything else before you die?

I don't know. What are my choices?

Sex, food, and comfort.

What about happiness?

Happiness comes after either sex, food, or comfort.

In years to come, lonely people will start advertising their loneliness and using the newspapers to solicit relief. Personal ads will become acceptable ways of meeting new people, after their first, sordid, laughable, naughty existence as "those personals in the back" of the *Barb*, the *Voice*, and all the other counterculture newspapers.

Obviously, the Primary Goal of those first counterculture-reading people will be Sex. When the personals will become respectable enough to move up into the back of the bus of the family newspapers, respectable people can also admit that their Primary Goal is Sex. Of course, they will have to use euphemisms and refer to "mate," "companion," and "significant other" when they talk about it, and the thing they will want most out of life will become diluted to "LTR" or "someone to share the rest of my life with."

Other people will want Fame. Show-business people will want Fame.

"What about 'Fortune'? Doesn't that always go hand in hand with 'Fame'? You always hear them together: 'Fame and Fortune.'"

Okay, not Fame so much as recognition, appreciation, love, an affirmation from somebody else that I exist and I'm standing here on this Earth. See me, God damn it. Listen to me, God damn it. Love me, God damn it. And for more than fifteen fucking minutes.

Some people will want Power. Business-business people will want Power. And that includes military-business people, as well, who are nothing more than business-business people with a more rigid uniform code and who use hand signals to demonstrate each other's power in public.

"What about 'Glory'? Doesn't that always go along with 'Power'?"

Okay, not Power so much as control, influence, respect, a proof to my ego that I exist and I can control my environment and the people around me, because I love me more than they do and more than I love them.

Some people will want Art. Some people's lives will be driven by an abstract obsession that transcends physical needs for sex, food, and comfort, that transcends needs of recognition, love, power, and self-love. Artists will be driven by a need for spiritual harmony, for creative exercise, for a love of humanity and a desire to make the lives of the rest of humanity a better existence, a contemplative beauty, a restful, lovely time on this Earth.

Some people will want a Cause, noble or ignoble. They will choose an objective to try to achieve, such as Save the Whales, Save the Snail Darter, Save the Planet, Save Ourselves. Or they will simply try to reaffirm their own beliefs by attempting to make everybody else believe the way they do. Ban the Bomb. Ban Abortions. Ban the Motherfuckers.

Some won't know. Some people will drift among the detritus of Life not making any self-commitment to a Primary Goal. They will just want to don't worry, be happy. Contented. At ease with themselves. At peace with the universe. In love with love.

But they will be the weak ones. They will need a crutch to get them through the nonexistence of life. Those will be the people who need drink to get them through the nonexistence of the day. Those will be the people who need drugs to get them through the nonexistence of their lives. Those will be the people who will believe that meaningless statements like "Today is the first day of the rest of your life" are the most profound statements in the world. What is the meaning of "meaning"?

Life can be a lot of things, even though they are all meaningless, perhaps, but, then, what does meaningless mean? What is the meaning of "meaningless"?

Life can be a lot of things, but death is nothing. Death is the absence of a thing where once a thing had been. I always hated the word "thing," but in some cases we have no other words to use. To go along with Shakespeare, a person plays a part, yes. We all play a role. We are characters in life. All the world's a stage, and all the people merely passengers. And then suddenly one character, one passenger, is not present anymore, gets off the stage, and all the other character actors have to play around that vacant part and ad-lib for the rest of the journey or the rest of the play, whichever comes first. We have to try to fill in that void somehow, but we can't, because no one else can fill that missing role. We must try to fill in around it as best we can. We all know the part, we can sit in the seat, we can utter the lines, but we can't portray it convincingly, because we all have our own parts to play, and our own self-consciousness comes into play to prevent us from playing anyone else. We just cannot fulfill someone else's part. And all the awkwardness about death comes from trying to fill the role, from our own selfishness and foolish attempts to keep our lives from changing because of someone else's death, from trying to make the dead person's part live on after that person is dead and gone, has left the stage, or in Elvis's case, the building.

We should just try to forget it. Life's a bitch, and then you die. Or else you marry one, one wag will add.

Death occurred occasionally on campus, sometimes very close to me. It happened once during the winter as we were driving home after a party at a fraternity brother's house. His parents lived in town, and he lived in a sort of barn-apartment behind their house. It was quite comfortable, and he decided to have a party at his place during a particularly bad off-season of entertainment. The party was typically quiet, about ten couples, bring-your-own drinks, music by records, dancing. It started quietly, built up to a subdued hum, and ended quietly.

Rape was there stag. He had tried and tried to get a date, but he had had no luck. He had had had a date originally with a freshman girl he had had had had taken out once before, but the day before the party she had called him and told him she had to go home to Denver that weekend, because her grandfather was going to be there, and he was very old and not too well, and this was probably going to be the last time she would ever get to see him alive. Her story was just odd enough to be true. 'Tis true 'tis odd. And odd 'tis 'tis true.

So, Rape called and called, and I called, and my date even tried to get him a date, but we all tried too late. The stage was gone.

So, Rape said, "What the hell," and he went stag. He had a reasonably good time, drinking with us, dancing with a few of the girls, playing the bongos along with the music. Listening to "Last Date" by Floyd Cramer. We didn't realize how drunk he was until we got into the car.

Because Rape was alone, he said he had plenty of room in his car, and he had driven my date and me and Bido and Myrna to the party. We had stayed late, and because my date was a freshman, we were hard pressed to get her to her dormitory on time. So, we roared off, and Rape was just drunk enough to think he was a race-car driver. He was always interested in sports-car racing and talked about it a lot, and he was just drunk enough that night to think that he was one.

The roads were slippery—snow had fallen the day before—and Rape decided to take the short cut through the campus to get my date to the dorms faster. We had about ten minutes to go. The road through the campus at that part winds around Varsity Lake. It is a one-way road. Rape went through the road taking racing corners and muttering to himself all the time, "Zoom, zoom, patow, patow-w-w!" in his rendition of a sports car taking corners. The road made a sharp curve to the left, ice was on the outside of the curve, the wheels hit the ice, Rape couldn't get the car to turn away from the tree. We all saw it coming, looming up in the glare of the headlights as if in a quiet, ear-shattering, mind-screaming nightmare.

Rape lay against the bent steering wheel, muttering over and over, "I couldn't turn . . . . I couldn't turn . . . . I couldn't turn . . . ."

My date, Marilyn, and I had been sitting in the front seat with Rape. Rape and I had put on a show before we left the party about being queer and in love with each other, and I sat next to him on the way home. Marilyn was next to the door, right where the car hit the tree. We tried everything we could think of, but nothing worked. No thing. She was dead.

Her death affected everyone strangely, I thought. Rape took it hard, blaming himself for the accident. He swore off everything for about three weeks—drinking, driving, even smoking. Bido was shocked, and Myrna went into hysterics. I felt sorry for Marilyn, and I was sorry it had happened. But her death was just one of those things, one of those crazy things that happen all the time. I couldn't get emotional about it. I hadn't cared a whole lot for her, but the victim could just as easily have been me. Or Myrna. Or any or all of us. We should actually have been relieved, even glad. I was sorry because of the inconvenience it caused, because of all the questioning and all, but all in all that was all.

Myrna got very upset with me about it.

"You're crazy, you know that? My God, you are insane. Have you no feelings?"

"Have I no feelings? Of course, I have feelings. But why do I have to get so worked up about it? You didn't even know the girl. Why are you getting all worked up about it? She's dead. She's not coming back, Myrna. She's dead and she's gone. Why make yourself miserable because of an unfortunate, chance occurrence? Everything in life is just one long series of chance occurrences, and this was one of them. What's happened happened. What's over's over. What's done is done. That's it. That's all she wrote. There ain't no more. There's nothing more *we* can do about it. The only thing we can do is to forget it and go on living for as long as we can. Her death was an unfortunate accident, but that's life. That's death. It shouldn't mean the end of *your* life just because it was the end of hers. Why can't other people see that? Why?"

"Can you ever get all shook up? Can you? Can you ever get all shook up about something? Anything?"

Perhaps I was too embarrassed to answer her.

FIFTEEN

I pull the car over to the side of the road

I pull the car over to the side of the road about six in the morning. We are some fifteen miles outside the city limits of Las Vegas, and the sun is just getting ready to come over the horizon.

"Wha—? Where are we? What's the matter?"

"Nothing's the matter. This is just where I'm getting off."

He pulls himself up out of the back seat and looks around. He shakes his head twice and rubs his eyes with his knuckles. He shows that sleeping in the back seat of a car isn't easy.

"What's the matter with you? Why didn't you wake me up at midnight? We're out in the middle of the desert, for Christ's sake. What do you mean, this is where you're getting off?"

"That's hard to explain. I just don't want to go into town right now. I just want to sit out here in the desert and do some thinking and watch the sun come up. I want to be alone. I want to forget."

I get out of the car and stand by the door. He stops to look at me before getting into the front seat.

"Kid, you're either crazy or on the lam. You look too smart to be crazy . . . . But, then, you look too smart to be on the lam, too. I can't figure you out."

"You and a lot of other people. Look, I appreciate the ride and all. Thanks. I'll hitch a ride the rest of the way in in an hour or so. I'm not crazy and I'm not running from anybody. At least, I don't think I am—on both counts."

He drives off shaking his head. *Boy, he has seen a lot of loonies, but Jesus Christ . . . .* I tramp about a hundred yards off the highway, through the still cool sand, find a quiet place among the rocks to sit where the sun will hit me when it wants to, and I sits and I thinks.

So, what is the matter with wanting to sit and rest easy for a while and watch nature at work? I have come a long way since I left Boulder. I am tired.

I am scared to go into Las Vegas.

Why?

I'm not scared of Las Vegas itself. Perhaps I'm scared of the fact that Las Vegas is the last jumping-off place before going on to California. Maybe that's why I'm reluctant. Perhaps I want to rest at the halfway point, gathering my energy before making that last spurt across the California desert to the ocean.

Perhaps I am just scared.

The sun peeps over the horizon, and the music from the "Grand Canyon Suite" starts buzzing in my brain. The air is still chilly, but my sweater and parka keep me warm. I just want to sit and think. I don't even know exactly what I want to think about.

Do I really know what I am doing? What am I trying to prove by going to California? Am I trying to prove something? Am I merely making an idealistic statement? I have no intentions whatsoever of staying out there. I am merely going out to take a look at the ocean, test the waters, and then turn around and go back. What's so crazy about that?

Well, that's a pretty idealistic thing to do. If seeing the ocean means so much, couldn't you have waited until after graduation before dropping out and zooming on?

I refuse to answer questions that begin with a negative.

Maybe I am crazy. Enough people certainly have been telling me that I am. They say that the people who *are* crazy are the ones who deny it the most. And the people who aren't sure whether or not they *are* crazy are the ones who are the most sane. But in that case, then I should be sane. Therefore, I'm *not* crazy. But, then, that's denying it again, so maybe I am.

So, I sit here in "El Houl," the desolate place, and think. Here I am in El Houl, the desolate place, on my way to Tlappallan, I think, therefore I am, lapsing into a philosophical literary mood. Here I sit in the Nevada desert on my way to the California coast. On my way to see the ocean, on my way to see the sea. And, by gods, I do *not* wish to return to the womb! I hate—. No, "hate" is too powerful a word. I am extremely annoyed by psychological catch-all diagnosis-like terms such as "return-to-the-womb" and "death wish" and "anal-personality" and all the ego, id, super ego business. I don't believe in them. The theories are too phony—too many easy and convenient tags and labels trying to describe life, trying to explain—to put some meaning into—life. Life is as complicated as the square of the number of people on the Earth. Yeah, that's it. Explain life mathematically, not psychologically. Now we're getting some wares.

I'm not neat and orderly because I had rigorous toilet training, which I don't even know if I had. I'm not pausing before going into Las Vegas because I have a younger brother, which I know I have. I'm not going to California because I secretly want to escape life, have sex with my mother, and return to the womb, where I wouldn't fit, anyway.

The womb's a fine and private place, but none, I think, do there embrace.

Stanley used to call his brother and himself "womb mates" all the time. Stanley was a shy guy, a Japanese-Hawaiian. He had trouble pronouncing the letter "l," just like in the movies, so we all called him "Stanrey," affectionately, just to bug him. He also had trouble with American sayings and idioms, always getting them confused and mixed together. But, then, when you think about them, they are pretty confusing, anyway.

One day we were walking along on the Hill, and Stanley saw a penny lying on the sidewalk in front of us. He swooped down, scooped it up, and put it in his pocket.

"For Christ's sake," I said, "it's just a lousy penny. You almost tripped me getting that lousy penny."

"Ah, but a penny saved is a drop in the bucket."

His version actually had a lot of truth in it, and now that I think about them, *all* of Stanley's mixed-up sayings had a lot of truth in them. In fact, probably more truth than what is intended in the original sayings. Perhaps that is how society changes, how language changes, how humanity changes. Someone sees a truth, changes it consciously or unconsciously to a newer truth, and we all—those of us who survive, anyway—accept the newer truth. Perhaps Stanley got them mixed up on purpose. Perhaps he saw through us all the time.

"Come on," he said. "Be daring for a change. Throw caution out the windows."

Once, he seemed to be pretty hot for a certain girl, and we kidded him about her, asking him when they were getting pinned, when they were getting married, if he was getting in . . . .

"Ah, no," he said. "Her? She means nothing to me. I just give her a little bus token of affection. She's just a flash in the pants."

Once, I asked him how his grades were coming along, and what he thought he was going to get at the end of the semester.

"Oh, I figure I'll get about a B average. Maybe a B minus, but that's just a horseback estimation."

"*What*? A horseback estimation? What the hell does that mean?"

"I don't know," he smiled. "It just sounds good."

Stanley also had trouble concentrating when he read his text books, so he bought *How to Read a Book*, hoping that it would help him to do better in his studies. T.K. thought that book was just hilarious. He thought that that was the funniest thing he had ever heard.

"*How to Read a Book*? That's great! That's really great. But if you don't know how to read a book in the first place, how can you read *How to Read a Book* in the second place? Hey! I think I'll write a book called *How to Read a 'How to Read a Book' Book*. Hey, Dayo! I'm going to write a book. Will you read it?"

"Sure. What's it called?"

"*How to Read a 'How to Read a Book' Book*."

"You know, T.K., you're dumber than you look . . . . I mean, you're not as dumb as you look . . . . I mean, nobody likes a wise guy, T.K."

"But, then, how can they read *my* book? I'll have to write another book first. *How to Read a 'How to Read a "How to Read a Book" Book' Book*."

"T.K., who don't you go home?"

"Wait a minute! I'm not sure I know how to write a whole book, anyway. Maybe I'll have to read *How to Write a Book* first."

T.K. was always like that. Funny things just happened whenever he was around. He loved life and was full of it. I don't think I've ever seen him despondent, but that doesn't mean that he can't ever be serious. He is one of the seriousest guys I know. Perhaps he just laughs all the time to cover up his own fear. Perhaps he just makes us laugh all the time to help us cover up our own fears.

No, perhaps he just laughs all the time because he's happy, god damn it.

"You've got to live," he said once. "You've either got to live or you've got to die. Now, I've never been dead, but I think it hurts. So, I've got to live. All right, now. I can either be happy or I can be sad. Being sad's no fun. So, I choose happy. That's why I'm happy all the time."

Sometimes I wish I could be more like T.K. Sometimes I wish I could just say, "All right, I've got a choice. I can be sad or I can be happy. So, I choose happy." However, with me, I never seem to want to get that personal with myself.

But, no matter whether or not you were happy or sad, whenever you were with T.K., you were happy. The times we've had . . . .

Once, T.K. and I went to Denver to see a play, a Broadway road-show engagement. We got there a bit early, and the doors hadn't opened yet. T.K.

went to stand in line to pick up our tickets, and I waited at the ticket box by the door for him. I was just standing there minding my own business—I wasn't doin' nuttin'—just looking at the people, and a guy came up and asked me a question. I didn't even catch the question, because it caught me off guard, but I realized that the guy thought I was the ticket taker. So, I said the first thing that came into my mind.

"I don't know."

He looked at me queerly, looked me up and down, and then walked away. I saw the makings of a game here. Another man walked up to me, a real old fuddy-duddy fat guy, the kind who likes to smoke fat, juicy, horribly smelly cigars, and I tried to act more like a ticket taker.

"Excuse me. What time does the performance start?"

"I don't know."

He took a second before he comprehended what I had answered. I just stood there staring at him with a blank expression tacked onto my face.

"I beg your pardon?"

You're pardoned, my son.

"I don't know."

He was completely deflated. He tried to say something else, but nothing would come out, and he finally walked away. I knew that T.K. would love this when I told him, and I began to plan the story. I brushed a bit of dust from the top of the ticket box.

A little old lady walked up, obviously somebody's grandmother. She was sweet and innocent and old and fragile and vulnerable. Pow! She probably went out once a month and this was it. Bam! Was she going to get it! Ka-BOOM!

"Excuse me, young man. Do you have a phone here?"

"I don't know."

She jerked, actually jerked, when I answered. The strangest look came over her face, and she stood there twisting her umbrella with her hands. She walked slowly away, turning to look at me every few steps, walked, turned, and joined a lady friend who was standing in line. She whispered to her friend, and they both looked at me, and I looked back at them. I even smiled. And the lady friend said something encouraging to the first lady. Shortly the little old lady shuttled back over to me.

"Look, young man, I really have to make a phone call. Can I get in?"

"I don't know."

She began to get angry and red in the face. She shook her arthritic finger at me.

"Look here, young man. I have to make an important phone call. It is very important. Do you have a phone in there?"

"I don't know."

She really got mad then, and she raised her voice, causing people to stare at us.

"Young man, where is the manager? I am going to—."

Just then, T.K. walked up with our tickets.

"Are you ready to go in?" he asked.

"Yeah, I'm ready. Let's go on in, okay?"

SIXTEEN

I go on in to Las Vegas

I go on in to Las Vegas. After waiting about ten minutes by the side of the highway, I catch a ride into town in an antiquish dirty pickup. The driver is an ancient, obvious Indian. He asks me no questions about how I got out into the desert at that time of the morning, or where I am from, or what my name is, or even where I am going. He picks me up, and that is it. It seems like months ago that I left Boulder in much the same type of pickup truck, but in actuality it has been only two days.

The Indian lets me out in downtown Las Vegas. This is the first time I have been here, and I am curious. The gamblers look as if they are just getting ready to relax, to take a breather from the night's activities. Bleary-eyed men and women stumble out of the entrances of the hustling gambling houses. It is still early in the morning.

There are also plenty of people walking around who look like tourists. You can always tell a tourist. "But not much!" T.K. would add.

You can always spot tourists. There is just something about them, and it isn't only the way they dress, either. It's the air about them of "Gee, isn't that something!" At any rate, a number of crudely dressed, Western-outfitted tourists wander around, trying out the slot machines and other games of damn-slim chance.

I go into one of the casinos to look around. After all, I am a tourist, too. I am amazed at the plushness of the place, thick red carpets, shining fixtures, the colorful scanty costumes of the girls walking around still getting drinks for the people at that hour in the morning. And the sounds are all money sounds, the clinking of silver dollars at the blackjack tables, the clacking of the roulette wheel against the little steel ball, the shoosh-bangings of the one-armed banditti. So this is Las Vegas. This is where the action is. This is where fortunes are made and lost. And women, too.

A number of men and women are working the slot machines, mostly women playing them for all they are worth. The way they go about continuously stroking and pulling down the levers reminds me of something obscene. I notice one tall woman, extremely pretty, playing, shoving the coins in one right after the other. She punches one in, pulls the slot lever, and has the next coin in before the rollers stop spinning. Then she begins working the machine next to hers at the same time, pushing the coin in the one while the other is still spinning round and round. Her drop-dead beauty makes her stand out and look out of place with all the other tourists, but she isn't dressed like a tourist. She's dressed like she belongs in this town. She sees me looking at her and smiles, and I smile back. I mentally wish her good luck, because she looks as if she will need it, but if looks were money, she'd be a millionaire.

I begin looking around for a place where I can get something to eat, and I just start off toward the back of the casino when someone touches me on the arm and says, "Excuse me?"

It is the beautiful woman I have just been watching playing the slots. I stare curiously into her clear blue eyes. This interests me, hot damn you all I swear. You bet.

"This is going to sound pretty strange," she says, smiling self-consciously, "and I wouldn't blame you if you just walked away, but I'm pretty desperate. I'll make you a proposition. I'm not trying to pick you up or anything, but if you'll pay my cab fare home, I'll take you home with me and cook you a real honest-to-goodness home-cooked breakfast."

Her voice is deep and husky and seductive. I just stand there looking at her, forcing my eyes to keep staring into hers and not drop to enjoy and caress her knockout body. Then I begin looking around, and then I look back at her. I must have a pretty dumb expression on my face.

"This has got to be a gag," I say. "Do I really look that out of place?"

"No, no. I'm serious. Honest. The thing is, I've lost all my money that I brought with me. I don't have any cab fare to get home on. But if you'll take me home, I'll cook you that breakfast. You look like you could use it. I mean, you know, you look unshaven and tired and all . . . . Well, you just look like you're tired and hungry. And besides, you look honest. And cute, too."

She smiles, and I smile.

"Well, I'll have to agree with you. I mean, I could use some breakfast. And a shave. And, well, what the hell. Why not?"

She takes my arm as we walk toward the street to look for a cab. I am feeling pretty good. Las Vegas. My kind of town.

"Oh, uh, I didn't mean to stare at you back there while you were playing the slot machines. It's just that this is all kind of new to me."

"Oh? I'm sorry. I didn't even see you. You were just the first person I saw when I ran out of money. I don't pay any attention to anything else when I'm playing. I'm sorry."

Well, there goes the old ego. Shot down again. *The big hurt.*

"I could just kick myself for being so stupid," she says in the cab on the way to her apartment. "But I just couldn't help it. I couldn't stop. I had put enough aside for cab fare in a secret compartment in my purse, but when I lost all I had allowed myself today, I was sure I could get it back. I had this feeling I was going to win. I have these good feelings sometimes, you know? Sort of like the feeling I had about you. I was arguing with myself whether or not to use it when a lady right next to me won a double jackpot, and that did it. I just *knew* if I played my cab fare, I was going to go home a winner. Maybe I am, anyway," she smiles at me coyly.

I smile back and think, *Please help me, I'm falling. Party doll.*

Her apartment is cool, and small, and neat, not like most places I've seen girls live in. She starts right in on the breakfast, and I stay in the kitchen with her to drink coffee and talk. She looks about thirty-five, but could possibly go as many as five years either way. She obviously has been conscious of her appearance since she was twenty, probably, because she is extremely good looking for a woman of any age. She says she is a showgirl in one of those big production numbers in one of the big hotels. Hot damn you all I swear again! I'll bet! *Good golly Miss Molly.*

"You know, I just stand around without hardly any costume on at all, just lots and lots of feathers, always turned toward the audience, and I smile all the time. It pays enough to take care of myself.... I used to have dreams about becoming a dancer or an actress, but I'm willing to be patient and wait for my big break, you know, if and when.... Anyway, I like Las Vegas.... Oh, I don't know, I imagine one day I'll hit a big jackpot and have enough so as not to worry, anyway. And then I can get away from all this. I can sing and dance, and I'm sure I can act. So, I don't worry about the future. I'm just waiting for my big break, whichever comes first. But, tell me about you. What are you doing?"

Her voice is like a cool mountain stream, and I could fall asleep just listening to it wash over me. I could also fall in love, I think, if she weren't so old. Hell, she's practically the establishment! *Come softly to me.*

"Well, to tell you the truth, I'm just bumming around the country right now. I suddenly dropped out of school for a couple of reasons and I'm going out to the coast for a while."

She flips the eggs.

"Where are you from? I mean, what school do you go to?"

"University of Colorado."

"What? You're kidding! Really? I went there, too!"

"You're kidding."

"No! No, really! My freshman year. I'm from Denver."

"No kidding! You really went to C.U.?"

"Yes. It was . . . oh, a few years ago. But I wasn't smart enough, and I quit before they kicked me out. So then I came to Las Vegas and managed to get a job . . . uh, dancing."

She adds bacon to the pan with the eggs. I notice that she's doing it backwards. *Lonely teardrops.*

"So, you went to C.U., too. Small world and all that, like They say. They always say that."

She finishes the eggs and bacon, gets the toast and some more coffee, and sits down at the little table with me. I realize that I have been studying her body in fascination as much as listening to her cool, rushing, mountain-stream voice.

"It's not much, but at least it's breakfast."

"Hey, this is great. You must be a good cook."

"Oh, all right, I guess. I like to cook, but it's no fun cooking for just one. Sometimes I simply shove a TV dinner in the stove and let it go at that."

I ask her what she does with herself in her non-working hours, for entertainment and all. *Talk to me, talk to me.*

"Well, there's always swimming at the pool here—or anywhere, for that matter, I guess. Practically every place you go around this town has a swimming pool. I make it a practice to carry a bathing suit around in my handbag all the time."

I think about the size of her small handbag and grin like an idiot, trying to keep my dirty thoughts to myself. I imagine her knockout body in an itsy bitsy teeny weeny yellow polka-dot bikini, and I am feeling myself getting turned on. *Could this be magic.*

"If I ever feel like going out when I'm not working, I just go swimming at the hotel pool and wait for some old goat to pick me up. You know, look pretty and smile and laugh a lot, throw a little bust out, and they all come running—at least as fast as they can make it. Sometimes I almost can't stand them, the lecherous old men with their hot, knobby, restless hands, but it's a free night's entertainment, and if I'm careful I don't have to do anything. I really have to keep from laughing sometimes at all the old worn-out lines and approaches the old geezers try. You know, 'My wife doesn't understand me' and all that. I'll bet I've heard them all, and then some."

I am shocked and disappointed. *You cheated.*

"Well, like you said, it's a free night's entertainment."

"And then there's the biggest entertainment of them all."

"Oh? . . . What's that?"

"What's that? Oh, I'll bet you know . . . . Or, there's always second best. What's Las Vegas famous for? Why do people come here? To gamble, what else?"

"Gamble, huh? You get a kick out of that, do you?"

"Oh, sure. Only sometimes I'm afraid it gets to be more like an addiction. Really, I have to allow myself only so much money a day to gamble and make sure I don't take any more with me than that. Otherwise I'd probably gamble away all my earnings."

She pours me some more coffee.

"You mean, you gamble a considerable amount every day?"

"Yes. Ten dollars."

"You gamble ten dollars every day? And every day you lose ten dollars?"

"Well . . . yes."

"How can you afford it? Why do you keep going back?"

"Well, because I just know that one of these days I'm going to hit it big. I have that good feeling. I know it. All around me I see other slobs hitting it rich and I figure it just might as well could be me as them. I've got just as much a chance as they have. All it is, is luck, and if I stick around long enough, some of that luck is bound to come out of my machine. Then when I get it, that's it. I quit."

"You've really got it bad, don't you?"

"No, of course not. I can quit any time I want to."

"Yeah. Sure. You've done it hundreds of times, right?"

"Okay," she laughs, "don't believe me. But *I* believe me, and that's all that counts."

"Okay, Diamond Lil, I believe you. But me, I've got too little in my pockets right now to risk losing it. I'm a gambler just like everybody else, I guess, but I don't need any more than I've got to get where I'm going. However, I *do* need what I've got. So I don't plan to do any gambling while I'm here."

"So, what are you going to do now?"

I rub my two-day chin and take a secret, tentative sniff at my armpit. *My prayer.*

"Well, I'll tell you. I haven't had a bath in over two days, nor a decent shave, and I sure would appreciate it if you would let me use your bathroom for about an hour."

"Of course," she smiles warmly. "You're welcome to use it. I'll get you a towel and a washcloth. You don't mind flowers on your towels, do you?"

"Not at all."

"I'll get them for you and clean up the kitchen while you're showering. Oh! By the way, I'm Lorraine Evans."

"Huh! That's right. I'm sorry. My name's Hud Holyoke."

"Pleased to meet you, Hud Holyoke," she says, taking my hand smoothly.

"I'm pleased to meet you, Lorraine Evans from Denver, Colorado."

In years to come, losing ten dollars a day gambling won't seem like much, especially when a couple of recently graduated college kids will blow that much at a quarter a pop on an electronic trivia game in their favorite bar in Oakland with no return other than a chance to put their names in the machine as the highest scorers. But when Dayo, Theo, and I can rent a two-bedroom house for ninety dollars a month, when we can put ten dollars apiece in the pot every month for groceries and still have money left over at the end of the month, then ten dollars a day gambled and lost is a lot of money. Especially when the money represents your dreams. When you gamble away your dreams every day, the losses are more bitter than just not putting your name in a machine.

As I shower, I keep trying to convince myself that Lorraine doesn't remind me of Diane, but I can't. She does. She could pass for Diane's mother or older sister easily, but there are other resemblances to Diane. She wears her hair the same way, her eyes have the same sparkle of delight when she sees something that pleases her, and her nose wrinkles the same way as Diane's did when she smiles, or when she frowns . . . . But I don't want to think about Diane. No, I say to myself as I rinse my hair, other than those things, she doesn't remind me of Diane at all.

I put my jeans back on after I finish, and I borrow a razor from Lorraine and some shaving cream. It is one of those little lady's razors and she laughs at the sight of me shaving with it.

"Do you mind if I watch?" she asks, leaning against the doorway of the bathroom.

"No . . . . Course not. You get a kick out of watching people shave, or something?"

"No, Silly. Just men. I like to watch a man shave. It's so . . . so manly."

"Yes, I guess you could call it that. And this razor is going to take me twice as long, so you ought to get twice as much pleasure out of it as usual."

She doesn't say anything, and I get the feeling that I've hurt her, but she watches me intently while I continue. Every so often I smile at her in the mirror. I feel as if I am shoveling Colorado snow with a Kansas hoe.

"Hud?"

"Hmmm?"

"How soon do you have to get out to the coast?"

"How soon? I don't have any deadline or anything. There's no time that I have to be out there. I'm just wandering. Why?"

"Oh . . . just wondering."

I smile at her and dry my face. She hands me a bottle of Old Spice she has been holding behind her back.

"Oh? What's this? You shave, too?"

"No, silly boy," she laughs. "And I don't use it on my legs, either. I just love the smell of it, so I always keep a bottle around. Sometimes when I'm lonely I put some on my pillow and go to sleep dreaming."

A memory hot-flashes through my head about going to sleep smelling perfume, smelling perfume and hoping to dream about . . . .

"Well, thank you very much. For letting me mess up your bathroom, too. I feel great now."

"Oh, it's no mess. I was going to clean it today, anyway."

"Yes. Well, thanks, anyway. And . . . I guess . . . . Well, I guess I might as well be taking off."

"Oh! Oh . . . . Hud?"

"Yes?"

"Do you really have to go to California now?"

"What do you mean?"

I can't keep my eyes off her body. *Baby it's you.*

"Well," she says with some embarrassment, "aren't you just a little bit tired from all that traveling you've done in the past two days? I mean, you must be exhausted. And especially after not getting any sleep last night, you said. Well, don't you think you should rest awhile? Get a little sleep? I mean . . . ."

She trails off, and I smile and say, "Just what are you suggesting?"

She smiles and blushes. It's strange to see an older woman blush. *Goodnite sweetheart, goodnite.*

"You saw through me, huh? Well, it's just that I've been so bored and lonely, and . . . and I like you, and . . . . Well, I'd just like to help you, especially since you're from home and all. I mean, we've got so much in common."

I put my shirt on and stare at her. Her body cries out to me, "Take me, take me." *Ooh baby baby.*

"You want to help me? And you're lonely? How can you be lonely in Las Vegas with all these people around here, and you can get a date any time you want one—?"

"Oh, sure. Yeah, a date any time I want one with an old lecher. A dirty old man who tries to act like he was forty again. Or else a younger stud who thinks more of himself than he does me. A girl gets tired of that. I'd like to go out with someone nice for a change. Someone who can talk to me about things *I* like. Someone who doesn't try to throw me in bed the very minute he picks me up. Look, you don't have to worry about money. I'll pay for everything."

"Pay? 'Pay for everything'? Pay for what? All you mentioned was just staying here awhile to get some sleep. What's this 'paying'?"

"Well, wouldn't you like to go out? You said you had never been to Las Vegas before. You said you should see what it has to offer."

"You know, I can't keep up with you? You keep me jumping ahead too fast."

"Well, don't try to keep up with me, then. But will you? Will you stay? Please? Pretty please? Pretty please with peaches and cream on it?"

"Okay!" I laugh. "Sure. I guess so. This is all too crazy, this whole morning. But, what the hell. Okay, if you really don't mind."

Who the hell am I kidding? *A wonderful dream.*

"Oh, I'm glad! You know, I guess I should really be ashamed of myself. I mean, I sort of did pick you up, didn't I? Well, I'm not sorry. I've never been sorry for anything I've ever done. Besides, you're such a good looking boy . . . . Look, you must be pretty tired. I'll make you a bed on the couch and you can just go to sleep and I'll be quiet while I clean the place and won't bother you at all. No, better yet, you can just use my bed. I'll tell you what: You go to bed and get a good night's—rather, a good *day's* sleep, and then maybe we can go out later on. I don't work tonight, and after you wake up, I'll show you Las Vegas the way it's meant to be seen. How does that sound?"

"Fine, fine. Just fine. Point me to it."

Hot damn you all I swear for the third time! Maybe dreams *do* come true! *Just a dream, just a dream.*

SEVENTEEN

Going over this unbelievable bit of business at the time, I can't help thinking about Bido

Going over this unbelievable bit of business at the time, I can't help thinking about Bido. Bido really would have loved this setup. He would have gone absolutely crazy, absolutely ape over it. He wouldn't have believed it had happened. Of course, it might not have happened with Bido. Not that Bido would have minded that Lorraine was probably almost twice as old as he was, but that Lorraine would have been able to see what was on his mind from the very beginning.

Only one thing was ever on Bido's mind, and that was sex. He was obsessed with sex and girls, in that order. In fact, T.K. coined the phrase we used to refer to Bido: he was "obsexed with girls." Sex was the only thing Bido was interested in in a girl. No consideration of intelligence, no consideration of charm, no consideration of religion—he cared about none of these. No, the only thing Bido cared about was whether or not he could get a piece of ass.

"Bido," I asked him once in all seriousness, "just what is it you're interested in when you take a girl out?"

"A piece of ass," he replied in all seriousness.

So, Bido went from one piece of ass to another. He wasn't the kind to love them and leave them, however. It was usually the other way around. He loved them and loved them and loved them, and then they got wise and left *him*. He had no misgivings at all about a girl who had forsaken her honor. In fact, he said he respected her all the more for it. He would continue to take her out just as long as she continued to go down for him. But eventually the girl would realize that sex was the only thing he cared about and that she was only a necessary piece of biological equipment for him. During the beginning, she might have faint hopes that eventually Bido might love her for her *self*, and not just for her body. But ten or twelve nights in a row of tumbles soon convinced her she was wrong and that he would never consider her anything more than a necessary means to an end—her end—a veritable screwing machine. No, the girls left Bido. He didn't leave them.

Except when he couldn't score. *Then* he would leave them. Yes, the only time Bido would leave a girl was when he couldn't get into her pants. He would dust of the formula he applied to a girl, and if he didn't get anywhere after a few dates, she never saw him again except around the campus.

"I don't have the time to screw around," Bido said, "figuratively speaking, of course. I figure that a human being has just so many lays stored up in his body. It's a crime against Mother Nature herself not to try to use them all up. Well, I'm just trying my darnedest to use all mine up. I might even write a paper some day. I've been keeping count of mine. 'The Life and Loves of a Man: Are You Keeping Count of Yours?'"

"How many?"

"Four hundred and twenty-nine."

"Is that individual girls or individual times?" T.K. asked.

"Individual times. And that's pretty good, considering I didn't even start until my freshman year. The same year I started drinking beer. And smoking a pipe. I've since given up smoking a pipe, but, of course, I haven't given up screwing. Or drinking beer."

"Bido," I said, "have you ever thought about meeting a special girl, falling in love with her, and getting married?"

"Oh, I hope not. No, really, I imagine that someday I'll meet someone special and fall in love. And we'll get married. But I'll tell you this: she'll have to be able to give a really good piece of ass. I think I'm sort of getting spoiled."

Bido also had a "secret weapon," as he called it. He said that he had heard about some good-old-boy, backwoods hick in Arkansas or Tennessee or someplace like that who would always get laid every time he went to one of those barn dances they're always having way down South in the land of Cotton, old times there are not forgotten. Bido said that when this good old young-boy's friends asked him what the secret of his success was, the kid didn't rightly know, but he thought it had something to do with his handkerchief. It seems that Chester—or whatever his name was—kept a handkerchief tucked in his armpit, and whenever his dance partner got all hot and sweaty, Chester would offer his handkerchief to her, something strange would come over her, she'd become hot and bothered, and the two of them would leave the dance and go outside for a roll in the hay.

Bido said he used his chemistry training, did some research, and decided this "trick of tricks" had something to do with what he called "pheromones," a chemical substance all animals produce that causes the opposite sex to be physically attracted to them—and sometimes uncontrollably. So, Bido bought a special white handkerchief, always kept it handy in his bathroom, and whenever he got sweaty, he would wipe the sweat off with that handkerchief. "Binky," he called it. Then, whenever Bido went out on a date—or else, whenever he went out and expected to pick up girls—Bido would always take Binky along, and whenever the opportunity arose, Bido would offer Binky to the girl, hoping that something else would rise, too.

When T.K. heard this story, he just had to try out some of those "fora-moans," too, especially when our fraternity had its annual Barn Dance in the fall. However, wouldn't you know it, T.K. forgot to bring along a handkerchief, and when he noticed that his date was sweaty—or "glowing," as the girls liked to call it—the only sweaty thing of his T.K. could think of that he could offer her was a sock. "At least it was *white*!" T.K. muttered afterwards. However, his date was naturally appalled, she left him right then, there, and th-th-that's all, Folks! and she went home with a girlfriend, who was there with Theo, and that didn't make Theo at all happy. Bido, meanwhile, was nowhere to be seen, and we figured that he and Binky were doing okay, thank you very much.

And then Bido met Myrna. We figured something was up—ho ho—when he took Myrna out for the fifteenth night in a row. That was the all-time record for the number of times a girl went out with Bido over any period of time. I had talked to Myrna, and I knew she wasn't a nymphomaniac—or a bimbo. I had even tried to see if maybe I could get a little piece of the action. Ha ha. But, no, it was love on her part. It had to be, since she could put up with him that long. And apparently Bido had fallen in love with her, too—or her ass, which was probably the same thing to Bido.

"Boy, can she really give a good piece of ass," he told me. Bido was never known for being discreet.

And then Myrna cut him off. She realized that things couldn't go on—or come off—the way they had been. Bido was too content to think about marriage on his own. So, she thought about it for him. Either they get married, she said, or he would no more share her bed.

Bido thought it over. He had heard this line before, and always before, the decision had been easy. There were plenty of other fish in the Sea of Love and all that. But Myrna was different from all the other humpbacks. Like Bido said, she could really give a good piece of ass.

So, they got married. They just had a Justice of the Peace marry them—which we all thought was Aura Lee appropriate, and punny, too—since neither of their parents lived anywhere near Colorado. However, they invited all their friends to attend the ceremony, just as if it were a regular church wedding. Myrna even had a couple of bridesmaids, and Theo was Bido's best man. The rest of us—except for T.K.—were groom's men and ushers, which was pretty ridiculous, because we didn't have anybody to ush. T.K. managed to talk Myrna into letting him be a bridesmaid, saying that this would probably be his only chance—he could always be a groom's man or an usher. Hell, even a movie theater would pay him to ush during the summer.

All we had to do, however, was stand around in the office of the J.P., and the J.P. was awfully confused as it was, trying to figure out what was going on. I suppose he didn't often have a couple show up to get married with about fifteen witnesses.

But the marriage went off with a hitch—hee hee—and we had a reception of sorts at the Lamp Post, although it was a buy-your-own. The bride and groom looked very lovely and happy, respectively, and everyone else was very happy, too. T.K. was the happiest of all.

"I'm so happy I could cry," T.K. said, actually sobbing into his eighth margarita. "I thought for sure that Bido would be the last of us to go. And instead, he's the first. Look at him over there, smiling and nodding, and accepting congratulations—I mean, best wishes—and getting her drinks . . . . He's had it, Boy. If anyone was ever going to be p.w.'d, he's the one. To think that Bido could do this to us 'tried and trued' bachelors. Our guiding light, our shining star . . . crashed and burned. Sob."

All T.K.'s melodramatics aside, Bido and Myrna did look as if they would be a very dedicated and devoted couple, even if Bido *would* tend to be a little pussy-whipped. Considering all the girls whom Bido had tried and who had discarded him, certainly the one he married would be someone extra special. And for any girl to marry Bido after the reputation he had acquired—and through hard work, mind you—well, she must have loved him an awful lot. Yes, theirs was a storybook romance.

Unfortunately, neither one of them had read the book. About a month after the marriage, rumors started running around that Bido was running around. I didn't believe them at first, because it was unthinkable. Bido loved sex—pure unadulterated sex, and adulterated, too, for that matter—so much, why would he go stepping out on his wife when he could get it every night at home? Assuming she wasn't too tired, or had that nasty headache, or had cut him off again. So, the first opportunity I had to bring it up with Bido—in a manner of speaking, or course—I asked him straight out, point blank, what was happening.

"Uh, how's it going, Bido?"

"Oh, great. Great. Really great. Thanks for asking. Couldn't be better."

"Uh, how's Myrna?"

"Myrna? Oh, she's great. Fine. Just fine. Couldn't be better. I'll tell her you asked about her."

It was F.A.C. and we were squeezed among scores of screaming college students at the Sink, partaking of the perennial golden brew.

"And, uh, how's the old married life?"

"Marriage? Swell. Wonderful. Just great."

"Couldn't be better?"

"Yeah, I was just about to say that."

"Well, is anything the matter? You seem to be a little down."

"Down? No, I'm not down. 'Out' is what I am. Down, I'm not. Out, I am."

"You're miserable, aren't you, Bido?"

"Yeah, I'm miserable, Hud. No . . . . No, actually, I'm not. I'm not really *miserable*. I mean, I don't mind being married to Myrna and all. It's just that I'm . . . . Well, I feel guilty, that's all."

"Really? Why do you feel guilty?"

"Well, Hud, I don't know if you know this, but . . . . I've been going out with other girls. Now, don't get upset! Of course, I take precaution. I take my wedding ring off first."

I tried to be nonchalant about it.

"Yes, I, uh, heard rumors about something like that. I mean, going out. Not the part about your wedding ring."

"I don't know what it is, Hud. I love Myrna. I really do. But . . . . Well, it's just that . . . . Well, it sounds stupid, but I'm afraid I'm getting tired of her. I don't get such a great big kick out of going to bed with her anymore. In fact, we haven't made love for about three weeks. For a while there it even got to be a chore, and—can you believe it? Once, I couldn't even get it up. Now, you know *that* never happened to me before. Not the Bido Bandito."

"Yes, that's for sure."

"I don't know. I can't help wondering if all married men don't get this way. Do you think that after a month or so all married men get tired of making love with their wives? You know, the thrill is gone and all that? And it's just too much trouble to get a divorce, or they figure that's the way it's supposed to be? I don't know. Maybe married life really isn't all it's cracked up to be. No pun intended."

"No pun taken. Well, I wouldn't judge all marriages by yours, Bido. There are a lot of people around who claim to have been happily married for years and years."

"Yeah. 'Claim.' Before, Hud, sex was wonderful. It was really wonderful. In fact, next to a beautiful girl, sex is the most wonderful thing in the world. Pun intended."

"Pun taken."

"It was also exciting, because there was always a touch of danger to it. You know, the girl might get pregnant or something. Also, it was something you weren't *supposed* to do, which made it all the more exciting, simply because you weren't supposed to do it. 'Forbidden Fruit,' and all that. And to find a girl who would do it, and actually *liked* to do it . . . wonder of wonders—or, as Johnny Mathis says, 'Wonderful Wonderful'—that was really something, because you can get awfully frustrated and tired of having to go through the whole societal mating routine of seducing a girl. And then, she's usually the type to cry all the way home afterwards, and you have to play the gentleman and be nice and say, 'There, there, Honey. I'm sorry. Please forgive me. I don't know what came over me. I'm a pig. I just couldn't help myself, you're so beautiful. It was all my fault.' And all that other crap. But, to find a girl who actually liked to do it and who wasn't afraid to do it, that was great, because you both knew you weren't supposed to, but you both liked to do it anyway."

Bido drank from his beer bottle, and his eyes misted as he thought about all the wonderful girls he had discovered who had actually liked to do it.

In years to come, the Sixties will also be known as the Sexual Revolution years. People will lose their hang-ups about sex. Group sex will become popular. Men will share their "ladies," and that will be "cool." Women won't feel surgically attached to their mates, and that will be cool, too. "Hi, how ya' doing? Want to fuck?" will actually succeed with strangers, as often as 2 times out of 10, at least one cocksman will claim, citing the 20-80 rule.

In more years to come, in a typical backlash against the times, the tide will turn, the pendulum will swing, the sands will fall, and Free Love won't be cool, anymore. The Me Decade will also be the You and Me Decade. Maybe fear of disease will have something to do with it. Maybe the War will have something to do with it. Maybe boredom with the current society will have something to do with it. At any rate, people will be searching for permanent partners once again instead of fleeting sex. Goodbye, Fifties. Hello, Sixties.

Hello, Fifties, again.

In even more years to come, the tide will roll out and take quite a few diseased heads with it, as AIDS will turn casual sex into a deadly losing game of Russian roulette with all the chambers loaded with premature, devastating, lingering death. "Hi, how ya' doing? Want to fuck?" "Not on my life, Buster! Sister! Whoever or whatever you are!" People will say "Do you really want to sleep with everyone your partner has ever slept with? And everyone they ever slept with, too?" and then you will start thinking of all the scuzbags you saw in the Sixties. The watchword of the moment will become "safe sex," as if it should ever have been anything otherwise. Goodbye, Fifties, again. Goodbye, goodbye. I'm going to leave you now. Take good care of my Baby Love.

"But then you get married," Bido continued. "Oh, don't get me wrong. Myrna's a wonderful girl. Sure, she liked to do it. I don't think it's any secret that we went to bed together a few times before we got married. But, after you get married, and you can get laid all the time, and it's all legal—*expected*, even—it's not so exciting anymore. I don't even have the desire anymore, Hud. I was really worried there, for a while. I thought that maybe it was the end of my sex life. For good. I thought maybe I'd already used up all my times. But, one night Myrna was at a sorority meeting, and I was bored, and I came down here to the Sink, and I met this freshman girl, and I took her back to her dorm.... Only I took her back by way of Flagstaff. Don't get me wrong! She was perfectly willing to go. In fact, she was actually the one who suggested it. And I discovered that I hadn't really lost the desire, after all. Boy, was she a good piece of ass! Those inexperienced little freshman girls are always willing and eager to please."

"Easy steady, big fellow."

"Yeah. So, I thought I was cured, and I could hardly wait for the next night with Myrna, but the next night came, and that was the only thing that did. And then I knew. I was tired of Myrna. I craved fresh nooky. So I started slipping out of Myrna—. I mean, slipping out *on* her! Hell, you know what I mean. Anyway, I really feel like an ass, Hud. I'm sure Myrna knows. At least, she must suspect something. She found Binky drying out in the bathroom, and I tried to cover it by saying I was getting him ready to try to help our own problem. I'm a dirty, no-good bastard to do this to her, but I can't help myself. Do you think I'm maybe addicted to illicit love like some people are to dope?"

"I don't know, Bido. It sounds awfully far-fetched, but, then, science is coming up with new far-fetched discoveries every day. The psychologists keep telling us how screwed up we are."

"Yeah, maybe I'll become famous for bringing attention to it, and they'll name it after me. The Bido Sex Syndrome."

"But what about Myrna?"

"Okay, okay! The Bido and Myrna Sex Syndrome."

"That's not what I meant."

"Yeah, yeah. I know."

Bido's smile fell onto the table, and he stared at it lying there among the beer rings. He was really sorry for what he was doing to her, but he honestly couldn't help himself.

"Hey, Bido, maybe if you kind of cut down with Myrna? You know, maybe you've been knocking it off too much with her. Cut it down. Take it easy. The old desire ought to come back then, don't you think?"

"I don't know. We haven't made love for three weeks now, and I don't feel any desire . . . . But take a look at that chick that just walked in! Over there. The one with the huge knockers!"

And that was—as They say—the beginning of the end of Bido's and Myrna's marriage. Bido tried; he honestly tried to keep it working. Ho ho. But it just gave out. His slippings-out increased in frequency until he was going out with other girls more often than he was staying in with Myrna. More often than he went out with her, too. We tried for a while to straighten things out between them. The girls all talked with Myrna; we all talked with Bido. At least, most of us tried to. Of course, T.K.'s advice was more along the lines of "Why don't you try and get something straight between you and Myrna?" And "Why don't you let Myrna sit on your lap and see if anything comes up?" Then T.K. ended up double-dating with Bido and another freshman girl, because Bido fixed him up with the girl's roommate.

Eventually everyone just gave up. Bido and Myrna didn't have the time or the money to go through with all the divorce proceedings that were legally necessary right then, so they just agreed to separate for a while, still legally married for all intents and purposes, but also still practically single for other intents and purposes. Bido went back to his old ways—he even moved back into his old apartment with his former roommate. He always referred to his marriage as the time when he was crazy—ha!

"Remember that party at my place? You know, back when I was crazy—ha!"

But he was the only one who mentioned it. All the rest of us avoided the subject. Myrna, of course, never ran around with us again. She stayed in school and I would see her on campus sometimes, and sometimes I would run into her before I saw her and could get across the street, and I would have to speak to her. I felt sorry for her, but there wasn't anything I could do. Eventually they got divorced, and Bido continued his old ways legally, or at least not illegally, still trying to prove the mathematicians wrong.

Diane and I argued quite a bit at that time about Bido and Myrna. She claimed that Bido's reasonings were absolutely absurd. She claimed that if he really loved Myrna, as he claimed he did, then it was impossible for him to act the way he did. She claimed that Bido didn't really love Myrna, because if he really loved her, he would have absolutely no desire whatsoever to be with another woman.

"Look," I told her, "it *is* possible. You know Bido. You know how he was before they got married. You know how long Bido and Myrna went together before they got married. They talked it over. They knew what they were getting into. I'm sure that they both loved each other very much. And I believe Bido. Haven't you ever had false ideas built up about something, and then when you actually encountered that something, it wasn't what you had expected, and you were disappointed?"

"What does that have to do with what we're talking about?"

"Look at what we're surrounded with these days. What's popular in the movies? What's popular on the best-seller lists? We're inundated up to our ears these days with popular misconceptions about love, marriage, and sex. How were you initiated into sex? Not by actual experience, I'll bet. No, I'll bet you became familiar with sex through a book. First by novels—sexy ones—the ones that used to be banned. Then, through books about sexual techniques. You know, *Sex without Complex*, and all that sort of thing. So, by the time you actually got around to having sex personally, you knew all about it. Or, at least you thought you did. You thought you knew what it was all about, what it felt like, how to go about it. But, I'll bet you something else, Baby. I'll bet you, you were surprised the first time, weren't you? And I'll bet you were a little disappointed, too, weren't you?"

"Hud, how can you be so disgusting at times? I don't want to continue this discussion any further."

I suppose I did go on a little too far, especially considering the fact I knew very well that Diane had had sex only one time, and that had been with me. But I hated to see a girl always take the injured girl's side, and I felt I had to stick up for Bido. Bido was far from being a saint, of course, but I believed what I had said to Diane. Ideal imaginary life has become so large a part of our existence that when we encounter "real" life, we tend to be disappointed. It doesn't measure up to our imaginary life, and we believed that the imaginary life was the real thing. Or, at least we thought we could make it the real thing. Things go better with Coke.

So, Diane and I dropped the subject of Bido and Myrna, and I didn't realize it at the time, but I can look back now and recall that the word "marriage" didn't pop up in Diane's conversation as often as it used to. I guess that that was the start of the deterioration of our relationship, but I was too stupid and blind to see it.

Or, did I see it and not care?

It took only about a month after I first met Diane until she seemed to start talking about marriage in general, that subtle way girls use when they like to drop hints. She probably wasn't actually seriously thinking about marriage at the time, but was only playing the part that all young girls in our society have been taught from birth. No, I guess actually she was just subconsciously starting to lay the foundation for what might could turn into something larger and more permanent, so to speak. Just to keep things on the right track, so to say.

I first met Diane at the swimming party Dayo threw at his parents' house in Fort Collins. Diane was Theo's date, and she had the most sexy two-piece blue-and-white checked bathing suit I had ever seen. What a body she had! I had never before seen a flatter stomach, even on Brigitte Bardot, which, of course, I had never actually seen personally, but like all young college men I had made it a point to see *And God Created Woman*, which was enough right there to make you believe in God. Anyway, Diane had a flatter stomach than Brigitte's. And her cute little buttocks were beautifully sculptured. What a fanny! I used to call her D.B.—Drag Butt—kiddingly. Either that or Chubby Cheeks. But, she wasn't the least bit chubby. Just wonderfully low slung.

We rode up to Fort Collins from Boulder three couples in the car, Theo and Diane, T.K. and his date, and me and my date. T.K. had fixed me up with a naive little freshman girl who must have never had a suggestive thought in her tiny, teeny brain. She not only didn't understand dirty jokes, she couldn't even get the clean ones. She didn't drink; she didn't smoke; she just sat around and looked and listened, and sometimes danced. The only reason I forgave T.K. for fixing me up with her was that it led to my meeting Diane.

T.K. drove up to Fort Collins from Boulder, and even though Diane sat in front and I was in the back seat, I was very aware of her. She was quiet, because the only one of us she knew was Theo, but she held my attention as if she had been sitting up there talking steadily right at me. However, at the time I thought she was more interested in Theo, because I knew that he had taken her out a couple of times. I knew that Theo didn't care much one way or the other, but I figured that she was hung up on him, Theo being an artist and all.

The party was a success. Dayo's parents were away for the weekend, and we had the place to ourselves. There were about fifteen couples, and there was lots of drinking, dancing, and swimming in the backyard pool. We swam in the afternoon, then dressed and ate, and afterwards some of us danced around the patio while others went back for some moonlight swimming. T.K. was bounding around in the pool, trying to act like a shark and attacking all the girl swimmers ("I'm a *woman*-eating shark!"), and trying to induce Theo to go swimming ("Come on in, the girls are fine!"). Theo was dancing, though, and he stood on the edge of the pool yelling at T.K. ("Watch out! Watch out! There's sharks in the pool!") So, I quietly walked up behind him and shoved him in, clothes and all.

"*You goddam dirty* BLUB!"

There was mass confusion, and T.K. attacked Theo, and Theo began swimming around with his clothes on, and then he started doing a strip under water. Then the next thing I knew, I was attacked by Dayo, T.K., Stanley, and Bido, with Theo leading them on wearing only his shorts.

"No mercy! No mercy! Down with witches!"

I kicked, clawed, twisted, yelled, and screamed as they carried me to the edge of the pool.

"I can't swim! I can't swim! My wallet! My wallet can't swim! Save my wallet! Save my baby! Save *me*! Help!"

I kept yelling about my wallet and my shoes, so they removed them from me—my wallet and my shoes, and then my pants while they were at it. And as I continued to yell and scream and protest, they tossed me tumbling into the warm water.

When I climbed out of the pool, Diane was the one who handed me the towel. No one was mad. It was all great soggy fun. I borrowed a pair of Bermudas and an old sweat shirt from Dayo, and Diane put my clothes into the dryer for me. My date was sitting by the table on the patio drinking a Coke and getting ready to go back swimming. She thought it was all "super" and was having a "golly swell" time. So, while Theo continued to swim in his shorts and chased T.K., who continued to chase the girls, Diane and I danced.

Going home that night, my date sat in the front seat with T.K. and his date, because going to the party Theo and Diane had been the ones to split up. My date slept all the way back with her head bumping against the door window. However, Theo wasn't going all the way back to Boulder. His parents lived in Longmont, between Boulder and Fort Collins, and he was going to spend the rest of the weekend at home. So, we let him out there, and that left Diane and me alone in the back seat. Right outside Longmont there is a long, sharp curve, where I, acting somewhat drunk, just kind of fell over into Diane's lap. She cradled my head and stroked my hair all the way back to Boulder. Unfortunately, though, I actually did fall asleep and didn't get anywhere.

It wasn't until a couple of months later that Diane confessed she knew all along that I wasn't drunk that night. She thought it was cute. After I got Theo's permission to ask her out and did, and after Diane accepted and we started seeing each other, we never went out with anyone else after that. Right up until the end.

EIGHTEEN

The two days I spend with Lorraine are wonderful

The two days I spend with Lorraine are wonderful. She comes home on the third morning after work about nine o'clock, while I am still in her bed. We have decided that I might as well use her bed on the days when she works, since she doesn't come home until early in the morning.

"Good morning, Lazybones," she smiles at me from the bedroom doorway.

"Hi. Aren't you a little late?"

"Yes, a little. Just a minute. I have to pay the cab driver."

She rummages through her chest of drawers, comes up with an envelope tucked inside a pair of red silk panties, and goes back outside. I kick the sleep out of my head and sit up. I'm wearing the scarlet pajamas with a golden Chinese dragon on the tops that Lorraine bought me, but she won't let me wear the tops. She reserved them for herself, saying, "It's sexier that way, for both of us."

She walks back into the bedroom.

"So, lost your cab money again, huh?"

"Yes," she says curtly as she hangs up her jacket. She is wearing a blastingly shocking pink blouse and very tight matching slacks which show off her generous, but neatly turned ass. It reminds me of Diane's. More and more things about Lorraine keep reminding me of Diane.

"I thought sure I was going to hit big this morning, Hud. I felt it all the way down to my bones, you know? All the way down to my toes. I really thought this was it. Big time. Escape City. But . . . I was wrong."

"Tell me something. Why did you have me take you home the other day? Why didn't you just do what you did this morning? Pay the cab driver when you got home."

I am having trouble keeping my train of thought, because Lorraine is running her warm hand up and down my bare chest, twisting the hair into little black curls.

"Oh, I don't know," she grins, affecting a little girl's voice. "I guess because I thought you were sexy, and I wanted to see what you looked like without your shirt on."

She runs her hand underneath the elastic of my pajamas.

"Hey! Cut that out," I say, embarrassed, pulling her hand out gently. "What are you trying to do? Cause something to come up between us?"

"Maybe," she continues with her little girl's voice. "I'm exhausted, Hud. Would you give me a back rub? Please?"

She suddenly takes off her blouse, and I am startled at the sudden sight of her brassiere, white and soft and lacy. She shucks her slacks and lies down on her stomach beside me. "Shall I undo my bra?" she asks, and she unsnaps it without waiting for my answer.

I don't say anything as I start massaging her back. Her flesh is smooth and clear, except for one small mole on her right shoulder blade, staring up at me like the Eye of God. Lorraine purrs and moans with pleasure, as my hands work their way up and down her back in slow, sensuous strokes. Every so often I let my fingers drop fleetingly to caress the sides of her breasts as if by accident, but I know that I am tempting my own weaknesses. I am also letting my hands slide down over her buttocks with pressure strokes and my gentle, fleeting fingertips kiss the inside of her thighs.

She rolls over on her back, holding the bra in place with her hands, and smiles up at me.

"Would you like to give me a front rub, too, Hud?"

I frown, say goodbye to temptation, and stand up beside the bed. I resist the desire to hold my hands out like giant grabbers.

It would be too painful.

"No."

"What? What's the matter?" she says in her normal voice. Then she smiles. "Did I do something wrong? What's the matter with me, Hud? Don't you think I'm pretty? Or, maybe you think I'm too old . . . ?"

"Of course I think you're pretty. I think you're beautiful. And I've never let age bother me, one way or the other. But I don't want to play around just for the sake of playing around. Besides, I thought you were against this sort of thing, remember? What was that you said about guys who wanted to throw you into bed right away?"

"Maybe I've changed my mind," she says, still smiling and affecting the little girl's voice again. As she talks, she slowly inches her bra down to let her nipples peep out at me, giving me a view of the soft flesh of her breasts. There are no tan marks on her body. "Besides, technically this isn't right away. You've been around for a couple of days now."

She stops pulling her bra down just below her nipples and slowly caresses them with her thumbs, watching my reaction. "And, besides, you're even sexier than I thought when I saw you in the casino."

I try to keep talking to her eyes.

"Oh, 'I see,' said the blind man, as he picked up his hammer and saw.' So, now you've decided that it's all right for me to seduce you? Is that it?"

"Well, my God! What the hell if it is? Look, I don't have to go around *begging* men to jump into my pants. I usually have to fight to keep them *out* of my bed!"

"Is that supposed to make me feel honored?" I ask quietly.

A pained, hurt expression covers her face.

"Look," I say, "strange as it might seem, I *don't* want to go to bed with you. I *am* flattered, but I don't want to go to bed with *anyone* right now." I begin to put my shirt on.

"Are you serious? What are you?" she says, back in her own voice again. "You're not queer, are you?"

"No. I'm not queer. I'm not carrying any torch, either. I'm just not in the mood for sex. I don't want to hurt you—. Believe me, I don't want to hurt you. As a matter of fact, I am extremely grateful to you, but I just don't believe in sex being used as a reward for favors. If I were going to be staying here in Vegas, I would jump at the chance to jump your bones, but I've got to be going, and I have other things to do."

She lies there, hurt, staring at me while I put my pants on, and in a last-ditch effort she flings her bra aside, exposing her breasts, which stand up proud and firm, even though she is lying on her back. I am glad I wore my underwear underneath my pajamas so I won't show her how she is really affecting me.

"*Besides* sex. *And* gambling. I would like to believe there are *some* people in the world who can refrain from pulling down their pants every time a woman decides she's ready for it. I prefer to wait until the time is *right*."

"You know something?" she says seriously. "I think you're crazy. Sexy, but crazy."

"No, Lorraine," I say as I finish dressing, "I don't think I'm crazy. In spite of what everyone's been telling me lately, sometimes I believe I'm the only sane person left in the world."

She is very quiet. Sad.

"Maybe you're right. But if that's the case, then you would still be crazy, because then everyone else would be the same. They would be alike, but you would be different.... I'm sorry, Hud. I'm really sorry. Will you forgive me? Come on. Here. Let me give *you* a back rub, okay?"

"Lorraine. Please understand. I don't want to go to bed with you. With you, or anybody. I ... don't ... want ... sex right now. Okay?"

She just lies there breasts up on the bed. She can't believe it. I am probably the first person ever to turn down the offer to seduce her.

I get my sweater and parka out of the closet. I start to leave the bedroom.

"No! No! Hud!"

She jumps out of the bed, ignoring her nakedness. She stops me and grabs my arm. I ignore her nakedness, too, as she starts to rub against me.

"Please, Hud. Don't go. Stay. Please. Stay, Hud. I'll make it up to you. I'll treat you real nice. Please, Hud. I'm sorry. Really. I didn't mean it. Please? Hud? Don't you want to stay with me just a little bit longer? I'll be good. I promise."

I gently remove her hands from me and don't look at her breasts or her honeypot hiding inside her damp panties.

"You've kept me long enough, Lorraine. Goodbye."

"Hud, please.... Hud, don't.... Please.... Hud!"

Alright, I say to myself outside, it's time to drink. It's forget-time again.

In years to come, men will have to be very careful where they let their eyes look, even when the women they are talking to are fully clothed and properly dressed for the office. Sexual harassment won't be in the eye of the beholder. It will be in the eye of the beheld. The business place will truly be an arena and change all the rules of society, because money will become more important than sex itself. Some people will believe that what's good for business is better than people. Look. I am a man. You are a woman. We have biological urges that are perfectly natural. Give in to them. Doesn't matter, Buster. You look at my breasts while we're discussing business, and I'll haul your ass into court. You ask me out, you make a joke, you so much as look at me funny, and if I don't want to play, if I'm not attracted to you, I'll make your life miserable and your past shameful. I've got the power *now*, Asshole. Look at 'em and weep.

At the bar I find, I soon discover that the drinks don't help the nagging memory in my brain. Besides, it's still too early to drink. I keep thinking about Diane. I try to wipe out my thoughts with liquor, but with nothing going on in the bar to distract me, all I can do is drink, think, and be mellow. So, I give up and decide to try a casino. At least in a casino I can drink while I am alone in the midst of a crowd. The action will take my mind off my thoughts.

The casino, however, isn't very crowded. There isn't much action to watch, and I certainly don't want to gamble away all my money to try to create some action. I try to decide what to do when I bump into Joe Hawkes.

"Hud Holyoke, you old son of a gun! What the hell are you doing in Las Vegas?"

"Joe! What do you say? I'm here on my way to California."

"You are? So am I! I'm going out with two other guys for spring vacation. Do you know Dick Hanks and Kent Davidson?"

"I know who they are. Don't know them personally."

"Yeah, well, we got Dick's station wagon. We left Boulder yesterday afternoon after classes and barreled through all night. Stopped off here for a bite, a drink, and a toss before we head on out."

"Hey, well, look: You got room for me, too?"

"Room? Sure. What's the matter? How'd you get *here*?"

"I've been hitchhiking. Taking it easy. I dropped out of school about a week ago."

"Really? I didn't know that. Well, sure, we can take you along. Dick's car's got plenty of room. You might have to pay for some gas. Where are you going in California?"

"I don't really care. I just want to get out there and see the ocean, is all."

"Well, we're headed for Oxnard. Dick's brother's roommate's from there. They're already there, Dick's brother and his roommate. They left a day early. We're staying there a couple of days and then going on down the coast. If you want, I'm sure it's okay to go out with us. I don't know about staying at Oxnard."

"Oh, that's okay. All I want's a ride out. I'm okay once I get there."

"Well, come on, then. Dick and Kent are in the cafeteria eating. I wanted to try the slot machines once just for luck."

Joe introduces me to Dick and Kent, and, sure, they are glad to have an extra body along. We've all seen each other around campus and know each other by name, but we've never met or talked or done anything together, except be on different intramural teams. The three of them are in the same fraternity, which is a rival of my fraternity, but Joe and I are friends from when we were freshmen in the same dormitory. And even though the two fraternities are rivals, they are friendly rivals, mostly on the sports fields. There are no hard feelings between us, usually, unless girls or sororities get involved.

Joe is right about Dick's car. They have plenty of room. In fact, the back seat is down and a sleeping bag laid out so that they can sleep stretched out at nights. Their suitcases, cameras, empty beer cans, and other junk are just piled to one side in the back. Dick and Kent sit in the front seat, Dick driving, and Joe and I sit in the back with the junk. We stop just before leaving the city limits and pick up two cases of ice-cold beer, because the sun has really started to hammer down and we have a long stretch of desert to cross. We put the tailgate down for circulation, open a can apiece, and we all settle down for some serious driving and drinking. I know, I know! It's dangerous, but what the hell? We're young and foolish. I have pussyfooted around long enough. I allowed myself to get distracted. I am really headed for California now. I am really going to see the sea.

Jesus is it hot! The hammer of God pounds on the anvil of mankind and makes us senseless. Of course, lapping up the brew as we are doing, and, in all the heat, it doesn't take too long before we are all pretty well blasted. Dick keeps the wagon busting along at ninety, the road is straight and smooth, and there isn't enough traffic to give us any trouble. We wave goodbye to Nevada as we cross the California line and all open another beer.

"Hit me!" Dick yells, as he tosses his empty into the back at Joe and me.

"So, man, what did you do in Las Vegas?" Joe asks me.

"You wouldn't believe me."

"Why'd you quit school?"

"A lot of reasons. I'd pretty well had it. I needed a good, long vacation."

"Weren't you going to graduate this June?"

"Yeah. But, so what? I got tired of all the bullshit."

The bleached countryside rolls past us, and it all looks the same: hot, dry, scorched. And empty. And dead.

"Man oh man oh man oh man," Kent wails. "We just gotta stop pretty soon for a piss call."

"Yeah, me, too!" Joe yells up front.

"Hold yourselves a bit longer," Dick yells back. "I've been seeing these signs advertising some kind of desert monster up ahead. We got about two more miles to go."

"What kind of monster?" I ask.

"A gila monster," Joe says.

"No, no!" yells Dick. "Not a gila monster. Some kind of rare prehistoric animal they found in the desert. They've got a souvenir stand and snake farm etcetera. They're bound to have a rest room, too. We can stop there, take a leak, and take a look at their goddam monster, too."

"Yeah, well, hurry," Kent says, "before I piss my pants."

"Here," I offer, handing him another can over the back of the seat. "This will take your mind off your troubles."

"What are you? Satan? That's the *cause* of my troubles, Boy! Hurry, Dick, God damn it!"

"Hey! If we were going any faster, we'd be flying!"

The place is pretty well run down. There are no other cars around. No other tourists are interested in looking at the desert monster. There are faded, well-worn, hand-painted signs and crude pictures tacked up haphazardly on the outside, advertising other attractions such as snakes and spiders, but apparently their main attraction is their rare prehistoric monster which is practically a dinosaur, for Christ's sake.

"For Christ's sake," Kent says when we stop. "They're charging a dollar to see their goddam monster."

"No monster's worth a dollar," I say.

"Yeah," Dick agrees. "Well, we can use the head, and buy a candy bar or something, and then take off."

The inside of the place is grungier than the outside, only more littered. There is a grimy counter of souvenirs, Indian arrow points, tom-toms, wooden spears, painted jackknives, and rocks all against one wall, along with the main attraction against the other. A door leads off into the museum and to the world-famous desert monster.

The oldest man in the world comes from around the counter where he has been reading a movie magazine and says, "Help you fellows?"

"Yeah," I say. "We want to use your rest room."

"Rest room's inside the museum," he says. "Museum tour costs a dollar."

"You mean, we have to pay a dollar to use the rest room?"

"That's right. Don't have no rest room outside."

"Forget it," Joe says, and we all turn and walk out.

"Do you think he pays himself a dollar every time he has to whiz?" Kent says outside.

"How about against his wall?" Dick suggests.

"No," I say, "let's go down the road a piece."

"No," Joe says, "let's go down the road a *piss*."

We drive down the highway about a hundred yards until we come to a culvert bridge. We race each other underneath the bridge and Joe wins. Dick comes staggering down with his camera and gets a couple of action shots before Kent starts aiming at the camera.

We retake our positions in the car, Dick and Kent up front, Joe and me in the back, our feet hanging over the open tailgate, and continue our driving and drinking. The sun pulsates with the beat of our brains and the tires' hum on the highway. Kent starts to play his guitar, and Joe decides to write a love letter to his girl.

"Hey, Joe," Dick says, "I didn't know you were in love with anyone."

"Since the day before yesterday," Joe yells up front. "That girl I borrowed the fifty bucks from."

"What girl?" I ask.

"Oh, I met a girl about a week ago. Had one date with her. I was fixed up. Anyway, I took her to F.A.C. last week, you know. She wasn't bad at all. I even got to mouse a little bit with her. Not the rat, mind you, not the big mouse, but enough to keep us both excited. Anyway, I told her I wanted to go to California for spring vacation, but the fifty bucks I had saved for it I had to give to a brother when I wrecked his car. You know, to pay the fifty-dollars deductible. So, I gave her my story, and darned if she didn't offer to loan me the fifty bucks. So, here I am on my way to California with her money, and she sits back in Boulder not able to go home, because she is broke. So, I figure the least I can do is write her a love letter."

"No, man!" Kent says. "The least you can do is never see her again. Maybe pay her back, but write her off. That's the least you can do."

"How's this sound?" Joe says. "'Dear Gloria: I love you madly, passionately, wonderfully, unfulfilledly, exquisitely, tremendously, Gloria-sly' (Do you get it?), 'and most joyously. I miss you more and more as each fleeing minute passes along the roadside. I wish you were here so I could show my appreciation in actions, and not in the cold, dead praises of a letter.' What do you think of that so far?"

"Too dry," Kent says. "You've got to be more personal."

"Hell! I only met her a week ago!"

"Yeah, but you two have already done the Little Dirty!"

"Oh, oh! Look alive, guys. Here comes a buzzard."

"What's the matter?"

"That sign said we got to pull up at a checking station a mile up the road," Dick says.

"A checking station?" Joe asks. "What the hell are they checking for? Bad checks? Illegal immigrants?"

"Fruit or something," I say. "Didn't you read *The Grapes of Wrath?*"

We drain the cans we are drinking and shove all the empties, a case-and-a-half's worth, into a pile back with Joe and me, and we cover the pile with a blanket. It isn't until we try to act sober that we realize how drunk we are. The station comes into view, and Dick starts slowing down. We stop under the canopy, and a man in uniform comes out of the building over to Dick's side.

"Hello," Dick says, trying to act very friendly and at ease, but even a blind man could see that he is drunk.

"Howdy. We have to check to make sure you aren't bringing anything into the state."

He opens the rear door.

"Whatcha got in here?"

He pulls the blanket back and exposes all the empty beer cans. None of us says anything.

"Well, you certainly aren't bringing any *fruit* in, that's for sure."

"No, Sir," laughs Dick. Falsely.

"Yeah," the inspector says. Cautiously.

"Say, Sir," Dick says. "Can you tell us the best way to get to Oxnard from here?"

"Well, I'll tell you. I think the best way would be for you boys to stop in Barstow, get a cup of coffee, and check a map."

"Yeah!"

"Sure thing!"

"Ha! Ha!"

"Thanks a lot!"

We all laugh and chuckle at the good joke and climb back into the car and drive off, not too fast, now, take it easy, don't draw any more attention, okay? Whew! We're safe.

"Man, I thought it was going to be worse than that," Kent says.

"Yes," I say, "but his idea wasn't really so bad. Let's stop and at least check the map."

At the coffee shop in Barstow we look at all the maps that Dick brought along, but they aren't detailed enough to really show us how we can get to Oxnard the fastest and the easiest. So, we decide the easiest and the fastest way is to take the freeway through Los Angeles. There should be plenty of signs to show us the way. About the only thing we can determine from our maps is that Oxnard isn't too far up the coast from Los Angeles.

Once back on the road, we are all still pretty well buzzed. Everything is nice and hazy to me, and we figure we might as well finish off the rest of the beer, even if the cans are warm. Kent is able to chug a whole beer in one smooth swallow.

"Say, weren't you involved somehow with that girl a couple of weeks back?" Joe asks me.

"Uh, yeah," I say. "You want another beer?"

"Sure. What was the story—?"

"Hey, you guys want another beer?"

In all the years, males have for some reason decided that their ability to drink large quantities of beer quickly and smoothly is a measure of their manhood. Being able to open your throat and just pour the beer down without gulping is a mark of honor. With the advent of the pop-top, some foolhardy fellow discovered that if you pierced a small hole in the bottom of a beer can, covered the hole with your mouth while holding the can above your head, and then pulled the top, the entire contents of the can would gush straight down into your stomach in one big alcoholic whoosh. At a party once, I even saw one guy lie down underneath a beer keg, stick the hose in his mouth as far down as possible, and turn on the spigot. He didn't walk away from the party. He didn't even see the rest of the party. He didn't even remember what he had done, and the story he would tell in years to come would come from someone else's memory, not his own.

We hit Los Angeles right at the afternoon rush hour. We have all heard about the driving in L.A., but none of us has ever actually experienced it before. We suddenly find ourselves zooming down a six-lane highway at eighty miles an hour, completely surrounded on all sides—right, left, front and back—by cars all tearing it up and switching lanes back and forth like maniacs. Dick is a nervous wreck, but the rest of us are still high enough not to care. Joe and I sit peacefully in the back, our feet hanging out the tailgate, making faces and waving to the people in the cars behind us.

"For Christ's sakes, you guys," Dick yells. "Keep a lookout for signs. I don't know where the hell we are!"

"We're in L.A., for Christ's sakes!" Joe yells back up front. "Can't you see the smog?"

"Jesus H. Christ!"

"*Mister* Christ to you! You don't know me that well."

"Listen, you guys," Kent says. "I don't give a shit where we are. I gotta take a piss pretty soon, or it'll be coming out my ears. We've got to stop someplace."

"*Stop*? I can't even slow down!"

We all agree we can afford to stop so we can relieve our bladders and maybe take another look at the map or ask someone for some directions. Dick manages to ease over into the right lane and pulls off at the next exit. We find a nice field of something green growing, with a worn-out shack in the middle. We stop beside the road and all run out to the shack as dusk starts to descend.

"Man, I needed that," Kent says, zipping up his jeans.

"Yeah? Then what'd you get rid of it for?" Dick wags, as we all run back toward the car. Joe and Kent both stumble on the way back, and Joe falls facedown in the dirt.

But no one is around to give us directions, and we head back for the freeway. At least we know we are driving north. Five minutes later we see an arrow that has "Oxnard" on it and we take that exit even though we aren't able to read all of the sign. Five minutes after that we are lost. We seem to still be in Los Angeles, and I am sure that Oxnard isn't a suburb. We get back to the highway and start over again. Again we see signs and arrows and words proclaiming "Oxnard" and "Ventura," and again we take the promising exit, and again we get lost five minutes later.

"You know what I think?" Kent says.

"I think we're lost."

"What?"

"I think these signs are pointing to goddam *streets*."

"You know what I think?" I say.

"What?"

"I think we ought to pick up that sailor and see if he knows where he's going and how to get there."

"Sure," the sailor says. "I'm going there, myself, at least as far as Ventura. That's right near Oxnard. You can take me there, and I can direct you the rest of the way."

"How about a beer? It's warm."

"Great. Don't mind at all."

Oxnard turns out to be about fifty or sixty miles on up the coast from Los Angeles. By the time we drop the sailor off, it is dark. He thanks us, gives us the directions, and wishes us luck. As it turns out, we need it. About ten minutes later, the argument starts.

"For Christ's sake, you took the wrong damn turn!" Kent yells.

"Look, I know where I'm going. I've got the damn address."

"Yeah, and you're still drunk out of your mind. The sailor said to turn *right* back there."

"Hey, quiet up there," Joe yells. "We're trying to sleep back here."

"Yeah, well, why don't you stay awake and try to help us find the goddam place?" Dick snaps.

"I thought you knew where it was, for Christ's sakes," Kent says.

Dick pulls in at a gas station to ask questions and fill up with gas. The station won't honor Dick's credit card, and Dick asks Kent to trade turns with him, saying that he'll pay for the next tank.

"Look, goddammit!" Kent says. "What's the matter with your damn wallet? What's wrong with cash? It's *your* turn."

"Why should I pay cash when I've got this credit card?"

"Because it's your dad's credit card and he's paying for it. So Joe and I are paying for gas, and you're paying for nothing. That doesn't seem fair to me, buddy."

"Oh, it doesn't, does it? Well, it's my goddam car!"

"Yeah, and you can just drive the godddam thing and pay for the goddam gas." Kent climbs over the seat into the back and lies down. "Wake me when we get there. If we get there."

"Look," I say to Dick. "I'll pay for the gas. I haven't paid anything yet, and I won't be with you after Oxnard, so let me buy it."

"Okay," Dick says. "Look, I'm kind of tired, too. Do you mind driving?"

We try again with fresh directions and a full tank of gas, but Dick and Kent keep it up, and Joe even jumps in every now and then. I try to remain a disinterested fourth party, but I am still feeling the effects of the beer and having trouble seeing straight. I am getting irritated at Dick's stubbornness and drunkenness, and I can't find the goddam address, either.

I pull over to the side of the road between two large cultivated areas.

"Hell, I give up. I can't see anymore, and I'm lost."

I climb over the seat and join Joe and Kent, leaving Dick in the front seat.

"God damn lousy . . . stinking . . . ." he mutters, driving off again. "What the . . . you'd think . . . don't even . . . well, that's . . . for you . . . ."

We leave the middle of the field as Dick takes us over railroad tracks, through alleys, and in and out of practically every god damn place in and out of town. I think we are still in Oxnard when he stops the car once again.

"Hey, are you guys hungry?"

We haven't eaten anything since noon, but none of us says anything. We just lie here in the back and try to go to sleep.

"Well, God damn . . . if that's . . . okay for . . . ."

Then Dick starts talking college Spanish out the window and a lady's voice answers. Dick has trouble, but eventually gets himself understood. I look out the back window and see a little old Mexican lady standing next to an open, portable barbecue oven. I don't know where we are, but we are obviously on the opposite side of the tracks from where we want to be. We are in a pretty shabby section of town. Raggedy-dressed Mexicans stand around in doorways and on curbs, talking, watching, playing. Dick manages to figure out how much she wants for her sick-looking tacos and starts off again.

"Hey, don't any of you guys want any tacos?"

We don't say anything, even though we can smell them.

"I've got more here than I want. They're good."

We still don't say anything.

"All right . . . . If that's the way you want it . . . . Sure seems a shame, though."

I lie back down and try to sleep. We are all getting to the hangover stage, and I try to sleep, swaying with the station wagon. Dick doesn't really seem to know where he is going, since he just keeps driving around and around, but it also doesn't seem to make much difference to him. I don't know if Joe and Kent are asleep or not.

"Hey, you girls want a ride somewhere?"

Dick has stopped the car and is talking out the window.

"Huh? You need a ride to some place? *Habla usted Ingles?*"

We hear girlish laughter, and with that all three of us pop up and look out. Dick is talking to two girls walking along the dark street, and he is driving slowly alongside them to keep up, trying to establish some sort of communication. The girls are Mexican, short, plump, and not interested.

"Jesus Christ on a stick," Kent says, "you can't even get a Mexican chick interested in you."

"Hell," Joe says, "you could at least try to get them a little thinner, couldn't you?"

"What the hell are you? Late at night, a pussy's a pussy."

"Yeah, but sometimes, a cigar is just a smoke."

"What the hell is that supposed to mean?"

"Beats the shit out of me, but I think it means something in psychology."

We are all happy again. Dick's lack of success has broken the ice.

"Next time, let me do the talking," Kent says, climbing back into the front seat. "I once knew a Spanish girl."

"Chinese Fire Drill!" Joe yells, and Dick stops the car abruptly at the stop sign. We all jump out and run once around the car before leaping back inside. We are all friends again and ready and eager to find wherever it is we're going.

We stop at a gas station for directions once more and find out that we are two blocks from the street we are looking for. In another ten minutes we find the right address and pull up in front of Dick's brother's roommate's parents' house.

"Now, let me do the talking," Dick says. "You bunch of drunks just try to stay in the background where it's dark and look sober. You all look a mess."

The three of us sit down on the doorstep and act silly. We don't have to try hard.

Dick's brother's roommate's mother comes to the door and is glad to see us. But Dick's brother and his roommate have gone out for the evening. They didn't expect us until tomorrow. She doesn't know where they went. She wishes she had room for all of us inside, but she doesn't. That's okay. We have a couple of sleeping bags, and we can sleep in the car. We don't mind at all. Besides, we are pretty tired and wouldn't mind going to bed right away, anyway. We will see Dick's brother and his roommate tomorrow. Good night.

NINETEEN

I realize that I still haven't seen the ocean

I realize that I still haven't seen the ocean as I pull a blanket around me in the back of the car and try to stretch out in my allotted two-feet width of sleeping area. Even though we drove through Los Angeles and up the coast, the highway didn't go close enough for me to be able to get a look at the Pacific. I am sure that we aren't too far from the ocean where we are now. Not too many blocks away, we drove by what looked like the beach. I try smelling the ocean, but I can't be sure if I can or not. I decide that the first thing I will do when I wake up in the morning is go take a look at it.

And then suddenly, without wanting to, I remember Diane. Sweet, lovely, gentle . . . soft Diane. I cared for her more than I ever did for any other girl . . . and yet . . . .

I want to keep from thinking about that day, but I can't. It's that damn white elephant again. My thoughts keep going back to that day, and to the night before, when we went to a fraternity party, and afterwards to the Twinburger for something to eat. We sat in the car underneath the trees, eating our double burgers, trying to avoid talking. I knew something was troubling her, but I was sure it would be better all around for all post-party parties if we didn't talk about it. I kept trying to change the subject whenever she started talking, but it wasn't doing any good.

"Why don't you want to talk about it?" she finally asked me.

"Talk about what?"

I was suddenly very interested in the radio. I had borrowed Theo's Volkswagen. *She Loves You.*

"About us. What's going to happen, Hud? Are we just going to go on like this forever? Never discussing anything important? Why don't you talk to me?"

195

"Because you're talking. How can I talk when you're talking?"

"You know what I mean, Hud. You . . . never talk to me. You sit there silently for minutes on end, deep in your own thoughts. Sometimes . . . sometimes I think you even forget I'm with you."

"Diane, how many times do you have to hear it? I'm the quiet type. I don't talk much. I never have. That's the way I am. My brother, now. He's the talkative one in the family. Never quiet. Never silent. Always singing, talking to himself—."

"Hud, do you love me?"

I finished my hamburger, slowly chewing the last bite, and I looked at her sitting close to me in the dark. *Nowhere Man.*

"Love you? Sure, I love you. You know that. I've told you that."

"Yes, just like you've told many other girls that you loved them. To you, love is like the word 'like.' You tell me you like me, that's all. Do you love me enough to want to marry me?"

I finished my milkshake. *Don't Think Twice, It's All Right.*

"Marry you? . . . I imagine that some day I might want—."

"*Some* day? *Some* day you might want to marry me? That's all I mean to you? Hud, I love you. I love you more than anything in the world. You mean even more to me than my family does. But I can't get through to you. You're too distant. I'm not so sure that you love me, even though you say you do. But you told me that the very first night we went out. Hud, do you even care for me more than any other girl?"

"Anything *else*."

"What?"

"Anything *else*. You should have said you love me more than anything *else* in the world. Otherwise, you'd love me more than me, and that would be logically impossible. Also, you should have said do I care for you more than *for* any other girl."

Diane started to cry. *You're Lost, Little Girl.*

"Baby, of course I do. How can I make you understand? I *love* you. Honest. Of course, I care for you more than for any other girl. The fact that I don't go out with anyone else proves that."

She wiped the tears from her eyes. *The Dangling Conversation.*

"Are you sure it isn't just that you know you always have a date when you want one? Why haven't you ever asked me to get pinned?"

"Pinned? Is that it? You want to get pinned? You want the tangible proof, the little symbol, the assurance that you've got a hold on me? I'm not the type that goes around pinning every girl I take out more than three times. I believe the pin means more than that. It's the next thing to being engaged."

"And you don't want that. You have no intentions of ever being engaged, is that it?"

"Oh, Baby, now, don't go getting started on that. Why do we even have to talk about it?"

"Because we *have* to, that's why. Because we can't go on like this anymore. Because we're both seniors and have to start thinking about the future. Because I love you and I want to marry you, that's why."

I made a funny. *Born to Be Wild.*

"You're not pregnant, are you?" I asked, mock scared, knowing full well that she wasn't. *Everybody's Talkin'.*

She looked at me, the hurt showing in her eyes. *Yesterday.*

"No. No, I am not pregnant. I . . . ."

She was crying again, and she turned, staring out the window on her side. Her shoulders shook gently with her sobs, and I could see the light from a neon sign catching in the tears as they slid down her face, tiny red sparkles sliding down her cheeks. She wiped her face with her fingers as they fell. I gave her my napkin, which she took without looking at me, and she wiped her eyes and blew her nose. She kept crying and breaking my heart. *All I Really Want to Do.*

"Baby, please don't cry. Please. I'm sorry. I'm sorry, Baby, but . . . ."

No. *A Hard Rain's a-Gonna Fall.*

I really didn't know what to say. *Leaving on a Jet Plane.*

My heart went out to her as it never had before. *Love Me Do.*

But I don't want to think about it now.

"Diane," I said softly, trying to sound meek and gentle and convincing all at once. "Diane, this isn't the way I wanted it to happen."

She didn't respond, but I knew she was listening. *The Sound of Silence.*

"I wanted it to be perfect, I wanted it to be romantic. I wanted it to be *right*. I wanted to get a ring and do it *proper*. But . . . how the hell do you propose in the front seat of a car at a drive-in restaurant that advertises two patties on every bun?"

She turned suddenly and looked at me, the crying stopped, the hurt turning to puzzlement, then tentative, hopeful joy. *Touch Me.*

"Hud?"

"Diane . . . let's get married?"

"Oh, Hud!"

The hurt gushed out of her, and she dove across the seat into my arms, laughing and crying both into my chest, still a bit afraid that it wasn't true, wanting me to hold her tightly and reassure her that it was. I freed my arm and enveloped her, crushed her into me and buried my face in her hair. *Under My Thumb.*

"Oh, Diane . . . Diane. I love you."

We kissed, passionately, and I truly loved her, as I never had before then. She was still in that happy euphoria between crying and laughing, combining both, perhaps too shocked to really believe it was true. I kissed the tears from her face and started the car. *Eve of Destruction.*

I took her home, and neither one of us said much more. We said good night and kissed once more at the door of her sorority house, just like always, but it wasn't the same. She kept the napkin and kept wiping her eyes all the time, but she smiled as if she owned the world. I drove home afterwards, cursing myself, I didn't really know for what, and fixed myself a good strong scotch and water, and sat in the dark and drank it. When I finished, I made another one and drank it. *Sympathy for the Devil.*

No. *Back Door Man.*

I picked up the phone and dialed the number of her sorority house. *You've Lost That Lovin' Feelin'.*

No. *Where Have All the Flowers Gone?*

I don't want to think about it. *Walk on By.*

Diane answered the phone. *She Said She Said.*

Don't think about it now. *If I Needed Someone.*

"Diane," I said softly, not wanting to wake Dayo and Theo in the next room. "Diane, this is Hud."

"Oh, Hud! How sweet! I'm so excited, I can't sleep. I'm just sitting here in the dark pinching myself, telling myself over and over again that it's true, that it's really true."

I groaned and plunged. *When the Music's Over.*

"Diane, listen to me. This is going to hurt, and I'm sorry. I'm really sorry, but I've got to be honest with you. You know how I pride myself on my honesty: 'Be honest even if it hurts, but don't be honest in order to hurt.'"

There was no sound from her end. I couldn't even hear her breathing. *Be My Baby.*

"But, I got to thinking on the way home, Diane, and I decided I've got to tell you before you get too involved in this thing."

"Hud?"

"Diane, I was lying. No, it wasn't lying; it was more like playing. I didn't want to hurt you, Diane. God, I didn't want to hurt you, and I could see that you were hurt. So, I said that to make you stop hurting. I didn't want you to cry. I can't stand to see a woman cry. I get all knotted up inside, and it hurts *me* to see a woman cry. So, I said that to make you stop crying. I don't want to get married now, Diane. I just don't feel right about it right now. Maybe I'm still too young . . . maybe I'm still too restless. There are some things I want to do first, before I get married, before I settle down, I mean."

Silence. *If You Go Away*.

"But, when I do want to get married, you're the one I want to marry, Diane. You're the one. I can't think of anyone I'd rather want to marry. *Else*. Because . . . I *love* you. You know that. I've told you that. I love you. Honest. I care for you more than for any other girl."

I couldn't hear anything from the other end. *Who Do You Love*.

"Diane? Diane, are you listening? Diane? Look, maybe I'd better go now. I'll see you tomorrow, okay? I'll pick you up and, and maybe we can go to a movie, okay? I'll see you tomorrow. Uh, I love you . . . ."

I heard the click in the receiver as she hung up. I put the phone back and fixed myself another scotch and water. *The Pusher*.

The next day I found out that Diane was dead. *Eleanor Rigby*.

She had taken sleeping pills, and her roommate didn't discover it until noon when she tried to wake Diane up for lunch. There wasn't a note or anything, just the shredded paper napkin in her mouth. Nothing looked wrong. She had undressed and put on her pajamas, had taken the sleeping pills, and she went to sleep. She had been having trouble sleeping lately, her roommate said, and the doctors decided that it could have been an accident. *White Rabbit*.

No one could ever see why in the world she had wanted to commit suicide, because it was just out of the question. So, it was decided by everyone that it must have been an accident. One of those truly sorry accidents that happen sometimes and you just can't believe that anything like that could ever really happen. They just occur in the newspapers sometimes, far far away. *Aquarius*.

Diane was pretty. She was popular. She didn't have any problems at all. She was making good grades in school. She wasn't pregnant. She had a wonderful relationship with her family. She had a wonderful relationship with a popular fraternity man. She had a promising future. There wasn't any reason at all why she should want to commit suicide. They just couldn't accept it. *People Are Strange*.

"I can't accept it," T.K. said.

"I can," I told him. "You know good and well she was too smart to make a stupid mistake like taking too many sleeping pills."

"Well, yes, I thought of that. But, why in the world would she want to commit suicide? Why?"

"I don't know, T.K. . . . I don't know."

"It sure seems like there's been an awful lot of death going on around here lately. Jeez, you can't even open the newspaper anymore without reading about somebody dying here, there, and everywhere."

"Yeah. Well, everybody dies, sooner or later. Some die sooner one way, some die later another. Some people die in an accident—a car accident, or . . . or by a machine gun. Some do it just by pooping out because of old age. A few die by their own hands, and some die inside only, T.K., and then they go around for the rest of their lives dead inside, and some of those poor slobs don't even know it. Every cause, no matter how noble it is, is bound to die in the end, sometimes after success, sometimes not. No matter what it is, no matter who a person is, or how powerful he is, or who he knows . . . . In the end, T.K., we're all going to die, aren't we? I guess that makes us all losers."

"Jesus H. Christ, you're awfully morbid today. You're not thinking of committing suicide or anything like that, yourself, are you, Hud?"

"No, T.K.," I smiled. "I'm not thinking of committing suicide or anything like that. There's been enough dying around here as it is. I was just giving you my moral of life."

I looked at him. *Riders on the Storm.*

"You know, T.K., I'm really going to miss her. I'll never forget her, but I'm really going to miss her. I really am."

"Yeah, me, too."

TWENTY

I am awake before any of the others

I am awake before any of the others. It is still early, but it is light out. I take care not to disturb anyone, and I carefully climb out the back of the car. We slept with the tailgate down to give us more leg room. I zip up my parka to keep out the cold, because it is chilly and there is a slight mist in the air. As I start walking down the street, I think about the morning I left Boulder in the fog, one morning that seems so very long ago now. I remember the apparition I saw in the fog that morning. The strange, wandering ghost that I wanted to believe in. I wonder if that ghost found what he was searching for or if he still has to keep wandering around in a fog. Maybe he found it, maybe he didn't, maybe he has just given up by now.

I am fairly sure in which direction the ocean is, and I start walking that way. No one else is around whom I can ask for help, so I has to pays my money and takes my chances on my own senses. I have gone maybe ten or twelve blocks when I can tell I am almost there. The residential sections give way to some agricultural fields which are growing small green plants, row on row of the same, leafy vegetable, I guess they are. Beyond that the road turns at right angles, and there is a low railing which runs out of sight to the right and the left. Beyond the railing the sand starts, but then drops down to the water, so that from where I am I still can't see the ocean.

I can hear it, though. An incessant rolling, washing, whispering, seductive sound in my ears, not like a shell held up to your ear at all, not like your own bodily noises accentuated and reverberating in the stiff carcass of some dead sea mollusk, not at all like that. This is the real thing, the real McCoy, the whole damn shootin' match. I force my hands deep into my parka to keep myself from breaking into a run. It waits for me just over that little rise beyond the railing.

The morning is overcast, and great huge gray clouds blend together until they completely cover the sky, blocking out the sun and its warmth. The wholeness of everything is gray, and the morning is still slightly cold, but I can tell that it will get warmer soon. I step over the railing and trudge across the sand. And then I come to the rise. And then I see it.

My first impression is that it is huge. It has a greater vastness to it than anything I have ever seen before, greater, even, than the mountains of Colorado. And I think, somewhat amused, that it looks just like it does in the movies, a black and white movie, only bigger. It rolls in constantly, and just before the waves reach the shore, the crest of each wave falls over, topping the ridge with white, foamy lace. Then the crippled wave crawls up onto the sand, strains to reach higher, and then it washes back out to sea, bubbling and frothing in frustration.

I stand there a moment, just over the rise, and smell the air. It smells like salty fish, like something rotten, something decaying. And then I walk on down to the water, stopping to look at some soggy seaweed sprawled about on the beach, looking like some kind of rubber plant bought in a dime store. I walk right up to where the water gives up on the shore, and I stop and look out at the sea. *Like a Rolling Stone.*

Lying beside me on the sand is some sort of jelly-like substance, shapeless and unknown to me. I don't know whether it is a plant or a fish. It is colorless, round, flat, somewhat shiny. I kick it and watch it. If it was ever alive before, it is dead now, probably washed up during the night from somewhere deep beneath the ocean's depths. *Salt of the Earth.*

I finally realize that there are other people on the beach this early in the morning. Five men are stretched out to my right, about twenty-five yards apart, standing there in their heavy coats, casting out into the sea with long poles. Most of them are Oriental, but the one closest to me is a big, black Negro, old, and grizzled with a pepper-salt beard of a day's growth. His pole is stuck into the sand at his feet, and he just stands there with his hands in the pockets of his pea jacket, staring out at the sea. I guess that even if you have lived by the ocean all your life, you can always find something fascinating in its expanse, in its emptiness, in its mysteriousness, and you can't keep from staring at it, looking out at the horizon, wanting to solve its secrets. *The Impossible Dream.*

The fisherman has on a woolen Army-green cap, pulled down almost past his ears, and he looks out with red, bloodshot eyes to where his line disappears into the surf. I walk up to him and am silent, just watching where he is watching. Then I ask him if he has caught anything, and he points to a bucket ten feet behind him. I walk over to it and look in, and I see two fish, slimy, gray, and gasping for seabreath. Their stench is powerful and shocking to me. The black man eyes me suspiciously while I stand there. I smile at him and nod, silently commenting on the niceness of his catch. Then I walk on down the beach. *Tell the Truth.*

I look back out at the sea. It doesn't have anything to tell me. So, this is the sea, I think, and I don't know if I am crying or not. I turn and start back, leaving only my footprints in the wet sand to show where I have been, knowing that they will be erased by the next high tide. I never look back, even at the top of the ridge as I start walking back toward the car and its little band of occupants, still sleeping, still dreaming, still still. *Get Off of My Cloud.*

I am crying now, but I don't know why, and I won't know why until after many more years to come. *Revolution.*

I am crying because of my lost opportunities. I am crying because of my failed expectations. I am crying because I lost my nerve, lost my confidence in my elf, and followed my head instead of my heart. *I Wish I Knew How It Would Feel to Be Free.*

I believe I will head back to Las Vegas. *Have You Ever Loved a Woman.*

I have seen the sea. *The End.*

Printed in the United States
115773LV00004B/32/P